# Professor Bernice Summerfield: Life During Wartime

## A Short-Story Collection
## Edited by
## Paul Cornell

Published by Big Finish Productions Ltd,
PO Box 1127
Maidenhead SL6 3LW

*www.bigfinish.com*

Range Editors: Gary Russell & Ian Farrington
Managing Editor: Jason Haigh-Ellery

Bernice Summerfield was created by Paul Cornell
Irving Braxiatel was created by Justin Richards
Jason Kane was created by Dave Stone
Bev Tarrant was created by Mike Tucker

ISBN 1-84435-062-2

Cover art by Adrian Salmon © 2003
Design by Clayton Hickman
Logo designed by Paul Vyse

First published September 2003

*The Fall* © Paul Cornell
*Careless Talk* © Justin Richards
*The Birthday Party* © Simon Guerrier
*Five Dimensional Thinking* © Nick Wallace
*Meanwhile, in a Small Room, a Small Boy...* © Robert Shearman
*Lockdown Conversations 1* © Paul Cornell
*The Price of Everything* © Gregg Smith
*Hit* © John Binns
*The Garden of Whispers* © Martin Day
*Lockdown Conversations 2* © Paul Cornell
*The Crystal Flower* © Cavan Scott & Mark Wright
*Midrash* © Ian Mond
*Fear of Corners* © Mark Stevens
*The Traitors* © Jonathan Morris
*Paths Not Taken* © Rupert Booth & Barry Williams
*Every Picture Tells a Story* © Jim Sangster
*Fluid Prejudice* © Paul Ebbs
*Suffer the Children* © Dave Stone
*Drinking With the Enemy* © Jonathan Blum
*Lockdown Conversations 3* © Paul Cornell
*Passing Storms* © Peter Anghelides
*Speaking Out* © Simon Guerrier
*The Peter Principle* © Kate Orman
*Lockdown Conversations 4* © Paul Cornell
*A Bell Ringing in an Empty Sky* © Jim Mortimore

The moral rights of the authors have been asserted.

All characters in this publication are fictitious and any resemblance to any persons, living or dead, is purely coincidental.

All rights reserved. No part of this publication may be reproduced or transmitted in any forms by any means, electronic or mechanical including photocopying, recording or any information retrieval system, without prior permission, in writing, from the publisher.

This book is sold subject to the condition that it shall not, by way of trade or otherwise, be lent, resold, hired out, or otherwise circulated without the publisher's prior consent in any form of binding or cover other than that in which it is published and without a similar condition including this condition being imposed on the subsequent purchaser.

Printed and bound in Great Britain by Biddles Ltd
*www.biddles.co.uk*

# CONTENTS

| | |
|---|---|
| The Braxiatel Collection | 1 |
| 1: The Fall | 3 |
| 2: Careless Talk | 9 |
| 3: The Birthday Party | 19 |
| 4: Five Dimensional Thinking | 25 |
| 5: Meanwhile, in a Small Room, a Small Boy... | 35 |
|    Lockdown Conversations: 1 | 41 |
| 6: The Price of Everything | 43 |
| 7: Hit | 51 |
| 8: The Garden of Whispers | 57 |
|    Lockdown Conversations: 2 | 67 |
| 9: The Crystal Flower | 69 |
| 10: Midrash | 77 |
| 11: Fear of Corners | 87 |
| 12: The Traitors | 97 |
| 13: Paths Not Taken | 107 |
| 14: Every Picture Tells a Story | 115 |
| 15: Fluid Prejudice | 121 |
| 16: Suffer the Children | 133 |
| 17: Drinking With the Enemy | 145 |
|    Lockdown Conversations: 3 | 155 |
| 18: Passing Storms | 157 |
| 19: Speaking Out | 163 |
| 20: The Peter Principle | 169 |
|    Lockdown Conversations: 4 | 179 |
| 21: A Bell Ringing in an Empty Sky | 183 |
|    Acknowledgements | 202 |

*For Mum and Dad*

*For bread and butter and honey*

# The Braxiatel Collection

'Collection of what?' is an invalid question. Arguably the finest and most extensive in the known universe, it is a collection of everything. The various departments of the Braxiatel Collection house antique artefacts, literature, playscripts, recordings of events and people and performances, geological specimens, software and hardware of days gone by... A permanent home for the Braxiatel Collection is currently under construction on a small planetoid formerly designated KS-159 – now known as the Braxiatel Collection. Fabulously rich, Irving Braxiatel is Renaissance Man for the new era. He is well read, extremely learned, an expert in almost everything, though in some matters he lacks practical experience. He does have a tendency to miss the details while looking at the big picture – details like how people actually feel about things, for example. He has built up his collection over the years – probably over the centuries. But how old he really is, whether or not he actually ever ages, is not something that it is polite to discuss.

Professor Bernice Summerfield is a guest of Irving Braxiatel. She is currently working (still) on the sequel to her best-selling coffee-table archaeology book *Down Among the Dead Men* (published originally in 2466, which is odd given it is now 2602). Wolsey is Benny's tabby tomcat. He is putting on a bit of weight now and slowing down. In fact, he's getting a bit lame in his back left leg. Joseph (so-called for historical and sentimental reasons) is Benny's personal digital assistant. He is an AI computer system linked to the Braxiatel Collection's main scheduling systems; roughly the size of a football. Personality-wise (and again for historical/sentimental reasons) Joseph has been programmed to be 'dry' and literal. Not surprisingly, he spends most of his time switched off.

Ms Jones (not Miss or Mrs, note) is in charge of Administration. This includes overseeing the construction work and the tending of the gardens and grounds. She is a lady of uncertain age and unspecified background. If it seems she has something to hide, it is probably because she does. She is six feet tall and seems almost as wide. She wears horn-rimmed glasses on a chain round her neck and woe-betide you if she has cause to put them on...

Mister Crofton is in charge of the grounds and gardens. He is a short, stocky man usually in his shirtsleeves and with a wheelbarrow close by. He is normally of a humorous and helpful disposition. But omit the 'Mister' ahead of his name and he immediately becomes surly and uncooperative. Ms Jones therefore always calls him 'Crofton.'

Adrian Wall is the construction manager. He is in charge of all the ongoing work at Braxiatel, and reports to Ms Jones. Like most of his workforce, Wall is a Killoran – a seven-foot-tall cross between an ape and an upright wolf complete with fangs, snout and claws.

Broderick Naismith is the Chief Public Relations Officer for the Collection. He is responsible for advertising, promotion, guide books and materials and all the notices. While Braxiatel is often detained at meetings with Naismith, nobody else has ever met him.

*Previously...*

Professor Bernice Summerfield is now the mother of a toddler called Peter, whose father is Adrian Wall. But they're not a couple, although Adrian would like them to be. Also present on the asteroid is Bernice's ex-husband, Jason Kane, a criminal and conman from the distant past. He gets by doing odd jobs for Brax, and is still close enough to Benny to babysit Peter while she's away. Also based on the Collection is Bev Tarrant, an adventurer and art-thief also stranded out of her own time, who is currently resting there after Benny saved her life.

At the end of the audio adventure *Professor Bernice Summerfield and the Poison Seas*, Bernice received an odd message from Braxiatel, encouraging her to head home at once...

# 1: The Fall

## By Paul Cornell

Planetoid KS-159 has a circumference of ten miles. That'd mean that, in normal circumstances, the escape velocity would be about eight miles per hour. Any cricket played on such a body would be timid, wasteful and brief.

So it's just as well for KS-159's three cricket leagues that the planetoid is home to the famous Braxiatel Collection, an esteemed pile of stuff. The Collection has an artificial gravity field that extends a long way into space, over four thousand miles about the planetoid's surface, to stop the atmosphere bleeding away. I gather that there are several levels of redundancy built into that. Actually, it's more accurate to say I suppose there are, because I've always been too terrified to ask.

That Earth-sized lump of gravity is difficult to park against. One's shuttle suddenly finds itself on the edge of a vertical gravity well. That's why there are navigational satellites that grab hold of one's controls and yell 'gently, gently!' at them.

Or there usually are. And today I was too preoccupied to check that said satellites were working. I was thinking of the scrambled message I'd got from Brax, the few words he'd managed to get through a blizzard of interference. He'd implied there was danger. On the Collection. Danger where my child is.

I was also looking at the hundreds of ships I'd come out of hyperspace amongst, that were hanging in space around the Collection. Warships. And I recognised that lightning bolt insignia. It was only a matter of seconds before one of them moved in to intercept my shuttle.

All that was why I'd suddenly found myself in free fall, my shuttle heading straight down at the green features of the planetoid, heat ripping at every surface. I think I might have seen that some of the buildings were damaged, caught a flash of smoke in my eyes.

I don't recall any thoughts I might have had in those few seconds. There was just an animal need inside me, a need to stay alive. For Peter.

I must have put my whole weight back against the stick.

They tell me the shuttle ploughed two waves of soil out of the cricket pitch. Like a stone splitting water from the surface of a lake.

I remember nothing of that.

I woke in a suspensor field, in a medical wing I recognised, but which looked different, being told I was fine. The fields in the shuttle had saved me. Sent me banging around the cabin in a little bubble.

I focussed on the uniforms. The guns. The looks of expectancy on their faces.

'You're Professor Summerfield, aren't you?' someone said, looking at an infopad and checking it against my bruised face. 'Bernice?'

I slurred something at them. I managed to ask where Brax was.

'Irving Braxiatel is under house arrest.'

'The Fifth Axis.' I finally managed to put a name to the insignia. Petty tyrants. A group of bullies who'd risen and then fallen back on a tiny front of worlds. A banana junta. We'd all thought they were over.

'Yes,' said the soldier, as my eyes grew wider and wider, because I was just realising what I couldn't ask them. The Fifth Axis didn't approve of humans breeding with other races. They didn't allow it. They carried out relocations and pogroms to stop it. So I wasn't going to ask about Peter, my beloved, my life... my half-human child. I wasn't going to ask about Adrian, his alien father.

I was not.

I let out a howl of something instead, with a mess of blood from my mouth.

The soldier wiped my face with his handkerchief and smiled. 'We're the authority here now.'

It was so quiet.

The cafés and bars on the Collection are normally filled with visiting academics and students, arguing with those resident here and each other. The Collection is a hub of intellectual debate, a meeting point for thought.

Was.

They'd let me go as soon as they'd checked my identity. They'd given me some new identification documents and a leaflet about what to expect under Axis occupation. In bold on the front were the times of the nightly curfew.

I hardly asked anything. I wanted my friends to tell me. I was told that someone would be in touch to talk about how my particular skills could be of use to the new administration.

The damage to the buildings was only skin deep, and was being rebuilt. Scaffolding everywhere. I smiled when I saw that someone had put up a fight: there were energy weapon scars on the walls every now and then.

I was trying to walk not towards Jason's accommodation, not towards Peter. I couldn't see any aliens around. The building crews were all human, not Killoran.

Which is when one of the soldiers caught up with me from behind, and gently put a hand on my arm. 'Professor Summerfield... It's about your son. I'm so sorry.'

\* \* \*

They took me to see a woman who sat behind a desk beside an empty swimming pool. 'I'm sorry to have to break the news to you,' she said. 'Your son... Peter, is dead.'
I felt for a moment that I was living in a parallel universe, and that thus this news meant nothing. It was simply wrong. 'No.' I smiled at her. 'No.' I was aware of a vast mass of pain, somewhere above me. It was going to descend. My body was already reacting, if I wasn't. My stomach had clenched so hard.
'Some missiles went astray during the initial barrage. There would have been no such assault had the Collection's automated systems not attempted to engage our craft. One of the missiles hit one of the accommodation areas. Peter is listed amongst the dead.'
They had no body for me to see.
I remember no more of that interview.

I felt afterwards that I should now go to Jason.
But I didn't. Doing that would make my son's death complete. I could hover between worlds. I still hadn't seen anyone I knew. I didn't realise at the time that, with the Axis in control of all communications channels, news of my return and crash would only gradually be leaking out through gossip.
I saw, in the distance, a man sitting at a table in the silence of one of the cafés, his hand raised. I only half knew him. Orst Gemayal. A translator of ancient Arabic. He and his brother kept a salon on Wednesday nights in their accommodation on the edge of the Garden of Whispers.
He didn't get up from his seat, he just kept smiling.
I didn't want to tell him my news. But there was a look in his eyes that said I had to go over. So finally I did.
'Bernice,' he said through his smile, glancing at the guards and the café owner. 'He's alive.'
'Who?' I asked, ridiculously.
He carefully kept his fingers over his mouth. 'Peter.'
So it was him I swore at, called him a stream of foul names, reached out and grabbed his hand and dug my nails into him.
He understood, held me up so it didn't look so strange, and just told me everything, kept telling me over and over.
The bombardment had happened, had killed thirty people, several young children, a Killoran baby and his mother, who were visiting someone in Applied Theology, and whose documents hadn't been processed when the Axis fired their initial EM pulse that locked the systems. The mother had been vaporised. The baby... well, enough remained.
The bombardment had destroyed Jason's rooms, where Peter was

supposed to be that evening. But Jason had wanted to go out that night, so, with ill grace I could imagine, had given Adrian the keys and asked him to look after him. The missile had landed... but Adrian had taken Peter out onto the grass. Adrian was slightly injured. Peter was fine.

Goddess be praised, I finally believed it.

As the first Axis transports landed, Adrian had run to the door of the Gemayal Brothers, had thrust the baby into their arms. He'd told them they were the best people he knew, and so this burden was theirs now, and there was no time.

Adrian knew all about the Axis.

He'd gone back to Jason and wailed in the ruins. He hadn't trusted Jason. Of course. I felt another jolt of pain at the thought of Jason thinking Peter was dead.

The Gemayals had set aside a room, and had camouflaged the door to it, and had quickly bought everything they needed before the Axis started to keep track of such things. The gap between grasping hand and closed fist had been around three days. Now the fist was closed, and when the sensor net was complete it would be fastened on the throat of the Collection.

I thanked the Goddess that I hadn't arrived a few days later.

I asked if I could see him.

Orst took my hands in his. He said that the Axis officers he'd been talking to had mentioned me a couple of times. That, for a while at least, he was sure I'd be watched. All the half-human children had been confined to a particular housing area. Their alien parents, and all completely alien children, had been rehoused in another. Everyone was certain this was a prelude to a 'relocation' offworld. The Killorans, who'd formed the majority of the work crews under Adrian, were now being redeployed to work under Axis team leaders. They, at least, might be allowed to stay a while.

Orst said that he and his brother had decided to die before they let the Axis get hold of Peter.

I looked into his eyes and finally nodded. 'Give him my love,' I said. 'Explain to him. Tell him his Mum...' But I couldn't find the rest of the words.

I would have gone to Jason, then, and found a place to tell him the truth. But before I left, Orst told me what had happened to everyone.

Braxiatel was confined to his private apartments. He'd been led away in chains, but he'd paid no attention to them. He'd just been shaking his head, talking to himself. I knew that Brax had access to time travel technology. He'd once told me he'd settled on this particular planetoid to house his Collection because he knew nothing dangerous would happen

in this area of space... ever.
 The Fifth Axis had surprised Brax. Which was a worldshaking horror in itself. It said that all bets were off. As someone who has had a small volume of prophecy written about her, who was to some extent, it turns out, unconsciously relying on it, I found that I had made one of those bets. I had to talk to Brax as soon as I could.

Bev Tarrant, who'd decided to hang around and work for Brax, collecting things for him from alien worlds, had remained tight lipped since the Axis had arrived. They didn't like what the records here said about her. But they had no excuse to arrest her. Yet. I saw her in the market, and made eye contact with her over the browning apples that in a few days would be mush and would not be replaced.
 Her look said to get the hell away from her, because sooner or later she was going to do something dangerous.

Ms Jones had moved from being a terrifying figure in Brax's bureaucracy to being a terrifying figure in the Axis bureaucracy. She put on a clipped smile when she saw me. The only thing I could see about her that was different was that she had a different shade of lipstick now.

Similarly, Mister Crofton was still tending the gardens. Only now he had explosion craters to fill in, and burnt plants to cut back and encourage. He just shook his head and sighed. He seemed older. He seemed like he had seen it all before.

I heard that when the Axis had first arrived, Broderick Naismith had tried to send a message – a cry for help perhaps, or a warning, to the Collection's friends and supporters in other sectors. The messages never got beyond the artificial atmosphere and he'd been the first victim of a public execution. I'd never, ever met Naismith, not after two and a bit years here. Of course I'd read his publicity brochures and heard Brax talking excitedly about some of the lectures Naismith had given on other worlds, encouraging the authorities of those places to send their brightest students (and most precious artworks) to the Collection. To be safe. And yet I felt something odd at hearing of his death – I felt like I'd lost a friend. He wasn't going to be he last, I guessed...

I glimpsed Adrian on a construction crew. I entertained the thought of running up to the wire and grabbing his fur to it and hugging my body to it in sacrifice. But I think they would have beaten me, and, more importantly, him.
 He loved me enough not to look at me, not to look up. Though I had

never loved him, never been his lover. We were parents together through a kind of magic accident, but I loved him as my dearest friend. I projected all I was through that wire to support him, and then I moved on.

And Jason...

Jason had changed. Perhaps it was the 'death' of Peter that had done it. Or perhaps he hadn't changed at all, and was just shown as himself now. He had led the first Axis troops around the Collection, deactivating all sorts of boobytraps that nobody had ever imagined could be there, but that Brax must have deployed at short notice. He had spent hours in conversation with the invading forces.

He had emerged, two days ago, in Axis uniform.

He didn't come to me. Perhaps he was wondering if he could look me in the eye. I didn't go to him. Even if it might unlock him, I didn't want him to know about Peter.

I found myself in the evenings not meeting with my fellow academics, not looking for the resistance which I assumed would be out there somewhere.

Nobody could enter and nobody could leave. Not yet.

And yet, I was alone now. I had returned to nothing.

When we're alone is when we learn who we are.

We were all of us going to learn who we were.

# 2: Careless Talk

## By Justin Richards

They met at night, in the cellars. Benny, of course, was late.

She had got the invite from Bev Tarrant, another encounter in the market. Only this time, Bev had rolled an apple into her hand. The apple had contained a message.

Bernice read the rice paper and ate it.

She didn't know if she should go. She hadn't had a chance to see Brax. She wasn't entirely sure who was in charge, didn't want to ask upwards through the bureaucracy so soon. It was said an Axis Governor was arriving soon.

It felt like fate held Peter as a hostage against her attending such meetings. She hoped the Gemayals would stay away, if they'd been asked. But what else could she do? She couldn't work. She couldn't read or write. She'd had a roster of visiting students in her charge, and had found that many of them, being aliens, had been separated from the minority of humans. She'd denied herself her friends. She woke every morning in a sort of shock at the changes.

So. Might as well join the resistance.

She decided to break the curfew dressed all in black. Given the choice between coordinated colours and staying alive, she settled for the less flattering option. She was ready to go on time. But five minutes before she was due to be off, someone cleared their throat, close behind her ear.

It made her jump in surprise, then whirl in anger.

'Joseph! Don't do that.'

'Apologies.' The small, spherical robot bobbed in the air as if bowing. She was sure that, post Occupation, he sounded sad too. 'I wished to alert you to my presence without alarming you.'

'Well, one out of two is... pretty average,' Benny told him. She found Wolsey where her sudden shock had startled him into the corner. Jason had continued feeding him after the Occupation, and had only stopped, without meeting her, without explanation, when she'd taken up her rooms again.

Joseph floated close to her. 'I have a message for you. From Braxiatel.'

'From Brax? How?'

'He sent a very simple electronic signal. I was to come to him after dark.'

'How is he?'

'Exactly the same. He programmed this message into my memory. The message is: the Axis know.'

'Know what?'

'About tonight's meeting.'
She thought about staying here. To her shame. Just for a second. Then she sighed. 'Gordon Bennett.' Then she ran.

There were about two dozen people crowded into the cellar, Bev noted with satisfaction. Academics, workers, support staff. Mister Crofton was standing as far from Ms Jones as was possible without actually being in a different room.

'There are one or two people still to arrive,' she said as the muttering died away. They all knew she meant Benny, of course. 'But under the circumstances, I suggest we get started. I thought it was worth getting together to talk through what we might be able to do to resist the Occupation.'

'Nothing,' Ms Jones said loudly. She put her glasses on and peered at Bev over the top of them, as if to make sure it was really her. 'Not if the staff act as they always have acted: a group of small children, bickering amongst themselves.'

On the other side of the room, Mister Crofton began to say something. His voice was cracked and quiet, and immediately interrupted by Ms Jones' stentorian tones.

'No, I will finish what I have to say before you try to shout me down.'

Mister Crofton seemed to recede into the background. In the dead silence following Ms Jones' admonishment, his muttered reply carried easily. 'I was going to agree with you, actually.'

Ms Jones seemed momentarily surprised by this. But she quickly recovered. 'Yes, well, ahem... You can do that in Any Other Business.'

An academic called Vosta stepped forward from the crowd. He had a look on his face that suggested he was bored by these proceedings. 'That was our right, in peacetime,' he said. 'It was what we liked to do. Now we have to do what we used to do to each other... but to them!'

'Oliver Norman,' said a youth, raising his hand. 'Visiting archaeology student. I was just wondering –'

'I have the floor, Mr Norman!' shouted Vosta.

Bev had an uncomfortable feeling that this was not going to be 'her' meeting for very much longer.

'Yes,' she called out, replying to Ms Jones. 'I think these sessions *should* run along more structured lines. So. Here's our strategy. Afterwards, I'll take questions.'

At that moment, Benny skidded into the room. 'Sorry,' she gasped.

'We have you under Apologies already,' said Ms Jones.

'Sorry,' Benny said again, less breathless and louder. 'But you have to get out of here. Now!'

There was a moment's silence, then people started to rush for the door.

Bev grabbed Benny amongst the milling people. 'How did they find out?' she yelled.

'I don't know. Brax sent me a warning.'

There was more confusion now as people ran back into the room.

'They're on their way,' Mister Crofton told them. 'Guards. Lots of them.'

The crowd was starting to panic. There was a general rush back into the cellar.

'There's a stairway up to the kitchen area. Go on!' Ms Jones pushed through and led the way, ushering the others in front of her like an impatient tour guide with tardy tourists.

Already Bev could hear the boots on the cellar steps. She pulled Benny into an alcove. 'Let's hope they don't find us,' she whispered.

'Oh yes, let's,' Benny hissed back.

She fell silent as the Axis guards entered the room. They looked quickly round, saw the other door, and ran for it.

'Through here,' one of them shouted back. 'They're through here!'

Bev waited a moment, then stepped out of the alcove.

But Benny pulled her back, just as two of the guards returned, dragging Vosta.

He was arguing with them, asking about wine, trying to make out he'd sneaked in here on his own. His tone of voice was imperial, withering, impatient.

Then one of the guards slapped him so hard that blood splashed from one corner of his mouth. He sagged. Then started up again, as if explaining to a very slow student.

So the guard slapped him again.

Benny and Bev held each other, as if holding each other back.

'Come on,' said the other guard. 'Outside'

They took him out. There was silence.

Bev waited for the gunshots. None came. The rest of the Axis guards filed back through the room. At first Bev thought that everyone else had escaped. But she felt Benny tense next to her, and followed the line of her sight... to see Jason, in uniform, walking calmly with the soldiers. He was saying something to the guard next to him, and in reply the guard laughed. Jason smiled too.

Bev watched the expression on Benny's face. It looked like she was the one who'd been slapped. 'How do you think,' she asked, 'they knew we were here?'

It had been the first time Bernice had seen Jason since her crash. He looked like he'd put on a few pounds. His uniform suited him. Horribly.

She found that her hands were shaking around the cup she was holding. And it wasn't just because of three nights without sleep and what those assembled in her rooms were saying to her. Or rather at her. This was supposed to be a lunchtime civic meeting about the rebuilding of the academic quarters. That was the cover.

But it was swiftly turning into a lynching.

'Vosta hasn't come out of his rooms since then,' Bev was saying. 'They let him go with a warning. Like all those who were caught that night. But it's like the reality of the situation has dawned on some of us. Our numbers are fewer now.'

There was no Ms Jones for a start. Only half of those who'd been there that night had come.

'Some of us have been arrested,' Oliver Norman reported. He was one of Bernice's students, but he wasn't looking her in the eye. 'Felix Johansen was while liberating some explosives from the construction shed. They were waiting. Only we knew about that.'

'You think it's to do with Jason,' Benny spoke up. 'To do with me and Jason.'

Bev took a deep breath. 'This always happens early on in the life of resistance cells. Before they really know each other. I think one of us is a traitor.'

Bernice found the appropriate authorities, and asked for permission to visit Brax. To her surprise, it was quite freely given. There was a search on the way in, the guards tapping her ribs with their sticks so hard they left bruises.

Benny entered to find him walking straight over to her, clasping her hands. Joseph had been wrong, then. He had changed. There was no distance from Brax now. He had been proved fallible, if not human.

'Bernice,' he said. 'This can't be happening.'

'No,' she shook her head. 'It's not.'

'In that case,' he said, gesturing to two armchairs. 'Let's have tea.'

At first Benny had felt self-conscious sitting drinking from an antique, probably priceless, china cup with a guard standing watching. Braxiatel was more at ease: after all, there was always a guard watching him. Over time it got easier. Benny tried to have coded conversations and drop subtle hints into the small-talk. But for the most part Braxiatel seemed to ignore them, or shook his head almost imperceptibly.

'And how's Joseph been?' he asked suddenly. 'You said he was playing up. Causing problems.'

'Oh, right. Yes. Much better, thank you,' she hazarded. The guard was taking no interest.

'But still problems, yes?' Somehow Braxiatel's eyebrows implied the correct answer.

'Oh yes,' Benny agreed, sipping furiously at her tea. 'Problems. I'll say. Tell me about it.' She forced a laugh.

At once Brax seemed at ease again, leaning back in his chair. 'Is there a problem with him right now?'

'Oh yes, I'll be trying to get him to do what I want as soon as I get back.'

Brax nodded.

Benny knew she had a channel of communication, but she needed something from him now that that channel couldn't give: actual, physical, support. 'Other people feel I've betrayed...' She had a form of words sorted out. Their trust in me. Over something academic.

'Never,' Brax cut in. And the look in his eyes gave her everything she needed. For now.

They were interrupted by a knock on the door.

Braxiatel sighed. 'I don't know why they bother,' he told Benny. Then louder, he called: 'Busy. Go away.'

The door opened to admit an Axis Officer, immaculate in his uniform. He had a small scar through his left eyebrow and perfect teeth. Benny recognised him as the current highest authority on the Planetoid, the officer who was always on the telecasts, but not offering himself as a leader. He was waiting for someone more senior.

Braxiatel gave Benny a 'see what I mean' look, and slumped back in his chair. 'Security Officer Klarzen, how nice.'

'Braxiatel.'

'I do wonder though, whether you have to knock in that rather Wagnerian manner? I imagine you are no stranger to just barging in when the mood takes you.'

Klarzen smiled thinly. 'I like to maintain a level of civility.'

He was looking at her with a great deal of interest. Bernice got to her feet, realising her time with Brax was over. 'I'll see you soon,' she told Brax, and leaned over to kiss him on the cheek. 'I'm sure you two have lots to talk about.'

'Well,' Braxiatel replied, 'one of us has. Klarzen will ask me where I've hidden something he wants, and I shall reply that I'm not going to tell him. We vary it a bit of course, but that's the gist.'

Klarzen shifted uncomfortably. 'You simplify things.'

'Oh I do indeed. There's so much that we leave unspoken, isn't there? Like the fact that you don't want it for yourself, or even really know what you are asking for. Like the fact that at some point whoever really wants it will get impatient and we shall drop even the pretence of civility. Like the fact that everything will change when Marshal Anson gets here. Like the fact that you think I don't know your men are opening up the Little Trianon because you think there's something you want in there.'

Benny was level with Klarzen as he caught his breath. She paused to watch his face deepen in colour.

'Don't look so surprised,' she told him. 'You can see the Small Trianon from Brax's bedroom window.' She raised her eyebrows and pursed her lips. 'Or so I believe.'

'Benny.' There was a hint of warning in Braxiatel's voice. 'See you soon.'

Nobody called it a trial. It was held in Vosta's rooms. He had called on everyone the previous day, bearing liquor, proudly displaying his facial bruises. He was determined, he said, to be part of the resistance once more.

Benny watched is if through a haze. She had to admit, as she heard more and more about Jason arriving with Axis guards at one arrest after another, that she was in the frame for this one. And then there came the killing blow.

'I told only Bernice about a second attempt to acquire explosives,' said Ashley Lawrence, a metaphysics student. 'There never was any such mission. But her old lover and the guards appeared at the site at the specified place and time.'

Bernice remembered the occasion. She had guessed what the information might have been for. It had been whispered to her in the market again. She had just nodded, dumbly, aware of the air from the axe on her neck.

They all looked at her now, some of them shifting awkwardly in their seats, some of them quite comfortable. Mister Crofton wasn't moving, for a start. His old eyes were fixed on her.

'I didn't do it,' Bernice said. 'But I see you can't believe that. What are you going to do to me?'

Bev got to her feet. 'This has to be now. There's no question of you being bugged. We've run all manner of sensors over you. I don't know why you haven't turned us all in. Perhaps you're playing favourites, perhaps you're seeing how far this will take you –'

'Perhaps I'm innocent!'

'So all the others should leave, and then I'm going to set up a suicide for you. Make it look like an accident. If you've still got any loyalty to the cause, you could write us a note...'

'No,' said Ashley. 'She could use code.'

'You're right,' Bev ran a hand through her hair. 'God help us, we haven't had to think about anything like this before.'

Bernice had found her eyes wandering the room, finding a print on the wall. That great wave breaking off Japan. She felt not threatened at all. The words were delivered so quietly. She felt like she'd been stunned on the way to the slaughterhouse.

Then she thought of Peter, and found the fear in her head that had been in her stomach all this time. She got to her feet.

Bev saw the look in her eyes and went for her.

The impact pinned Bernice to the ground. She tried to scream something, but suddenly they were all on her. Fingers pulled at her clothes and face. They were scuffling with her in silence, trying to take their rage out on her without making a noise. It felt horribly playground. There were fingers of her friends in her eyes –

Vosta pulled them off her with shouted words. He grabbed her and pulled her to her feet, sobbing, stumbling in his arms. 'Leave her alone! It isn't her! It can't be!' He looked into her eyes. 'God, I look at her and I know it can't be! How can we lose that?! Look at what they've done to us!'

They let her go.

She had been planning to tell them the contents of Brax's message, the one she'd received via Joseph after she'd sent the robot to go and see Brax that night.

But now she thought it wouldn't be safe to tell them. And now, damn it, she just didn't want to.

She had terrible suspicions of her own.

Which was why she found Vosta in the market the next morning, held him and thanked him profusely for her life, and then whispered to him something only she now knew.

'What?!' he said. 'It exists? It's here? In the Small Trianon all this time and Brax never told anyone?'

'Look, the Oracle of the Lost predicts the future. That's what Brax was trying to tell me the other day, only I thought he was on about something else. But anyway, you lot, the Resistance, whatever they're called, have to stop the Axis getting advance information from the Oracle. If they can ask the right questions, they could conquer everything, rule forever. That might even be how they're getting their information about your group.'

'We have to destroy it,' Vosta said. 'I'll let them know. But I won't say where I got this information. Thank you.'

Bernice watched him go. The poor man trusted her completely.

The ruins of the ancient temple were enclosed and hidden within the Small Trianon. Until the Axis had blown open the sealed doors. Bev could just make out the huge seated figure, apparently watching her and her team. The figure said nothing, but Bev had learned that when it did speak it would only be in answer – albeit cryptic answer – to a question, and that its voice would be sweet as honey, lilting and musical.

'I'm sorry,' she said quietly as they laid the charges round the base of the huge carved chair. And it seemed to her that the Oracle smiled sadly and inclined her head.

'What do you think you are doing?!' The words echoed round the huge space. At the same moment massive arc lights came on, flooding the temple with light. Braxiatel was standing in the centre of the building. Behind him was Klarzen and a group of Axis guards.

Braxiatel's voice was shaking with anger. 'Pirates! Vandals! How dare you?!'

But his voice was soon drowned out in an exchange of gunfire. Guards and resistors fell, blood splattering the temple.

Bev sprinted for the roof, and leapt into the darkness.

She hit tree branches, then the ground.

And found that she had the freedom to run off into the night.

She hit the activator button in her pocket as she ran. But they'd already cut the link to the charges.

Bernice stood apart from Bev's group in the Square. Klarzen stood behind Braxiatel, who'd been given leave for the day to address them all via a microphone that had been erected on a rough stage. Everyone on the Collection had been ordered to attend. Every human, that seemed to mean. The Square was full to bursting, other people crowding in with guards at their backs on the avenues that led to it.

Brax tapped the mike, then blew into it. 'There seems to be some interference,' he muttered. He looked back to Klarzen. 'Is there some sort of electronic field operating here?'

Klarzen looked steadily back at him.

Brax shrugged and turned back to the mike. 'Nothing justifies this outrage,' he told the audience. 'Nothing justifies damage to a valuable historical artefact. No matter how much you might think the powers of the Oracle are of use to the Axis, no matter how much you might believe in what you are doing, it is not worth the destruction of something this historically important.' His voice rose still further. 'I will do whatever it takes to preserve the Oracle.'

The next day, she saw Brax again in his rooms. The first thing he did was wink at her. He never did that.

She couldn't ask him about it. There was no guard with them now.

Brax went to where the guard had always stood previously, and winked at her again. 'As above, so below.' He picked up the tea tray and brought it back to their chairs.

By which he meant, she was sure, that they were still under surveillance. And perhaps, taking his words from the podium into account...

'I thought it was Vosta,' she said, sitting down. 'The author of this text we've been talking about.'

'The author of much good work. Not that one.' He was about to say more, but the doors suddenly crashed open.

In strode Klarzen, laughing. 'Very emphatic,' he said. 'That speech of yours yesterday. Very persuasive.' He stopped and leaned on the back of Bernice's chair, his attention focussed on Brax. 'Our scientific team has been testing the Oracle for several days now. Feeding it questions and recording the answers. These answers are then analysed so as to determine their veracity and utility. Of course the questions are controlled, but even so we have to wait a while for the predictions to come true.' He met Braxiatel's level gaze. 'Or not. And just now I was given a full report on the usefulness of this archaeological marvel. Or whatever it really is.'

'What do you mean?' Benny said.

Braxiatel shook his head. 'He doesn't appreciate the unique qualities of the Oracle, doesn't realise what he has there.'

'You think so?' Klarzen's smile was deeper than before. 'The report shows that the Oracle is useless. She predicts nothing. The answers are random. Or rather...' He walked round the chair and took Braxiatel's chin in his hand, turning his head so Brax was forced to look at him. 'Or rather, the answers to some questions are quite carefully phrased to endanger future Axis plans and strategies. Almost as if this "archaeological marvel" was setting us up.' He peered closely into Braxiatel's face. 'Where is it?' he snapped.

Brax didn't tell them, but they found it anyway: winking lights, circuitry, micro-processors. Concealed in the leg of the 'Oracle'.

'I set the Oracle up to lead them astray,' Braxiatel told Benny and Klarzen, later that day. 'To feed them false information, deceive them...'

'But...' Benny looked at him. 'But she told the future. I know she did. She told *me*. All that time ago.'

'No. It was a trick. It was always a trick. I knew that one day...' Braxiatel sighed. 'But it's over now. I thought that if you and the others really believed, then it might work. But Klarzen was too clever for me.' He turned to face the soldier, his shoulders bowed in defeat. 'What will you do? Destroy it?'

Klarzen shook his head. 'I think not. I shall seal the building up again and leave it there. So you will always know that I defeated you. Every time you see the Small Trianon from your bedroom window you will be forced to remember.'

He laughed again, and it was not a pleasant sound.

They asked her back to one of the lunchtime meetings. A smaller gathering. Vosta and Bev and a handful of helpers.

Bev embraced her. Bernice made herself not push her away. There were many words of apology. But when Bernice saw Vosta, she couldn't find it in her to apologise to him in turn.

Not that he seemed to have thought about why she had told him alone her privileged information. 'It's a planetary sensor net,' he said. 'They can listen and watch almost every corner. As Brax indicated. It came fully online just the other day. It relies on human operators, so Bev managed to escape from the Oracle in the darkness. But there are gaps created simply by the laws of physics. Including, fortunately, these rooms. There are others. I will work on this.'

Bev put a hand to her eyes. 'Those who got arrested gave themselves or each other away,' she said. 'We've been working back through everything that was said and where. We think they now have everyone they're going to get.'

'Unless those arrested crack under torture,' said Oliver.

'And they don't have much if they do,' Bev finished. 'Some names, grounds for suspicion. And I suspect they have that about us already.'

Bernice nodded numbly. And then asked about where in her own rooms was safe from the sensor net.

She got Joseph to run her a bath that night. And had him stick around while she splashed loudly.

'You were gone quite a long time when I sent you to see Brax that night,' she said. 'Did he get you to do anything else?'

'Indeed,' replied the Porter. 'I was told to make myself useful before the Axis sensor net rendered me redundant. I accessed the Axis database and changed the results of the probability tests concerning the Oracle. I also entered the Oracle itself and...'

'I can guess. So the Oracle of the Lost remains an incredibly powerful, sentient, predictor of future events that should on no account be allowed to fall into enemy hands?'

'Which, as I believe he told everyone, Mr Braxiatel will do whatever it takes to preserve,' replied Joseph.

'Erase your database on the subject of what happened that night, Joseph,' said Benny. 'Erase every moment.'

And she sunk under, thinking about her comrades of the Occupation as the water closed over her head. Of what sort of suicide Bev might have had in mind for her.

Joseph made a small noise indicating that he had forgotten it all. If only it was as easy for her.

# 3: The Birthday Party
## By Simon Guerrier

Benny scrutinised the mirror. Women have been doing this for thousands of years, she thought. And it doesn't get any easier. Shit. She should have bought something, or at least gone for a look. And somehow she had ended up in black again. Only this time it wasn't for stealth. Was black too boring? Or too morbid? Did she look too tarty, showing her shoulders? What would other people be wearing? When was the last time she had had a night out? She decided to keep the black in the end. It suited what was inside.

It only made things worse that the party had been organised at the last minute. Anyway, circumstances didn't make shopping trips a priority. No, there were few excuses for dressing up these days.

And nor did it help, of course, that the birthday boy was dead.

This new Marshal, Mushtaq Anson, had taken an office in what used to be the Collection's administrative wing. Only Braxiatel would have given what was essentially a team of filers, appointment-makers and accountants such elegant furnishings, and there was no doubt why the man had wanted his office amongst them.

Benny had waited for him under a Masaccio fresco, painstakingly restored from scattered fragments and dust after a Florentine earthquake had destroyed the original. The chaise longue she sat on had been chosen specifically to offset the fresco, the gilt in the wood and the colours in the fabric exquisitely matching Masaccio's palette. Even the coffee table made a neat, if anachronistic comparison. This mix-and-match history was entirely Brax's style. She was surprised that under the new regime the pieces hadn't been separated.

'Originally a bedside table,' said a good-looking man who had crept up on her, 'for the Kreaqpolt's retreat on Europa.' He was dressed in the stark uniform of the Axis, the coloured dots and dashes on his breast declaring his seniority. Goddess, he looked good. Dangerously so. He was only slightly taller than she was, with dark skin and darker eyes, his hair a mature play on what might have been a youthful roguish quiff. He held out his hand. 'Mushtaq Anson,' he said. 'You must be Ms Summerfield.'

Benny stood, took his hand and shook it firmly. '*Professor*, actually,' she said. 'But, yes.'

Anson pulled a face, all horror. 'I do apologise, Professor Summerfield. I really should have checked that. What can I do for you? Shall we sit down?'

When she had seated herself, he plumped down into the armchair opposite. One of the admin robots wheeled over and took an order for tea. Benny had never seen the machines so diffident, so polite. Normally any request for references took weeks. Had they been reprogrammed? Were they *scared*?

Benny fished in her bag and produced the papers. 'I've come about Oliver Norman,' she said.

Anson didn't seem to recognise the name. Was that an act?

'He was shot last week,' she went on. 'He was one of my students, so I'm responsible for the paperwork. But none of your lot will tell me why he was killed and I can't get his Jay-one-one-eight signed.'

Anson looked over the papers. 'I can get this arranged for you,' he said, matter-of-factly. 'Ah, here's our tea.'

The robot had everything on a finely etched silver tray. Benny took a biscuit, and when the robot had gone she asked the question.

'So you can tell me *why* Oliver was shot?'

'I can get the Jay-one-one-eight signed,' he said, not unkindly. 'Don't worry any more about it.' He sipped his tea.

'And the funeral?' asked Benny, keeping conversational. If she pushed him, he might well have *her* executed. 'Can that go ahead?'

Anson peered at her over his tea cup. 'The funeral?'

'You've not allowed a funeral for Oliver because the forms aren't signed. A lot of people would like to say goodbye.'

Anson shook his head, as if answering a child. 'Professor, the boy was executed, therefore he must have been a criminal.' A hardness crept into his tone. 'You know the law. Criminals forfeit their rights to... the usual social niceties.'

Benny dunked half a biscuit into her tea, as casually as she could. 'So what did he actually do?'

He glanced down, furtively, before discipline overcame this involuntary confession. He looked up at her, held her gaze. 'I obviously don't have that information to hand.'

'Are there that many executions?' Benny asked, eager to sound awed. She almost had him.

'There's been very little lawlessness over all. But there have been some unfortunate characters who –'

'But you said you didn't recognise Oliver's name,' said Benny. 'And yet you signed the docket refusing the funeral yourself, Marshal. So you must have –'

Anson held up his free hand. He leant forward in his seat conspiratorially. 'Professor Summerfield,' he said. 'Oliver Norman was executed as a criminal. That is all you need concern yourself with. I advise you to drop this. Disturbing the status quo is also, as I'm sure you're well

aware, a criminal offence.'
He sat back and calmly finished his tea.

She could have done with some time to compose herself, go over all that was said. Especially before having to face Luke. But as Benny left the building, she found him waiting for her.

With his wispy beard and pale complexion, Luke was now the only student she had left. He had been a quiet, back-of-the-class sort, only doing Applied History because his wealthy Ma and Pa had made him, on attachment to the Collection to further his studies. He had expressed nothing but indifference for the Collection in all the time he had been there, and made no secret of his longing for the end of the placement. Now things had changed. Maybe it was just the Axis extending his stay that he really resented. But since Benny's three non-human students had been taken away, he had become possessed, openly discussing his ideas to bring the Axis down. And now Oliver was dead.

'You saw him?' Luke asked.

'Yes,' said Benny. 'He didn't have anything to say.'

'He didn't know anything?'

'He didn't say anything. I couldn't push him, Luke.'

'You did ask him about the rumours, though?' he said.

'Luke, I couldn't confront him. What was I going to say? Do you think Anson would say so to me, if Oliver really had been having an affair with one of the sentries? Or dealing drugs? Do you? He threatened me enough, just for asking about the form.'

Luke shook his head in despair. 'They've killed another one, Benny.'

'What? Who?'

'I don't know who she was. I don't think she even knew Oliver, not when he was alive. They caught her out after curfew, and she'd sprayed "Olly lives!" on the wall of one of the Stewart buildings. Shot through the head.'

'It's getting worse,' said Benny.

'And they still dare to claim the moral high ground!' Luke took Benny by the hand. His palms were clammy and he couldn't keep still. 'There's going to be a party, Professor,' he told her. 'For Oliver. It's his birthday soon...'

Benny pulled away. She hadn't seen any of the Resistance since the matter of the Oracle. Unless Brax counted, and she didn't think he did. 'They'll *kill* you, all of you. Don't you understand that?'

Luke's whole body sagged. 'I thought you'd be better than this. You were his tutor. We have to do *something!*'

Benny nodded. 'We will do something,' she said.

\* \* \*

They had tea again under the Masaccio. Anson declined to see her again at first, but she made her reasons plain in an email, and he found ten minutes he could spare. The admin robot didn't need asking this time, and brought the tea over as soon as they sat down. The biscuits were better, too. Maybe Anson had had words.

'You said, Professor, that you didn't want more people killed. Perhaps you'd like to explain that remark to me.'

'Three people have now been shot just for mentioning Oliver Norman's name.'

'He turns out to have been a revolutionary,' Anson said, sadly. 'It's unfortunate. We're endeavouring to round up his accomplices.'

Benny took a deep breath. They weren't. Not the right ones, anyway. But she couldn't say that. 'You don't really believe that.'

'Oh don't I?' asked Anson, with a disturbing glint in his eye.

'The Axis is keen on the rule of law,' she said. 'It likes everything in its proper place. So if the paperwork isn't being done, something's not right. I've been puzzling it over. I think you made a mistake.'

Anson said nothing, just letting his eyes drift over the beauty around them. Would he shoot her himself?

'Well?' she said, unable to bear the silence.

And then he sighed.

'I've been doing my own homework, Professor, and your reputation doesn't do you justice. It was his earring, apparently. It was unusual, threading through the top of his ear. One of the soldiers made a joke about it. Said it looked "rebellious". Maybe he was just scared. I can see why he might have been. Oliver talked back. You don't know what it's like to be a soldier in an occupying force. Always expecting the worst. You try and keep alert, but you can't stop it getting to you.' He looked away. 'The matter has been dealt with. Internally.'

He had said all he was going to. 'There should be a court martial,' she said.

Anson actually laughed. 'Well, there isn't going to be. Think what that would do to morale.'

'Aren't you meant to be in the right?'

He shook his head, still calm. 'Oh. Easier said than done.'

She hadn't told anyone else. What good would it do? None. Or worse, it could get more people shot, herself included. Instead, she had found Luke and got the details of the party.

The bell rang as Benny slipped into her final choice of shoes. She hurried over to the door, worried she would pay for her decision in days of blisters. Was her hair okay? She hadn't checked. Was this even a good idea?

Sod it, she thought, and opened the door.
'You look beautiful,' said Anson.
'Thank you,' said Benny.
He had brought her flowers.

Some hours later, Benny allowed Anson to lead her on to the makeshift dance floor. She would never have done that were she sober. It had been so long since she had been out drinking, the alcohol probably hit her harder. That's what she'd tell herself afterwards.

Oliver Norman's birthday party had gone ahead, and Anson had even made a singular exception to the curfew. They could all stay out until eleven.

It hadn't made him welcome.

Anson leaned in close, and she turned her head so he couldn't kiss her. But he wanted to talk to her, or that's how he made it seem.

'Are these all Oliver's friends?' he asked.

Benny glanced around. There was nobody there from the Resistance as she knew it now. Just as well. 'I can't believe he knew so many people. But since he died... it's like everyone was friends with him.'

She realised Anson didn't look pleased by this.

'It was the right thing to do,' she told him. 'I think it's been cathartic for them, just to do something.'

'They don't seem best pleased with you, though.'

People watched them. Nobody said anything. No one dared. It was always possible there were other soldiers in the room. You wouldn't recognise them out of uniform. Not yet. The Collection had always been full of strangers.

Had Anson heard what Luke had said about them, over by the drinks table? If he had, Anson hadn't acted on it. Not that she'd seen anyway. Maybe Luke would wake up dead tomorrow. Another criminal. Maybe she would, too. Or worse, she'd be alive, the traitor who sold them all out. By dancing, now.

Anson must have guessed what she was thinking. 'What you've done saved all these people's lives,' he said.

Dancing, she didn't answer.

# 4: Five Dimensional Thinking

## By Nick Wallace

What you don't know can't hurt you, they tell children. Only as a child you never believe it. Because it's almost always what you don't know, what you can't see or understand, that does hurt you.

When I was a child, if Rebecca had ever been naughty, I used to shut her in a closet. Alone in the dark, not knowing. Just because Rebecca was only a doll, it didn't make it any less cruel of a punishment.

Somehow Anson knows about Rebecca.

Braxiatel has been hard to see of late. Anson's arrival seems to have meant an increase in the tempo of his interrogation. When I asked Anson about it, he commented that Braxiatel had been shut away like my doll. The surprise must have shown on my face, because he just laughed and said: 'We know everything about you, Professor Summerfield.'

In contrast to a closet, Brax's confinement is understandable, I suppose, because Irving is the most dangerous man on this rock, just by being that much smarter than anyone else.

It's what we've seen every time Anson's visited Brax in the Mansionhouse. Going in with the confident stride of a man determined; coming out with the look of a cuckolded rhinoceros.

It doesn't take much figuring out. Anson's been trying to take Irving on. Most likely some verbal cat and mouse; figuring Brax out, understanding him. He has, of course, been failing miserably.

But while there's an element of understanding to Brax's absence from our lives, there's also that worry of the unknown. What has been going on with him and Anson? Is he okay? Is he all right?

Of course, by rights, Braxiatel should be fine. Because, like I said, it's what you don't know that hurts you. And Braxiatel knows pretty much everything.

Whatever Anson wants from Braxiatel, though, he isn't getting it. Which is why he's sending me in to talk to him again. It's a seemingly friendly offer and an obvious charade. I know it, and Brax knows it.

But it means I can see him. And straight away, as soon as the door opens, some of that worry evaporates. All those unknown fears of unspeakable tortures and disfigurements come to nothing. His skin is unblemished, his hair unruffled, and all appendages remain utterly attached. You'd never even think he'd had major facial surgery in the last year. The two chairs are where they were last time.

It's a chance for us to share a cup of tea and a gossip, to forget about the bigger unknowns surrounding us. It's what I'm hoping for, it's what I want from Brax, what I need to happen right now. A moment of humanity. But I'm not feeling the love.

Brax smiles when I tell him about Oliver Norman's party.

He smiles, but it's not a good smile. It's the vacant smile of a mind on other things. I soon find out what.

'Marshal Anson,' Brax says, 'is a surprising man.'

'Yes,' I say. 'He compared you to the doll I used to own. The one I used to lock in a closet? That story you swore you'd never repeat to another soul, not ever, not never?'

'Ah,' Brax says.

'Of course,' I continue, 'one of the downsides of a lifetime of alcoholic dissolution is finding I've told *everyone* all the details of my life and then sworn them *all* to secrecy.'

Brax has been looking at me the whole time, keeping the tea a millimetre from his lips.

Then he quickly sips, one hand juddering a little with the saucer. 'He's looking for the time machine he believes I possess.'

We both know there are probably people listening to this. So I carefully spray some Earl Grey across the table, spluttering laughter. 'A time machine?!'

All the time thinking: has he actually got it back? Because if he has, why hasn't he used it? Is it just out of his reach, now he's stuck in here? And there's no way I can ask, because it's suddenly obvious exactly what information Anson was looking for when he sent me in here. He must have looked at the sensor logs from last time I was here and realised there was something he was missing.

'I can't imagine why they think I might have one. Is there anything about me to suggest I might own such a device? I mean, if I did, why don't I own every single *objet d'art* that I ever desired to possess?'

It's very hard not to say that I'd always assumed that was the case.

'It's odd,' says Brax, 'that Marshal Anson should be on this wild goose chase, because otherwise he's a very capable and intelligent man. He led the conquest of Hulzarr Prime, devising the battle plans, implementing the strategy. The planet fell within fourteen hours.'

And then there's a guard at the door, telling me my time's up. They're obviously going to be doing this by degrees. Keep us on our toes.

I'm more worried about him now than I was before.

It's what you don't know that hurts you.

\* \* \*

Wandering back through the grounds, I find a new thing to worry about. Bev Tarrant.

Clipboard in hand, Bev's making notes, peering over her glasses at the fountains and mosaics.

Both glasses and clipboard are new additions. Bev had trouble convincing the guards of her academic credentials (non-existent, of course, but that should never stop you), until she took up glasses and clipboard. Instant intellectual cred, and no more trouble. Degree scrolls offer no validation as strong as a pair of half moon specs.

A casual glance shows her copying mosaics onto graph paper for further study. A less casual glance reveals patrol routes in among the patterns.

'Don't say a word,' Bev warns me. And I don't know if she's speaking about the sensor net or her ability to trust until she walks a few steps and has me follow her.

But I still don't say a word. I stand here, watching, until her jaw sets, mouth disappearing into a straight line. It only takes a bit more watching before Bev snaps. 'Look, we're still active, okay?! The Oracle can't be the end of it! Just because you don't want to know –'

'Didn't say a word.'

'As you may have noticed, I don't do passive resistance very well.'

I nod at the clipboard. 'You'll get yourself killed, and you'll get others killed trying.'

'Look,' Bev hisses, 'you weren't here when they came. You were off adventuring and you weren't here. We had no chance. They were too quick and we were unprepared. We never even got to put up a fight.'

The vehemence stings, but I ignore it. 'And that's what you want, is it? Another fight?'

'Yes. I want a bloody fight. I want to have a proper go and see what these super-confident bastards are made of.' Bev turns a circle, waving her hand at the buildings surrounding the gardens. 'The Collection is all the advantage we need. They haven't got a clue about half the stuff here. The historic weapons, the contemporary weapons, the futuristic weapons, the fish.'

'The fish?'

'The two carp in that fountain over there? They secrete nerve toxins effective on almost all mammalian life-forms. Brax had me collect them from Hulzarr. If we could synthesise some of those toxins and –'

A guard's approaching, so I take Bev's elbow and steer her around, making big, (hopefully) academic-looking gestures at the grounds as I conversationally say: 'The first step to out-fighting these people is out-thinking them. And for that, we need Brax.'

Bev nods impressively at one of my hand gestures. 'So?'

'So Brax is keeping secrets right now.'
Bev shakes her head. 'He'd never collaborate.'
'No,' I agree, 'he wouldn't. What's so bad he won't tell me?'

They let me see him again a couple of days later. There's no tea this time. Anson's guards are searching his rooms again.

Brax doesn't seem interested in talking.

There's half a dozen holograms swarming around him: an opera, a soap opera, a classical romance, a couple of period tragedies, and a boy band. Though I suppose that last could qualify as a period tragedy too. Floating in between the holograms are view-screens, each one showing schematics of battles. Minutes tick over in green, rolling columns of red numbers count the dead.

And slowly turning on the spot in the centre of this cacophony of sound and vision is Braxiatel.

Around him, guards keep on tearing books from shelves, artefacts from the walls, paintings from frames. And somehow Brax keeps all this vandalism out. Instead, his eyes focus on the screens and the holograms, inhaling each and every scrap of detail.

A guard passes, and Brax's hand flicks out, taking a book, flicking to a mid-point. He reads for a half second, then tosses the volume to the floor, and keeps on turning.

'Brax,' I ask, 'what are you doing?'

'Marshal Anson suggested that I revise my opinion of the Axis.'

I look at the view-screens. Ytaxia, Belsas, Hulzarr Prime, the Solar Colonies. The Fifth Axis' sudden sweep across this part of the galaxy.

A guard bumps into me, the ceremonial mace he was carrying slipping from his grasp. I catch it before it hits the ground. The guard takes a long look at me, then vanishes, scurrying away to another room.

Before me, Brax shuts his eyes, and in a voice little more than a whisper, says something. But the hologram of the opera woman has started singing soprano and I don't hear it.

'What?' I ask.

'Do you see it?' He repeats. 'The pattern?'

I tune out the holograms, focus on the view-screens. I'm not a military strategist, but I know a bit. Not enough, though. 'No,' I answer. 'No, I don't. Beyond the aggressors, there don't look to be many commonalties.'

Brax's eyes snap open. 'Precisely. There's no historical context to make any sense of this.'

He snatches the mace from me and swings around, bringing it down on one of the view-screens. Glass shatters, electronics explode in a shower of sparks.

'Brax!' I cry, reaching in to stop him. But he swings around again

'No.' Swing, crash. 'Context.' Thrust, explosion. 'Whatsoever.' Pivot, bang.

He's gone mad. A whirlwind of anger, jacket flapping, hair coming unkempt, eyes unseeing, intent on destruction. View-screens gone, mace slicing through the holograms to their transmitters, destroying them too. The rage begins to drain away, his limbs sag, the violence abates. The opera woman is the last one to be hit. Brax bats the transmitter from the air, and it rolls to a stop by my feet. The music and singing have cut out, but the purple-skinned singer keeps on flickering in and out of existence next to me.

The guards continue their search around us. They've been told to ignore what he does.

Brax sinks to his knees, and only his hold on the mace stops him falling further. I make to help him, but his look stops me dead in my tracks.

'Leave, Benny. Leave now.'

To my shame, I do. I grab the holo-transmitter, and I run.

Braxiatel is cooking the next time I see him. And this time, he is a picture of calm. Pans steaming, lemons sliced, rind grated. And Brax, quietly humming to himself.

They let me in this time to make sure he's as okay as they think he is.

'I hope you don't mind,' I say. 'But I kept the holo-transmitter. I also accessed some of those files you were viewing.'

Brax just waves his hand, idly dismissing my words. 'I should never have reacted that way. Frustration, Bernice. It's poison for an agile mind. Looking for patterns that aren't there.' A sad pause, then he whispers. 'So two-dimensional of me.'

He tastes a finger of sauce, then asks me to pass the salt.

'The thing is,' I say, 'there may *be* a pattern. The Axis, their campaigns. There's very few commonalties. But, work with me here, I think that's the commonality.'

Brax raises an eyebrow and continues stirring.

'I took a long look at it all, and it seems almost... familiar. Like something you or I might have thought of.'

He grunts an ironic laugh.

'Their strategies aren't built around their own philosophies, but those of their opponents. Their histories, their cultures, their weaknesses. Axis forces don't overwhelm their opponents' tactics, they circumvent them.'

Brax keeps silent, and I start looking around for an open bottle of wine, rapidly losing confidence in my theory and hoping to bolster my own confidence with alcohol. The only thing I can find is cooking sherry, and there are limits. 'It's very clever, very psychological. And not remotely the Blitzkrieg you'd expect.'

I'm beginning to understand how my silent treatment unnerved Bev. It's exactly what Braxiatel's doing to me now.

'All of which just seems a bit...'
Brax smiles at me.
'...odd.'
'An interesting theory,' he answers. 'But you've nothing to test it against.' Shaking his head, he returns his attention to the stove. 'You're more like me than you think, Benny. Two-dimensional thinking. Things could still get worse here. You'll need to do better than that.'
There's something in the way he says it. Something so sad.

Five hours later, and it's getting dark, and I've been studying this Hulzarrian opera again. Trying to figure out what it is that's gnawing at Brax. Because when he was watching this thing, just before he went mad, he saw something. I'm sure of it. Something beyond that two-dimensional thinking he was talking about.
And I just can't see it.
It's what you don't know that hurts you.
But Braxiatel knows pretty much everything. He's bigger than we are. He goes beyond two dimensions. Well, beyond three, but you know what I mean.
All I know is that there's a fat opera singer so pissed off with her master's attitude that she's getting ready to kill him, and I'm approaching that same violence threshold Brax passed the other day.
There's a knock at the door.
It's Bev, holding that graph paper and wearing a triumphant smile: 'It worked. I got around the patrols. With that and the sensor log, which is nearly complete, we can beat the curfew. Your whole living space is now off the sensors, by the way. Which is weird. With a bit of time we can gain access to...'
My thoughts don't give me time to tell her I didn't invite her to come here. I snatch the graph paper from her, looking hard at the patterns there. There are patrol routes hidden here, but I'm interested in the wood around the trees. Fountains and Hulzarrian carp.
Because I've figured out what Brax saw in that opera, and a night where we drank until dawn, and what I told him then. And a whole host of other realisations follow on behind those.
'Oh,' I say. 'Oh wank.'

Eyes wide, his hands at his throat, Anson is dying on the floor when I reach the dining room. Bev's map did the trick, getting me through the grounds unnoticed and all the way through the Mansionhouse. But it's too late. Even slow baked in lemon sauce, the Hulzarrian carp still induce an anaphylactic reaction. Anson's airway is contracting, and there's nothing that hand at his throat can do about it.

Brax is seated, a sheen on his forehead. He's got a stronger constitution, but it's only a matter of time before he succumbs. And he's just watching Anson die. He doesn't even jump up in shock when I burst in. He glances at me, then returns his attention to Anson. 'Give me the name.' I get the feeling he's asked that a lot in the last couple of minutes.

'Stop this,' I say.

'Now, wait, Benny,' Brax replies, 'this is important.'

Anson's concentrating, slowing his breathing, trying to delay the reaction. 'They will...' A coarse whisper. 'They'll kill you for this. Kill you all.'

I sink to the floor, cradling Anson, and take hold of his hand and squeeze. Because no one deserves to die without the comfort of a human touch. No matter what the Axis might think about the survival of the fittest.

Ten days ago, we were dancing.

'...kill you...' Anson manages again, eyes fixed on Brax.

'He knows that,' I say to Anson. 'He's counting on it.' And then I look at Brax. 'Aren't you?'

Braxiatel produces a handkerchief, dabs his forehead. 'Please leave.'

'You already know the name, or you think you do. You just want it confirmed.'

'What name do you think it is I know?'

'The person orchestrating the impossible rise of the Axis. Someone with knowledge of temporal mechanics and the ability to plan on this scale. The only person I once told about locking a doll in a closet.' There's a sadness in his eyes; shame and just a hint of pride. 'You already know his name. You think it's you.'

Brax says nothing; a twitch of his lips, then his eyes shy away from mine.

Anson's passed out, and Brax nods at him: 'He led the taking of Hulzarr Prime. If he'd drawn up those battle plans himself, he would have known not to eat the fish. Even after I'd taken the first bite.'

'Because that opera's a cultural archetype on Hulzarr. A commonplace. The fear of the attack from within. The concubine who poisons her master with exactly this sort of fish supper.' I look at the remnants of the meal Brax cooked. 'And this is what you test the theory up against.'

Braxiatel says nothing.

'Five dimensional thinking,' I offer. 'It's not what happened or is happening, but what might be. You think they don't want your time machine for themselves, but to stop you from interfering in your own future. Because your future is tied up with their past.'

'It's the best answer I've been able to come up with.' A hint of the desperation he must be feeling creeps into his voice. 'The only answer that fits. How can they have surprised me when I know the future? How did Jason bring himself to deactivate my booby traps?'

'You don't know Jason.'

'In some ways I know him better than you do. Perhaps I was just careless with him.'

'What?'

'Never mind.' He looks at Anson. 'I had to know.'

'If he dies, you die too.'

'If I am responsible, if I someday travel back to create all this, then everything that's happening now exists in a temporal bubble.'

'And if you die now, the bubble bursts. History reverts to its natural course. I know the theory, but paradoxes aren't always as clever as you think they are.'

'My temporal physiognomy is different to yours; it should survive the collapse. I die in this timeline, I die in that timeline. There's no paradox here.' He mops his forehead again, breathing quicker. 'It's the only answer I have to offer, the only action open to me.'

'And if it's wrong?' I ask. 'Because you're not behind the Axis. The man I know, the man who'd literally kill himself before helping them, couldn't be.'

Brax blinks sweat from his eyes. 'I might be... a different person, then.'

'I've seen that, too, and while some things might change, they mostly stay the same. You're a good man, Irving. Condescending, patronising, frustrated that we don't match up to your expectations. But a good man. We've been through too much, and I know you too well. If you do this, they win.'

Whether it's the carp or my words, there's indecision on Brax's face.

'Five dimensional thinking. Cause and effect. It's not just your "temporal physiognomy" that's different. Your body can cope with extreme trauma and even death. What if *this* is the first step to fulfilling your own prophecy? Premeditated murder just to satisfy your own curiosity.'

The double pulse is beating hard in Brax's throat now. There's only a whisper of air reaching Anson's lungs. I'm running out of time.

'Where's the antidote, Brax?' I demand. 'I know you'll have prepared one. Where is it?'

'I... I don't –'

'He's dying, Irving.'

'I –'

'The antidote. Now.'

Brax shrugs back in his chair, head sinking into his chest. And he waves at the table. 'Angel Delight,' he says. 'The dessert. The antidote is in the Angel Delight.'

It takes a bit of massaging, but I get Anson to swallow some. The effect as it passes through his throat is almost immediate.

Brax has a spoonful in his hand, just studying it. 'Such a simple pleasure,' he offers. 'Milk and a chocolate powder.'

'The simple solutions are often the best ones.'

He nods, and takes a mouthful.

Anson's eyelids are flickering. I haven't got long before he wakes. 'We'll beat them, Irving. We'll figure it out together, and we'll beat them. I promise you.'

Brax nods at Anson. 'What do you think he'll do?'

'He knows you wanted to die, so I doubt he'll oblige.' I shrug my shoulders. 'At a guess, a month of solitary.'

Anson jerks free of my lap, his digestive system finally rejecting the fish in a sloppy pool on the floor.

'A month alone,' I say to Brax. 'Enough time to figure out a way to overthrow an empire of space fascists?'

'Undoubtedly,' Braxiatel replies. And finally, weary though it is, there's a hint of a smile in his eyes. 'But what will I do with the other three weeks?'

# 5: Meanwhile, in a Small Room, a Small Boy...
## By Robert Shearman

...sat waiting.

Sometimes he stood waiting, never slouching, always as if to attention. Sometimes he lay down waiting, though he tended to confine those bits of waiting to his sleeping hours. But as a rule he sat waiting. He found it to be the most comfortable of the positions on offer.

Sometimes he was waiting for food: sometimes breakfast, sometimes lunch, sometimes a cooked evening meal. Sometimes he was waiting for the shadows to creep across the floor of his room, or the little patch of sunlight by the door to blacken and fade and then disappear altogether. (Sometimes he liked to watch the day go by like this, minute by minute, hour by long hour. Sometimes he didn't like it at all, and would shed tears in frustration at its monotony.)

Sometimes he was waiting to find out what mood he was in today: either the sort which likes to watch the sunlight fade, or the sort which sheds tears in frustration. Discovering which one was a genuine surprise, and he treasured it.

Whatever else he was waiting for, there was something else above it all, something that was always on his mind. But the small boy tried hard not to think of it directly. He suspected, with a thrill of superstitious fear, that if he ever waited for it too *obviously*, that if he drew too much attention to it, that it would never happen. That all the other waiting, the superficial waiting, the *practice* waiting, would be in vain. But he couldn't help think of it, once a day, no, be honest, several times a day, he tried hard but couldn't stop himself. He got angry at the injustice of it all, and he bunched his hands into tight fists. He was just a little boy, it was too difficult, how could he *not*, just a little boy, how could he *not* think of her, they said he was a strong boy, they said he was a brave boy, they said he had to be strong *and* brave, his mother had said that, but it was sometimes too much, he couldn't help it, he was waiting, how could he *not*, he was always waiting, waiting for his mother. There, it was out. He was waiting for his mother. Where was she? Be strong, she said, be brave, she said, I'll see you soon, *I'll see you soon.*

In a small room, a small boy was waiting for his mother.

\* \* \*

He realised that this was a day in which he cried with frustration, rather than be bothered with all that sunlight and shadow stuff. He secretly rather preferred the crying-with-frustration days, and was so pleased that he forgot for a whole minute how unhappy he was meant to be.
 When he cried, he made no noise at all. And there was barely a tear to be seen in his eyes. But he knew he was crying, oh yes.
 Outside his room there were two men. He had been told their names, but hadn't even tried to remember them. His brain was far too full already, waiting for things and not thinking about waiting for other things. They were friends of his mother, he knew that, they fed him and kept him well like his mother would, but he could never find any trace of her in their faces or voices, and had long stopped looking for any. One of them always tried to chat to him, make jokes. He said he wanted to be his friend, but he did it so awkwardly it suggested to the boy that this tall man was really rather frightened of him. The other man never said much, did what he had to do, fed him, washed him, whatever, he would always leave as soon as possible. The boy preferred the second man. He was so much less effort.

One of them would bring him breakfast soon. There was a gnawing in the boy's belly which told him so. And the shadows were creeping somewhere near the wardrobe, too.

Since he was thinking about his mother anyway – and he was, he was, there was no point denying it – he decided to play a game. He only played the game on special occasions, which was pretty much whenever he thought of it. He would count how long it took for one of the men to bring him in breakfast. He would count slowly, deliberately, that would be good. And he'd make a bet with himself. If the breakfast arrived before he reached a thousand, he'd see his mother today. He'd see his mother *this very day.*
 He began to count. One, two, three. Slow. Deliberate.
 Come on, he thought. Hurry up with my breakfast.
 Two hundred and sixteen. Two hundred and seventeen.
 He counted silently, watching the numbers in his head pass one by one. So many of them, but slipping past too quickly.
 Five hundred and seven. Five hundred and eight.
 Bring me my breakfast! (I want my mother.) I want my breakfast!
 Seven hundred and eighty-four. Seven hundred and eighty-five.
 Bring it, bring it, bring it, bring it, bring it.
 Eight hundred and ninety-nine. Nine hundred. Oh dear.
 He was tempted to slow down, stop the numbers marching on, give the men outside more time, give his mother more time. But he knew that

would be cheating. And if he cheated, he lost by default.
Breakfast, breakfast, breakfast, oh, mother, mother, *mother*!

When he reached a thousand, he felt a pang of disappointment. So she wouldn't come today after all. She might have been on her way, she might have been outside the room that very moment, about to turn the doorknob and come in, come in to hug him and take him away. But because of the gamble he'd made, she would now turn around and go back to where she'd come from. He carried on counting anyway. It seemed silly to stop now. On two thousand three hundred and eleven the door opened and the breakfast arrived. He saw it was the man who tried to be chatty, and his heart sank that smidgen lower.

'Good morning, Peter, good morning, how are you today? Did you sleep well? I have your breakfast. Doesn't it look nice?'

It didn't particularly. The boy wondered why the man always used to bombard him with questions he had no intention of answering.

'What are you going to do today? Are you going to play with your toys?'

Something like a shrug.

'You know, Peter. I've been thinking.' The man's voice dipped almost an entire octave in concern. 'Well, not just me, we've both been thinking, ha ha, we both have!' Another joke, the boy didn't get it. 'It's really not healthy for you to spend so much time in this room. Why don't you come out into the rest of the house?' The boy saw spittle on the nervous man's lips. 'It's perfectly safe. So long as we don't go outside.' The spittle wobbled as it hung there. The boy waited for it to fall off. 'You should have more...' Going... '...than these four walls...' Going... '...to look at.' Gone! Hurrah!

But it was *his* room. It was his. And they couldn't take it away from him. They had taken so much else, but not this.

The man seemed unhappy. He was already backing out of the room, as if frightened the boy would chase after and bite him. 'Well, it's up to you.' The boy watched him wring his hands. 'It's up to you, of course.' The boy wondered whether the two men made bets with themselves, too, playing for which one got stuck with bringing his breakfast. He wondered whether this frightened, door-backing, hand-wringing spittle-forming man had lost this morning. 'Up to you. You play with your toys instead.' And he was gone.

The boy had been smuggled away so hastily there hadn't been time for him to select any toys. Instead, the adults had plonked into his arms a random assortment, kissed him on the cheek, and off he went. He wanted to tell them these weren't his favourite toys, not a single one of them – but they all looked so close to tears already and he didn't want to make them even more unhappy. Now in his room, worlds away from his mother, he couldn't remember what his favourite toys actually were, but he held a certain resentment towards the second rate ones he'd been left to make do with.

There was a red rubber ball, but it didn't bounce very high. The boy was young, but astute enough to realise that there was nothing in the world more useless than a ball without much bounce to it. Sometimes he'd roll it along the floor listlessly. Sometimes he'd roll it through his breakfast. But he'd never try to bounce it. What was the point?

There was a board game, snakes and ladders. A wooden board marked with a hundred squares, complete with dice. In the early days the boy had played this quite a lot, sometimes even with the men outside the room. But they hadn't worked out what the point of the game was. They had always tried to reach one hundred, whereas the boy knew if you kept sliding down the snakes you need never reach the end, you could go on and on forever. One day the boy realised it didn't matter whether you were trying to reach one hundred or trying to avoid it, the dice would take you there eventually all the same. You had no choice about what happened to you. And in despair he hadn't touched the game since.

He had more important games to play now. Games with consequences. Games that would decide his destiny, and the destiny of his missing, much-missed mother.

He looked at the porridge without enthusiasm. He had tried using it in the games once: his mother would come for him so long as he never ate again. This had greatly alarmed the men outside the room, and for a while after he lost that game he also lost his privacy, one or the other standing over him as he chewed and swallowed what they brought him. No, better he should eat it. It would give him the added strength needed for him to win the next game he'd play. He decided what it would be as the tasteless paste went down his throat.

He'd hold his breath. If he could hold it until he reached a thousand, then his mother would come. Not today, that was already forfeit. But soon. This week. She'd come this week. He vaguely wondered whether not breathing for a count of a thousand would kill him, and decided he'd do it for nine hundred instead.

It was easy to begin with. He took a deep breath, and puffed out his cheeks with all the air he could find. He counted in his head as his mouth clamped tightly shut.

His lungs began to ache. Or perhaps he just imagined his lungs were aching. He wondered if he was turning red, and, if he were, whether he was brighter than the rubber ball. He began to feel sick, then, curiously, to feel nothing at all.

He wasn't at a hundred and fifty yet! He couldn't stop. Wouldn't stop.

Did stop, though. His mouth popped open, against all his firmest instructions, and he took in a whoosh of air, panting, coughing.

He'd failed again. He'd doomed himself to at least another seven days in this room, waiting for all the little somethings and the Big Something. In anger he kicked over his porridge bowl, then he kicked over his toys, then he kicked the bowl again, just for good measure. Outside the room the chatty man dithered whether to go inside or not, before deciding that discretion was the better part of valour. As the boy kicked, the wooden dice spun across the room, hit the wall, and fell on to the floor.

The boy stopped dead. He looked at it, walked over to it. Then without thinking, he snatched it up into his hot, angry little fist.

Right, he thought. Right. One more game. Just one more. I shall try to throw a six. No, I shall try to throw three sixes, one after the other. And if I do, then my mother shall come for me, this cancels out all the other games, she'll be here before I know it, she'll hold me in her arms and I'll be safe. And if I fail. If I fail. If the dice shows anything else. Even two sixes and a five... Then she's dead.

He felt numb. But continued.

Yes, she'll be dead. That's right. You'll never see her again. Not ever, no way. And she never loved you at all, or else why does she leave you with these men, one who smiles too much, one who doesn't smile at all, she put you in a world of finding patches of sunlight and tasteless porridge and balls that don't bounce. If you don't throw three sixes, and *throw them right now*, she's dead and nothing and she *hated* you. And the war that the men outside speak about in such hushed voices, they think you won't hear but you do, you *do*, the war will be lost and everything will be lost and you, you, Peter Summerfield, you will be lost forever.

Oddly calm, in spite of what's at stake – perhaps because of it – the boy stands up. He doesn't slouch, he stands as if to attention. This is important. And he throws the dice.

It is a six.

He lets out a huge sigh. He's not sure whether it's relief or not. He'd thrown it defiantly, as if to show he didn't care, but he did care, didn't he? He must have done, because look at him now, the sigh winds him, and he has to get his breath back before he can pick up the dice again.

Second throw. Six, six, six. Come on. Six, six, six.

It leaves his hand. And as it does, the boy realises he should have given it one more shake. Another one for luck, for his mother's sake, for his own. He tries to catch it, take it back again, but it's too late. The dice hits the floor.

It is a six.

Peter's head spins. He feels nauseous, and he realises that the porridge did have a taste after all, his mouth is full of it, and all the swallowing in the world won't change matters. He thinks for a moment he might black out, but he has no such luck, he *has* to bend down, he *has* to pick up the wooden cube, he *has* to straighten up again.

He now knows without question it's not a game any more. This throw of the dice will decide the lives of countless people. It's no longer just about himself.

And for just a moment, he hates his mother. It's just a brief flash of anger, but it happened, he can't undo it. He hates her for making this his responsibility. He hates her that she's made him grow up too fast, too soon. And although he wouldn't be able to find the words for it, he understands that he'll never quite trust her the same way again. If he sees her again – he will, he *will*, throw the six and see! – he'll love her, of course he will. But never as unhesitatingly, there will always be that moment of hatred getting in the way. He bites his lip and tastes blood. He is crying, and this time the tears are wet, his cheeks are wet, it's all wet. He's changed irrevocably, become a different person. And his mother wasn't there to see it happen.

Hardly knowing what he's doing, his fingers let go of the dice. It makes no more noise as it clatters to the floor than it did before, indeed, it possibly makes less, because it's thrown with such little force. But at that very moment Peter catches his breath, and the sound of wooden dice striking wooden floor is all he can hear.

Is she alive or dead? Did she ever really love him?

The dice has the answer. He backs away from it. He doesn't have to see. It's all decided now. It's either a six or it isn't. But he doesn't have to know what he's done. Whether he's saved her or killed her, he's only a little boy!

He sits on the floor, at a distance from it, and turns away. He dries his eyes, he dries his cheeks. At some point one of the men will come in. They'll clear up after him, as they always do. They'll put his toys away. And he'll never find out what the dice said. So long as he doesn't give in to temptation, and go to look. So long as he sits here, nice and still, and doesn't move until it's safe.

He waits for someone to come in.

In a small room, a small boy sits waiting.

# Lockdown Conversations: 1
## By Paul Cornell

She let them back into her rooms in the end because she needed someone to talk to. About everything, not just the limited subjects she could discuss with Brax or Anson or the hesitant crowds who returned to the cafés. The two of them brought sleeping mats and stayed after curfew.

It was her first real encounter with Jason that she mainly needed to talk to them about. She'd made an effort to start some work, had taken a pad out into the park.

She'd found Jason directing a work party of aliens, Thoolmids, ploughing up a specific area of parkland and planting seeds. She watched him from a distance for a while. He was definitely getting heavier. He directed the Thoolmids without rancour, but without kindness. There was an offhand distance between them. He could never be like them, simply didn't understand how heavy that plough was for them.

And this while he thought he was unobserved.

He saw her after a while, and to her horror, came over.

'I'm sorry I haven't seen you, Benny,' he said, and his voice was just the same, his smile just the same. 'I've been really busy.'

'I noticed. The fascist thing.'

He inclined his head. 'People don't understand. This is just a glitch in history. After a bit, the rest of the universe will see through all that.'

Bernice had made quick excuses and left. And had been upset all afternoon. And had finally decided she needed to talk about it.

'He was in the sensor net,' said Bev.

'I know, but...' Bernice took Wolsey into her arms. 'I could just see it in his face. He has a home now. He's like all of them, solved by the Fifth Axis. It makes sense for him.'

'Dangerous,' said Vosta. 'I've been reading the histories. They arose out of an anti-globalisation movement on one of Earth's older colonies. One global market, of course, the usual galactic liberal economics has that as a socialist ideal, because no matter what expansive imperial power creates such a market, they find themselves generating true democracy, an end to planetary currency, and low level world government as emergent properties. But to the Fifth Axis, that was anathema. They persist with trade barriers and tariffs even amongst systems they've completely conquered. They preach what we'd see as failed globalisation as a positive force, a way to keep humans competing with each other, because only in competition do we find satisfaction.'

'I see their point,' murmured Bev. 'Kind of.'

'And unlike the Nazi party, in which the cult of a single charismatic leader made every drone want to be special, and thus the system was rife with egotism and corruption, the Axis have deeply reasonable support systems. Their leader, Gator, is avowedly a figurehead, their third one, whose term will be up next year. His successor will be appointed by a vote amongst "qualified" Axis staff. There's the reward for working hard and knowing your place.'

'And this is all that it took?' Benny asked. 'One day they're a tiny political movement, the next an invading force that hijacks a few worlds and gets kicked out, and then suddenly... woosh! They're conquering a spiral arm and breaking the historical rules of the universe?'

'No.' Bev shook her head. 'There's something else there. They keep it hidden, but there are some instances of technology far in advance of what they should have.'

'They don't like time research, for one thing,' added Vosta. 'They tend to grab it and swallow it up. And that sensor net was better than it should be. And look at this.' He brought up a map of the Collection on his pad. 'Under one of the old accommodation blocks, they're building something. The sensor net is perfect around it. It's some sort of control centre. Quite small. Lots of antennae on top. If there's a place where Anson gets his orders from on high... that'll be it.'

Bernice looked at the map for a moment and found that her eyes hurt. 'Well,' she said. 'Good luck with all your plans.'

'*Our* plans?' asked Bev.

Benny nodded.

'You and I both have an associate who sorts this kind of thing out.'

'But I don't have any way of contacting him, and neither do you, and if Brax could have, I'm sure he would. So I don't find his continuing existence a reason to join the Resistance. Goddess, that's almost the first line of a musical.'

'This is because of Peter, isn't it? You're still in mourning.'

Bernice had still not told them. Had made sure the Gemayals didn't in one of her random encounters with them in the cafés of the Collection. Though it hurt like hell every day, she was not going to let anything get out about her child.

So she nodded. And didn't add that she still sometimes felt the fingers of the Resistance in her face.

Vosta sighed and picked up his glass. 'To good,' he said. 'As opposed to evil. We all know where the difference lies.'

'To someone to save us,' said Bev. 'And in the meantime to us saving ourselves.'

'To life,' said Bernice, quietly. 'Long may it continue.'

# 6: The Price of Everything
## By Gregg Smith

Throughout the many space wars, there have been two constants of humanity's inter-stellar age: commerce and tourism. These two abide because almost all intelligent species, and all human factions, observe the rule of free ports. *You* may well be forbidden from travelling to Axis worlds, but, for now, you can still travel through Axis space, and utilise orbitals designated as free ports.

Abadron is one such port, orbiting a world of the same name, in a system on the traditional border between two territorial blocks. Spinward from this system, the recently conquered Astral Hellenic Alliance is now part of the Occupied Territories of the Fifth Axis; towards the Galactic core lies an expanse of space that Earth seized from the Tilda-Grant corporation a decade ago.

Though now under its ownership, the Axis' recent arrival has had little effect on the running of Abadron. It takes a share of the profits, an occasional look at the travel records, but the staff has been left largely unmolested. Few workers have tried to seek employment away from this busy travel hub.

Lounge 12B, on a pylon extending from the anterial quarter of the station, has the same dark blue décor as the main concourse and waiting zones, though not the bright white murals. It is sterile and impeccable, a waiting area for more exclusive shuttle routes. One of the most exclusive, a journey undertaken by invitation only, is to the planetoid KS-159, terraformed home of the Braxiatel Collection. Only a dozen people are booked on the next flight to KS-159, all approved by the Axis, and only three of them are not partaking of Abadron's various diversions. And only one of those waits here out of choice.

Leo Didas has no interest in the exhibitions or immersion games, no desire to browse in the shops or learn about the various exciting destinations he could visit at half price this week only. He has no taste for the rich food available in Abadron's famous restaurants (some virtually destinations in themselves), nor the gambling opportunities in its sizeable casino (where Irving Braxiatel allegedly won KS-159 at Pontoon).

This man is smartly dressed and carries his five decades sternly. His two escorts, Axis soldiers with broad shoulders, stand on the threshold to the rest of the station, amusing themselves by harassing a family of four Killorans who made the mistake of walking past. They're passing through Axis space. Didas smiles as the parents hustle their crying children away. He smiles even more as he spies the shivering attendant retreat behind a door marked Private.

He stands, alone in the Lounge, and wanders over to a window that looks down onto the docking platform.

'You.' A whisper, but he jumps. He turns to his left. The two Axis guards are still outside, chatting to a girl. He swings round. He is still alone in the lounge. He swings full circle, then he sees it: a movement in the shadows behind the bulkhead, on the right of the window. A blank, humanoid shape steps forward. It must have been there all along.

Before he can speak, he feels a sharp pain in his stomach. He looks. A black blade, extending from the creature's right arm into his gut.

He can't make out any features. He staggers, and then the shadow grabs his shoulder. He blinks, trying to focus on a face or clothes. It has clothes. A dark brown coat, a black tunic and trousers. Those are *his* clothes. He looks at the face. It is fluid, blurred. He blinks. Now it's solid. That's his face, his short grey hair and trimmed grey beard.

His head is throbbing. He squints. Yes, his own face staring back at him, his own blue eyes, looking back in a manner he recognises, a manner he's worked so hard to create.

His body falls limp as this new-made clone drags him into the shadows, reaching for the bio-coded plasti-disc in his pocket.

Benny is dreaming of her fairy godfather, appearing in a cloud to dispense the goblins that had her tied to a stake, and then unfurling his umbrella to protect her from the fiery hailstones, when the crunch of boots on paving stones invades her sleep. She screws her eyes shut against the sunlight. Throwing back her covers, she swings her legs onto the floor. Her right foot splashes into a bowl of warm cereal. It feels quite nice.

'Joseph, I've warned you about this,' she says lightly. With no reply, she concludes he isn't in the room.

She lifts her foot and shakes it, then struggles into something approximating a standing position. She risks opening her eyes again, but it's still too bright. She stumbles forward, blind but knowing exactly what she is stepping on: half a dozen books, a number of periodicals and papers, three dirty plates and a pair of dead gin bottles. After six or seven strides, she puts out her hands. They land gently on the glass of the tall window.

Shielding her eyes with her right hand, she squints at the terrace. Four neat rows of Axis soldiers are square-bashing under a squat, skin-headed drill sergeant. Again. She has mentioned this to Anson. Several times. He must have them doing it on purpose: the best way of making sure she gets up in the morning.

The sergeant barks and the soldiers halt. A couple of boys in the front row catch sight of Benny and grin. She looks down. She is naked, framed by the window. She scowls and snaps the drapes shut.

As she struggles back to bed, she hears the sergeant laying into the two distracted soldiers. She smiles with faint satisfaction, then feels guilty at the thought of the beating they'll get.

She lies back down and closes her eyes. The marching resumes. She stuffs her head under her pillow with a groan. Then her door creaks open, and Joseph floats through with a buzz.

'Good morning, Professor,' he trills.

'Go away.'

'You really must get up.'

'Joseph, how many times do we have to go through this?'

No response. Benny sighs and concentrates on getting back to sleep. Then something prods at her shoulder.

'Bernice.'

'Joseph?'

'Bernice, get up.' It's coming from Joseph, but it isn't his voice.

Benny throws the pillow away. It bounces off the end of the bed as she grabs Joseph.

'Brax, is that you?'

'Yes, of course.'

'Where are you? How did you…?'

'You must listen. I've managed to improve my communications to Joseph. I don't have much time.'

Benny keeps a tight grip on Joseph's small, round shell, as Brax explains.

Though under close guard, he has managed to contact an agent of his, a reliable and resourceful individual, albeit a very eccentric one, with full access to certain of Brax's off-world accounts.

'He is arriving today, disguised as a personal guest of the Marshal. It's something Anson has been trying to set up for a while. I've made it possible. He doesn't know that, of course.'

'Who is this guest?'

'An artist. You must rendezvous with him, show him around the Mansionhouse. He'll know what to look for.' He paused. 'I have to go, they're coming. Good luck, Bernice.'

Joseph beeps a few times, then starts to vibrate in her hands.

'Professor, please let me go.' He squeaks, pushing out of her grip.

Benny washes and dresses hurriedly.

She thinks back to the previous night, remembers dinner with Anson in the Hall of Mirrors. Oysters, gammon, and several bottles of white. Somehow she seems to have become Brax's regent under the Occupation, guardian of the Collection and its staff. Anson is treating her like a trustee, in both senses. After branding her dress morbid and threatening to assign her a maid, Anson had boasted to Benny of his impending guest: the famously reclusive sculptor, Leo Didas.

Renowned as much for his xenophobia as his art, Didas' severe, neo-neo-classical style, patented as *Didasticism*, is perfect for the Axis, and Anson is a particular fan.

Benny had let slip that she had met Didas four years ago, in his Sirius studio. Menlove Stokes, who as always had no concept of how art could have anything to do with such concepts as 'good' or 'bad' (well, 'good', anyway), had been granted a rare opportunity to record the artist at work, and took Benny along. Anson was surprised and delighted. Being one of the few people to have enjoyed the honour of meeting Didas was almost as special as being the man himself. Not that she wasn't special anyway, he told her. And now he was going to meet Didas, and he would be special too. Didas' studio had turned out to be a bare grey room and Benny hadn't warmed to him on any level, but she didn't mention this to Anson.

Freshened and dressed, she rushes through to her study. Through the bay window, she can see three men outside the Reception Area, a shuttle touching down behind them.

The Marshal proffers his hand to Didas as the artist walks through the doors of Reception. A robotic porter trundles behind, balancing a large trunk and two cases, and the escort troopers head for the mess.

'Mushtaq Anson. I'm the Marshal.' Two firm shakes and a brief hold. 'It's a great honour.'

'Yes,' says Didas.

'This is Mickelthwaite, my Aesthetic Attaché. And Jason Kane, our Resources man. He'll make sure you have everything you need.' Anson looks over Didas' shoulder to the porter. 'Take Mr. Didas' luggage to his guest room,' he instructs it.

'Pleased as I am to be working for your noble organisation, Marshal Anson, now that I'm here I would like to know what this commission is for.'

Anson frowns at Mickelthwaite, then turns back to Didas.

'I do apologise. I understood you desired not to know anything about it until you saw the location.'

'Really?' Didas frowns now. 'A breakdown in communication, I suppose. I...'

'Good morning, Marshal Anson,' Benny calls as she jogs up the path towards them. 'Ah, I see your guest has arrived.'

'Of course,' says Anson. 'You two know each other.'

'Well, Mr Didas might not remember me. Professor Bernice Summerfield. We met a few years back.'

'Oh yes,' Didas replies flatly, shaking her hand. 'You were with...'

'Menlove Stokes,' she interjects. 'That's right.'

'Yes. *He's* not here, is he?'

'No, you're quite safe. Well, how about a tour of the Mansionhouse? Anson can show you the jewel in the Axis' meritocratic crown?'

Anson looks between them, a little nonplussed. 'Well, unless you want to get straight to work...'

'No, no,' says Didas, raising his eyebrows. 'If the Professor wishes to give me a tour, that sounds... acceptable.'

As they head for the Mansionhouse, Jason flashes Benny a puzzled look. He slips in behind her on the path.

'Something up your sleeve?' he asks. He's gained so much weight since joining the Axis. He's soon going to need the next size of uniform. It's only just starting to show in his face.

'Why should you care?' She walks away quickly, placing herself between Anson and Didas.

The tour of the Mansionhouse turns out to be somewhat repetitive.

As they walk through the corridors and galleries, Anson or Benny point out one item of interest or another, and Didas ridicules it. The décor is opulent, gaudy, tasteless. This artefact is decadent third-rate tat, that one is so alien and has no value.

Jason is quite perplexed by Benny's compliance, her thoughtful nods when Didas speaks. She hates guided tours almost as much as she hates the Axis. He grows impatient with her insistence that Didas be shown every gallery and display.

Once finished in the Mansionhouse, the small party heads onto the terrace. Anson directs their attention down to the Avenue of Fountains.

'Each fountain has an individual sculpture. You'll see them better up close. Some are objectionable, but we're keeping them for now. With one exception.' He points to the last statue on the West Side. 'That one is uncarved, still rough stone.'

'Why?' Didas asks.

'Brax called it, The Future,' Benny explains.

'Exactly,' smiles Anson. 'I would like you to sculpt it into the form of an Axis soldier.'

'I see,' says Didas. 'I approve. It will be a bold, inspiring piece. A vision of perfection.'

Mickelthwaite creeps forward, producing a small, black folder. 'I have some photos and rough designs,' he says in a thin voice. 'Just suggestions.'

'Not now.' Didas waves him away. 'I want to see the medium.'

'Of course,' says Anson. 'Shall we...'

'No. I must concentrate. The Professor's company is all I desire. She clearly knows when to stay quiet.'

Anson deflates visibly. Benny almost feels sorry for him as she follows Didas.

'Very well,' Anson calls. 'The kitchens have prepared a variety of dishes for lunch, when you're ready.' He doesn't get a response.

Benny and Didas wander between the fountains. They both glance up at the Mansion house. Anson has already gone back in, Jason now follows, glancing back at Benny over his shoulder.

'We're safe exactly here,' says Benny. 'Don't get too close to the statues.'

'Better keep up appearances.' He points across the garden. 'Pretend you're telling me about the Grand Trianon.'

The artist's flat tones have given way to a more cultured register. His features are softer. His body language is the same – stiff and superior – but Benny finds herself talking to a different person.

'My name is Kellarn.'

'You do this a lot?' She makes a grand, sweeping gesture toward the Garden of Whispers.

'Yes, for various employers. I particularly like working for Brax, acquiring pieces for his collection. Covert work is about all I'm good at.'

'Not that good.' She grins. 'You don't look much like Didas.'

'He's a professional recluse, Professor. He's never allowed a public recording of his appearance. He even made your friend Stokes limit himself to a series of sketches. And obviously they don't help much. Who knows what he looks like?'

'Call me Benny.'

'Brax managed to establish contact with me just before the Axis touched down,' Kellarn tells her. 'He gave me the authority and the access to his bank accounts necessary to set up a full-scale operation. A fleet of mercenary ships is in hyperspace, ready to evacuate the residents.'

'Evacuate?'

'The strike will happen at oh eight hundred tomorrow. After I evacuate Brax from the Mansionhouse, cruise missiles will blow out the third and fifth floors, bringing the building down. I've already painted the appropriate locations with guide markers. There are also missiles targeted to bring down the defence management system the Axis has installed. Now – and this is my favourite bit – in my trunk, I've got fifteen floating holograph units. They will project the images of invading aliens. All the ones the Axis are particularly afraid of. The real bogeymen, like the Martians. The Axis security will rush to combat them, whilst their commanders try to figure out where the hell they came from. It'll be chaos.

'To top this off, an automated gunship will bombard the two Trianons on the other side of the asteroid. This is all a distraction, of course. Whilst the Axis forces are defending the major buildings, my other ships will land near the Hamlet. We will evacuate all the inhabitants. As they struggle to protect the collection, the soldiers won't be bothered with the inhabitants. They'll be falling back to defensive positions, thinking this is a full scale assault with the aim of taking the planetoid. We'll be in and out before they even know what's going on. The lift off and escape will be the last thing they expect.'

He waits for Benny to respond with her thoughts. She doesn't. He turns to face her.

'Well?' he asks.

'Not really. Are you insane? You'll destroy the Collection.'

'My mission is to save the people.'

'With high casualties along the way! Brax can't have told you to do this.'

'He asked me to help. He didn't have time to construct a plan himself. This is how I help.'

'But can't we do something similar that doesn't harm the artefacts?'

'Harming the artefacts is part of the plan. Do you know why I've spent all this time helping Brax add to the Collection? Because I like the idea of removing this clutter from the rest of the galaxy. Brax kept it locked away and limited access to academics. Art is the past. The leftovers of the dead. The Axis, being in love with death and tradition, love art. They want to show it off. Now I can be rid of it.'

Benny frowns, utterly dumbfounded. 'What are you talking about?'

'Do the poor and weak ever rush to the defence of art? Of course not. They've got more important things to worry about. Maybe a painting looks nice to one person, if they can afford it, and a story entertains another, if they understand it. This Collection is just decadent nonsense. The only good thing is that –' He points to the blank lump of stone. 'The future.'

'I won't let you do this.'

'You really don't care about the people you work with?'

'I do. They're my friends... my family.'

'Then you know what you have to do. Or will you put your job first?'

'It's more than that. Brax wouldn't want this.'

'I *need* your help.' His tone is menacing now, and he almost loses control of his body language. 'You must decide. If you back out, you're condemning everyone here. If you're in, meet me at the entrance to the east wing after dinner.' He turns and strides for the Mansionhouse.

Back in her rooms, Benny is torn. She misses lunch. Joseph brings her something light for dinner, but she only picks at it.

If it were one artefact, a dozen, maybe even a hundred, she'd make the sacrifice. But so many treasures?

She can see them, burning and broken. Everything here, all the work and research, the last remains of cultures long dead and periods passed.

She can see them, burning and broken. The people she loves, and those she doesn't even like.

Help Kellarn destroy the Collection, or leave her friends and family to the mercy of the Axis? No choice at all.

Benny is waiting for Kellarn when he comes down from his guestroom.

'Good,' he says. 'You made the right choice. It's all set. I've got Brax's location and...' he pauses. 'What's wrong?'

'I can't do it.' Her voice is a whisper. 'You have to go.'

'You'd sacrifice the people here, pay that price? You'd side with the Axis?'

'If I have to.'

Kellarn walks a few paces away from her. She turns, waiting for him to say something.

Then she hears the double doors to the Theatre opening.

'Congratulations, Professor Summerfield.' It's Anson. 'You made the right choice.'

She doesn't turn around, just lets her shoulders sag.

'We had Braxiatel's accounts monitored. We knew immediately there was movement, and we easily traced this Kellarn. He was intercepted before he got here, his fleet destroyed.' He reaches round Benny's right shoulder, presses a spot on Didas/Kellarn's forehead, then steps back. The face and body Benny has been looking at melt away, leaving a black, featureless humanoid. 'Something our techs have developed.'

Benny thinks for a moment that such technology is far beyond anything the Axis have shown her so far. Far beyond Earth's scientists, let alone human colonials. But she lets the thought drift.

'Why did you do this?'

'Some of my people say you're untrustworthy. They mentioned a certain conversation between you and the man Vosta. But I saw no great guilt in it. So I decided to show you what you're capable of. You know what's right, just like us. You're a gifted academic, Bernice, a brilliant archaeologist...' he trails off as she still refuses to look at him. 'A divine dancer. The Axis would cherish your talents, Professor. *I* would cherish them.'

Bernice stood looking at him for a long time.

Then she turned and walked away.

# 7: Hit

## By John Binns

For a split second after Bernice heard the bomb go off in the Ministry building, she felt as if she had caused the explosion herself.

The Junior Information Minister, on a flying visit from somewhere closer to the Axis' centres of power to the latest tiny branch of his Ministry, had just finished one of his longer tirades about the importance of genetic purity, and the need to get people like Bernice on board the Axis's 'project'. She felt like she'd heard all of this so many times before, but it was uncomfortable to hear it spouted with such conviction by someone so intelligent, so young. It seemed that Anson had wanted her to meet with a real ideologue, someone who wouldn't just laugh like he did at all the awkward points. All part of grooming her, she thought. Like Anson was doing with all the academics. Please let it not just be her.

The Minister – she tried not to think of him by his name, which the compulsory name-tag on his shirt told her was Paul Thomas Gale – had long blond hair and smooth, slightly freckled skin. His accent was educated without sounding snobbish, and she could have listened to it for hours if it hadn't been intoning the most terrible, poisonous nonsense. For what could have been no more than twenty minutes, he'd leaned across the table in this rather shabby, makeshift office in what had been a housing block for visiting alien students (the building was strictly temporary, so the Ministry had claimed, but it was an irony of the Information Ministry that no one ever believed a word it said), with the crude intention of converting her to the cause.

Perhaps Anson had been obliged to arrange this meeting. Because Bernice was sure he'd know as well as she did that this was never going to work.

The point he'd been trying to put to her for the minute or so before the bomb was that the Axis's concerns were simply for the next few generations of humanity, who would be growing up in a chaotic galaxy where other worlds and races presented an ever greater threat. Without a concerted effort from those in authority to improve the chances of 'our' children, he said (and he used the word, she noticed, with not the slightest hint of irony), they'd be at a competitive disadvantage, and prone – over several generations, admittedly – to extinction. Surely, he told her with a raised voice – a cutting motion across the table for emphasis with one slender, jewellery-free hand – there was a moral imperative 'on all of us' to make sure the human race prospered. That extended to the research and education in which the Ministry was currently engaged, and in which he felt prominent academic voices would be crucial.

There had been a silence after that, perhaps ten seconds, while Bernice made an attempt to formulate her thoughts into words. If she'd been calmer, less riled by Gale's invective, she might have asked him why his own extensive research hadn't shown up the fact that her contribution to the next generation of humans had been condemned by the Axis as unhelpful to the human gene pool and wouldn't, in an ideal universe, have been allowed to breed. She was on the verge of putting into words her gut instinct that what the Minister was describing as the modified next generation didn't sound much like the human race at all, or that the constant battle for survival he saw as inevitable really didn't sound like fun, and probably wouldn't to the majority of aliens either. But Bernice was angry, and the jumble of thoughts in her mind wasn't coalescing into coherent sentences so much as it was steadily rising in a bilious tide of rage.

It was just as that tide was about to spill over into something loud, vocal and probably obscene that a loud bang cut in from somewhere behind, below and uncomfortably close to where she was sitting. The Minister, who had been looking expectantly across his desk while she formulated her reply, suddenly took on an expression of shock which she imagined mirrored her own. For a few seconds, the building around them actually trembled, with enough force and for enough time to convince them that this was actually happening, that they were sitting in a bombed building. A split second after the explosion itself, the even louder and closer blaring noise of an electronic siren – obviously the Ministry's fire alarm – began its persistent, deafening and entirely superfluous message.

A curtain of dust broke from the roof and descended on them.

The Minister let out a curse and got up from his chair. Bernice's first thought, she would be ashamed to admit later, was to kick herself for having agreed to meet Gale at all, and for actually suggesting this particular date and time. If she hadn't been open-minded enough to agree to listen to the Minister's proposals, if she hadn't let her curiosity get the better of her, she wouldn't be here on the fifth floor of a building at the exact time someone had decided to put a bomb in it. She couldn't help but feel some annoyance that whoever was targeting the Fifth Axis had managed to get her as well: she, surely, didn't deserve it.

By the time she'd angrily dismissed this thought from her head, the Minister was in the doorway of his office, holding the door open for her to come through. 'Any idea what that was?' she said.

'I have a suspicion,' he said. He started leading her along the long corridor, which she remembered led to the stairs: she'd had to walk up five flights of them to get here, after waiting what seemed like an age for the one lift to arrive. The half-dozen or so doors to the offices along the corridor were all open now, with men and women coming out of them in various states of alarm and distress. There was a general hubbub of confused, urgent conversation. In the background of one of the offices to Bernice's left, she could hear the sound of a young woman crying.

She realised she had missed the start of what Gale had been saying: it was something about intelligence reports on terrorist action, which came in all the time from sources both reliable and unreliable. 'Humans. Can you believe it? All across the sector. They're confined to their individual worlds, obviously, but they must be getting their weapons from somewhere.' He looked back at her as they walked. She got the feeling that he'd left his Axis Minister's voice behind him in the office, that the impact of the explosion had somehow dislodged it. Now he sounded candid, riled, somewhat bitter and altogether more human.

As they turned the corner towards the stairs, now a group of a dozen or so, Bernice was alarmed to see the thick clouds of smoke coming towards them from the top of the staircase. A young man in shirt-sleeves had already grabbed a fire extinguisher and had started moving forward: it was just about possible, through the smoke, to see the blaze coming up from the floor below. The staircase was narrow, and even though the young man fired off the extinguisher with all its force, there was no way the fire was really abating. In fact, as she craned her neck to look down to the lower flights, Bernice could see that the fire covered at least two floors of the staircase, and was spreading.

'We need another way out,' she found herself shouting harshly. As she turned round, she was shocked to see how frightened the people in her group were, and how young: with a start, she realised she was probably the oldest among them. Many of these people, she supposed, would be junior administrative staff, some of them temps, some recruited very recently and shipped here. The Axis, after all, hadn't been here long enough to build up a very senior or experienced staff.

'This way,' Gale was saying, and he started leading their group back down the corridor. The pace of their progress was deeply uncomfortable, the briskness and urgency of their walking betraying the fact that they would all rather be running. It was Gale who set the pace though, and she could well understand that at this stage it was more important that they keep order and stick together.

They walked like this through the building for what seemed like an age, the steady rhythm of the fire alarm bashing relentlessly at their consciousness like an aural version of Chinese water torture. They walked down two flights of stairs, in a disused part of the building that looked as if it hadn't been cleaned for years. Another, smaller group joined them on the fourth floor: again, all fairly young men and women; again, obviously, all humans.

When they reached the third floor, the noises of panicked shouting and the smell of smoke seemed closer. Bernice felt an awful sense of realisation as she remembered something the Minister's aide had shown her earlier. The third floor contained a vast processing centre now, an open-plan hall of a hundred or so people whose job it was to gather and analyse data from this sector of the Axis worlds. Part of the Axis bureaucracy that was naturally suited to the Collection, because of its educational commitment. If there was any part of this building that was 'significant' enough to be a target, in the Minister's words, Bernice guessed that was it.

A few of their party were already on their way down the stairs to the second floor, but Gale had stopped: it seemed the same thought had occurred to him. Together they looked through the double doors to the corridor that led to the processing centre. The glass in the doors had shattered. A young girl – maybe nineteen – was running towards them with her face in her hands: they could make out some blood between her fingers. As she came through the doors, hardly stopping to acknowledge them as she rushed past, Bernice could see some tiny shards of glass embedded just below the girl's right eye.

'You keep going,' Gale was telling her, stabbing his finger in the direction of the staircase. She didn't bother to argue with him, but followed him through the double doors anyway. Mercifully, at that point the fire alarm stopped abruptly. 'They've hit the processing centre,' Gale said. 'This is going to be nasty.'

She nodded as they ran. 'I know.'

As it turned out, there wasn't a lot they could do in the processing centre. The thick black smoke made it very difficult to see anything, and most of what they could see was a chaotic mess of small fires and twisted metal. Where there were signs of people either trapped or struggling to get out, there were already paramedics moving in to help them: thankfully, Bernice reflected, the Ministry building was only a few kilometres away from the medical facilities.

Dimly noticing that Gale had rushed off to help one of the medics, Bernice spent a short while moving clumsily through the wreckage, trying to see if there was anything she could do. But in the mean time, she could feel her breathing getting steadily more strained as a result of the smoke. Eventually, one of the medics led her, protesting only slightly, back down the corridor and down the stairs.

Dozens of people now were evacuating via this stairway. Bernice wondered how many people actually worked here, how many would know some of the people who had died. She wondered whether anyone else, like her, had just been visiting the building, and how many of those who did work there would defend the Axis and its politics as strongly as Paul Thomas Gale.

Worse, she wondered who the people were who had planted the bomb, where they were, what they were thinking. Whether any of them had actually been in the building, whether they'd lived or died, whether they were evacuating now with the rest of them. Whether, in such a small community as this, she'd actually seen them, met them, talked to them, perhaps. Whether any of them were her friends.

She joined the mass of people filing out through the fire exit on the ground floor, and felt with them a sense of relief and safety as she emerged into the open air. The street was filled with parked ambulances and medics tending to the injured. A crowd of people was being kept at a distance by a group of Axis soldiers. Bernice looked into the crowd, but didn't recognise any faces.

Coughing a little as she gulped the fresh air, Bernice noticed a small group of the researchers from the fifth floor on the other side of the street. One of the medics was handing out cups of water, and they were sipping it gratefully as they stood and sat together, watching the exit doors as if waiting for friends to emerge.

Realising then how tired and thirsty she was, Bernice hurriedly crossed the street to join them.

Somehow, she didn't feel ready to go home just yet.

# 8: The Garden of Whispers
## By Martin Day

Lieutenant Bernard Moskof of Axis Criminal Investigations stood waiting on the steps to the Summer House, weight shifted onto one foot as if preparing to flee. As always, he looked uncomfortable outside. The zephyrs that played over the lake were as artificial as everything else on Braxiatel, but, even so, Moskof was a man better used to interiors, to poorly-lit rooms, enclosed cells, and a recycled atmosphere. He was rumpled, untidy, ill at ease in his uniform. His dark hair was turning grey before its time.

He made himself breathe deeply, giving in, just for a moment, to the fantasy in which he found himself: the orange streamers of cloud that mottled the horizon, the lengthening shadows, the soft lapping of the water at the lake's shoreline. The single red rose that his lover would bring.

Moskof had come to Braxiatel to police the Fifth Axis's latest acquisition, and instead had – it was the only phrase that came close to expressing the reality of his feelings – *fallen in love*. The words were ludicrous perhaps, but something was going on, deep inside him. A ravenous ache, balanced by an almost euphoric delight at the simplest of things: a passing butterfly, the warmth of sunlight on his neck. The beauty of an empty in-tray.

'I trust you have not been standing here long?'

Moskof turned. For a large woman – who hated the insincere blindness of flattery even more than plain old rudeness – Ms Jones was incredibly light on her feet. Moskof often wondered if her formidable interpersonal skills, allied to her deft self-control, weren't wasted on administration. There were worse officers than her in the Criminal Investigations Unit.

'No,' he lied. 'Only just got here.'

'My apologies, in any case,' said Ms Jones. 'Especially in times such as these, free time is precious. I do not fritter it away lightly.'

'I'm sure,' said Moskof. He pecked her on the cheek.

She handed over the rose.

It was their little ritual, a sign that the working day was at last over. 'Shall we go?' He held out his arm, which Ms Jones took, and they strolled down towards the lake, passing a statue of a pair of blindfolded nymphs, their arms and bodies interwoven and indivisible. An appropriate image, thought Moskof: two beings finding succour in each other, but utterly ignorant of the future.

'I wonder what the lake will tell us tonight?' said Ms Jones. Her voice, usually so thin and spare, sounded warm and full to Moskof.

'Well, whatever it is,' he said, smiling, 'we'll be the only ones to hear it.'
Ms Jones arched her eyebrow. 'You haven't been... *leaning* on people again, have you?'
Moskof shook his head. 'I'm a very private man, Ms Jones. You of all people should know that.' He ran a hand through his greying hair, only too aware of Ms Jones's accusing gaze. 'I have the surveillance devices deactivated for our walks. And I suppose, from time to time, I might remind certain people of my relative position, and...' He started fiddling with his collar, like a cartoon character trying to let off steam.
Ms Jones chuckled. 'Well, I approve of the peace and quiet, if not perhaps of your methods...'
'Listen!' Moskof raised a hand suddenly, his eyes eager. 'Did you hear that?'
'What?'
'Words on the wind!'
'Really? What do they say?'
'I think they're saying...' Now, it was Moskof's turn to smile. '"Ssssssssssucker".'

Bernice burst into Ms Jones's office, trying simultaneously to pull on a T-shirt and read the details of the hard-copy report that had brought her here, and barely succeeding in either. 'Have you heard...?'
Ms Jones nodded. 'I thought I might see you.' She nodded towards the desk, where a cup of strong coffee sat. 'I took the liberty...'
Bernice gulped it down: it was just right, not too hot, not too much milk, spoons and spoons of sugar. The woman was a star. 'I know you can sometimes tell me things others can't,' she said. 'Tell me everything, right now.'
'The blast occurred shortly after midnight,' said Ms Jones, already cognisant with the facts of the matter. 'The damage caused was superficial, but symbolic. Rumour has it that there are those on the planetoid that would rather see the Collection destroyed than remain under the control of the Fifth Axis.'
'"Rumour has it"?' queried Bernice. 'So you *are* seeing Moskof?'
'I beg your pardon?'
'Everyone knows. How could they not? Just thought you should be aware.'
Ms Jones coughed lightly, staring intently at something in the middle distance. 'He... He's a good man, Bernice.'
'Didn't say he wasn't.'
Ms Jones reached into a desk drawer, pulled out an old buff envelope. She slid it across to Bernice. 'It has nothing to do with why you came here, but since you know, I think I should like to show you this. Somebody's idea of satire, I think. It was waiting for me this morning.'

Bernice opened the envelope carefully. Inside was a cheap pad, the sort that you usually found on market stalls, downloaded with illegal copies of the latest bonkbuster or a manual on how to cheat on the wife and get away with it. A light glowed at its side, showing that it was full.

'The complete works of Sylvia Plath,' said Ms Jones before Bernice could press the button to bring up the contents page. 'I imagine you'll be familiar with her work.'

Bernice shook her head. 'I didn't need dead poetry to make my teenage years any more miserable.'

'My anonymous friend has highlighted certain poems,' continued Ms Jones. 'They appear to be about women who secretly want to be dominated by Nazis.' Her voice was as calm as usual, but Bernice could sense an underlying tension. 'I think the point is clear enough.'

'They say love is blind,' noted Bernice. 'Seems to me, it lacks any sort of sensory apparatus whatsoever.' She put down her coffee mug. 'I mean, have you seen my track record?'

Ms Jones smiled for the first time, grateful for Bernice's support. 'I have heard some interesting reports. Mainly from you, I should point out.'

Bernice stuffed the pad back into the envelope. 'You get a better quality of threatening note on KS-159.'

'I'm not overreacting, then?' said Ms Jones. 'To see it in negative terms?'

'Well, they're hardly saying "Good on yer".'

Bernice wanted to say more but Ms Jones brought a picture of the damaged Theatre onto her desktop, effectively ending that part of their conversation. 'About the bomb blast,' she said. 'You can see that the outer façade bore the brunt of the damage. Nothing structural at all.'

'A small bomb, then,' said Bernice. 'Or a larger one that didn't detonate properly.'

'Indeed. But a potent message all the same.'

'How has Anson reacted?'

Ms Jones waited for a moment before replying, and Bernice felt her heart sink. Ms Jones had been trying to delay her hearing this, she realised. 'He's ordered that a group of Killoran interned workers be placed in solitary confinement. Any subsequent attacks will be followed by the execution of a number of hostages.'

Benny felt her mouth tense, lines of force that went through her jaw and skull. 'What the hell's it got to do with the Killorans?'

'Not much, I'd have thought,' said Ms Jones. 'And I don't know who has been selected. But that's the point. He wants to use sentiment against the terrorists. One more attack and an innocent dies. Another, and two will die. Yet another and, well, you get the picture. If he runs out of Killorans then he'll start on another well-liked species of slave... of interned workers.'

Bernice made for the door.

'He won't listen,' said Ms Jones, stopping Bernice in her tracks. 'Believe me.'

Bernice made a growling noise at the back of her throat, balling her fists in exasperation. 'I've got to do *something*,' she said.

Ms Jones glanced down to delete the picture of the damaged Theatre before adding, quite casually, 'I believe Bernard is in charge of the investigation.' She paused, straightening the items on her desk. 'You might want to have a word...'

Moskof stood watching a small group of Killorans erecting scaffolding across the wound in the side of the Theatre. They seemed even more surly than usual, which was hardly surprising. News travels fast, especially on a rock the size of the Braxiatel Collection.

'I expected better than this from Marshal Anson.'

Moskof turned. Bernice Summerfield stood behind him, hands on hips. As if it was all *his* fault.

'I assume you're talking about the hostages?'

Bernice snorted. 'I'm hardly talking about the songs we're getting on Braxiatel FM.'

'I thought you'd approve,' said Moskof. 'From what I've heard concerning you. This is about society, about shared responsibilities.' He paused, watching as another plastiglass walkway was secured against the Theatre. 'Still, if it makes you happy... I'm only following the orders of Commander Spang, who, as his first act in charge of security on this planetoid, made the decision to take them. I plead guilty to the charge of... whatever it is you're accusing me of... and ask for about a million other crimes to be taken into consideration.'

'This is serious!'

Moskof turned towards Bernice. 'I know. But it needn't be. If this attack is just a one-off, nobody need get hurt.'

'Hurt? This Spang is going to execute innocent people for something they weren't even involved in!'

'You look me in the eye and say you wouldn't approve of terrorism against the Fifth Axis.'

Bernice glanced away. 'This is so wrong.'

Moskof lowered his voice. 'The answer to the question you haven't been asking is yes. The father of your deceased child is amongst those imprisoned.'

'He hasn't done anything.'

'That's the point. Neither had the guards who were injured by the bomb.' Moskof bent down, a plastic bag in one hand, to retrieve something from the concrete: a spec of meaningless incongruity, from before. He found that it made him terribly sad to see it here.

He clipped the bag shut and straightened. 'It looks like it might have been based on a low-yield industrial mine, though it's of a type that's got our boys scratching their heads.'

'Low yield?'

Moskof nodded. 'Fits with our assessment, that it's a shot across the bows rather than anything else. Wouldn't be surprised if they target some of the Collection proper next time.' He paused, holding the plastic bag up to the light. 'A rather civilised form of terrorism,' he muttered.

'If you say so,' said Bernice quietly.

'What I can't figure out is how they placed the bomb,' said Moskof, his brow furrowed. 'Security's so tight you can't belch without it setting off an alarm somewhere. We've got hidden bugs, infra-red cameras...' He stopped himself from mentioning the audio net. 'I've checked them all.'

'And found nothing?'

Moskof nodded. 'It's like the bomb appeared out of nowhere.'

Bernice indicated the bag in Moskof's hand. 'May I?'

Moskof hurriedly slipped it into an inner pocket. 'I think I've been quite forthcoming, don't you? In order to try and put some very polite pressure on a possible source of information. But I have my limits.'

'There is no source of information here. I have no contact or influence with those who planted this bomb. Please believe me.'

He found himself believing that look on her face. Not that it mattered. 'All right,' he said.

Moskof watched Bernice head off towards the Mansionhouse, then he turned towards the Killorans who were awaiting further instruction. 'Begin the repairs,' he said, looking at the damaged theatre one last time. 'I've seen enough.'

'This is strictly off-the-record,' said Ms Jones.

'Right,' said Bernice. There was no humour in her now. She had woken to news of another blast, this time at the Small Stables. Artefacts had been destroyed. Worse still, by the time Bernice had finally been allowed to see Anson, the first execution had already taken place.

It hadn't been Adrian.

'Same methodology as the first attack,' said Ms Jones. 'The explosion happened about an hour earlier.'

'I didn't hear anything.'

Ms Jones rolled her eyes heavenwards. 'They're not using gunpowder, you know.'

'When I saw Moskof yesterday he suggested a modified industrial explosive. Of low power. An odd choice of weapon.'

Ms Jones nodded. 'Frankly, I don't think Bernard's men have a clue.'

'I know,' said Bernice. 'But I think I do. It helped me strike a deal with Anson.'

'What sort of deal?'

'I saw him a few minutes ago. I got him to show me certain files. I told him that I thought I could put a stop to the attacks. If he gave me time.'

She'd been ready to do anything. Had gone expecting to get to the point of offering sexual favours. There had been no conflict in her about that. Anson being as he was, she had even allowed herself to fantasise about it. Up to a certain point. She had reached that stage, as women in wars are made to, so quickly. It was like they'd all got used to a certain level of threat. But then that level increased. It kept increasing. In increments.

She kept dreaming about Guernsey.

But Anson had listened to her first idea, her first line of defence. He hadn't seemed ashamed, but perhaps he was, because he'd allowed her to accuse one of his men of something... one of his men or the woman he loved. But she wasn't going to tell Ms Jones that.

Ms Jones seemed distracted, rearranging the few items on her desk. 'Do you think...' She shook her head slowly. 'Do you think it right that I see Bernard Moskof?'

'It's not for me to judge,' said Bernice too loudly.

Ms Jones looked away. 'I still cannot believe... I still cannot believe that he might have feelings for me. I find it hard enough on that level. Add in the complication of what other people think...'

'That's never bothered you before.'

'But the father of your child is threatened. Don't imagine for one moment that I believe that *this*...' Her broad hands encompassed the planetoid, its Collection, the occupying forces. 'I *can't* accept this as the *status quo*. Can you?'

Bernice shook her head quickly. Her eyes were fixed on Ms Jones, interrogating her gestures.

'It does not help that I find the very idea of romance somewhat puzzling.' Ms Jones looked aside. 'I am never sure what to say, what to do. I give him roses. Neither of us seem quite sure of the rules. What they would have been before, never mind now.'

'Life during wartime.' Bernice reached into her rucksack. 'I have something for you.' She removed the pad from the day before and slid it across the desk. 'I left some of the poems, the novel, deleted other bits. Made room for something else.'

Ms Jones switched on the pad. 'Roland Barthes?'

'*A Lover's Discourse*. It's about the language of love, its inadequacy, its loneliness.'

'And this will help me how, exactly?'

'It's just to show that I understand,' said Bernice carefully, 'some of the disguises that we find ourselves adopting. As I hope you'll understand... what love sometimes makes us do.'

That night, Ms Jones waited in the gardens once again, clutching a rose.

Moskof hailed her from far off, met her by the lake.

'You're early,' she said.

'So are you.'

They kissed, he took the rose, completing the ritual, but for once they talked of work.

'It's not going well,' he admitted. 'The forensic information, the security records... They don't seem to be pointing anywhere right now. Perhaps I'm missing something under my nose... I just hope there isn't another attack tonight. For all sorts of reasons.'

'You've had no communication from the terrorists?' asked Ms Jones.

Moskof shook his head. 'Nothing. No notes, no threats, no "Leave the Collection or we blow it sky-high".'

'Perhaps it's not about the Collection at all.'

'Perhaps. But if it's a grudge... Who? There's nobody in common between the blast casualties. And the bombs have gone off when there aren't many people around, in exterior locations. Never mind about work now, anyway.' He took a sniff of the rose. 'I love your roses.'

'I've always wondered. You never said anything before.'

'Well, I should have.'

'I just thought... That's what I ought to do. In a situation like this. One of Crofton's gardeners finds me the best ones.'

'I just wish I could take them home, or back to work. But... someone would see them.'

'People see us now.'

'Perhaps. But openly keeping one of these would be a statement. Someone might feel they had to make a statement in return.'

'What do you do with them?'

'I confess I wait until after you've gone, then I just leave them behind, for some other random person to enjoy.'

'Such honesty.'

'With you I can be honest.' Moskof's eyes fixed on a point ahead of them. 'What?'

Ms Jones looked up. A figure was running towards them.

Moskof went for his gun. The rose fell to the ground.

'The rose!' Bernice was shouting. 'Get away from the rose!'

Ms Jones looked between the running figure and the flower on the ground.

Then, before Moskof could say anything, she grabbed it, ran towards the lake, and hurled it away.

The resultant explosion, though almost silent, threw up a torrent of grey water and a flurry of surprised and dead fish. The swans, sitting at the far side of the lake, rose as one into the air, hooting in alarm.

Bernice ran into Ms Jones, knocking her down, putting her own body in the way of the wave of heat and debris that blossomed over the shoreline.

They looked up, dazed, when Moskof arrived a moment later.

'On my recommendation,' Bernice gasped at him, 'Anson just sent men to arrest a particular gardener. He was already gone. Mister Crofton knows nothing about it. They were working on the timing mechanism. I didn't know where you'd gone, couldn't get hold of you.' She paused, sucking in lungfuls of acrid air. 'They were trying to assassinate you.'

Ms Jones stared at her, carefully getting to her feet. 'You thought it was me,' she said.

'Or him,' Bernice nodded at Moskof. 'Some kind of deep cover agent.' She climbed to her feet, and gently took the front of Moskof's uniform in her shaking hands. 'Please notice: I saved your lives. I want a life back in return.'

Moskof stared at her in shock. 'I think we need to talk,' he said.

The next day Bernice found Ms Jones alone in the summerhouse, watching the now still waters of the lake. A heron, emboldened by the quantity of free food, was picking its way through the pile of fish that had washed onto the shore.

'Are you all right?' asked Bernice.

Ms Jones paused, choosing her words carefully. Her eyes were still on the lake. 'I'm... unhurt,' she said. 'Physically, I mean.' She smiled. 'Amazing what they can do nowadays. Miniaturisation, nanotechnology, genetic manipulation, what have you.' There was a rose in her pale hands, slender and blood red. 'I've had to source my flowers from elsewhere,' she said lightly. Then she looked Bernice in the eyes for the first time. 'How did you know?'

'I couldn't work out why they were using such small bombs to target the Collection. Then I realised they were actually targeting a person.'

Ms Jones nodded slowly.

'I noticed gaps in the files when I came to look at them yesterday. It must have been common knowledge that Moskof was in the habit of turning off the security bugs when you met. Three nights ago you ended your walk near the Theatre, the day after that you passed by the Small Stables. What clinched it was a petal Moskof found at one of the blast sites. But he didn't think twice about it. He knew he'd left a rose there. I got Anson to let me get the petal analysed. The results came through a few minutes before I thought you were going to meet Moskof. Only you were both early.'

'If it had been me, trying to kill him, for whatever motive, would you have let me?'

'If I could have made a good enough show of trying to get there in time… Perhaps.'

'The Killorans have been released, haven't they?'

'All of them have been returned to work duties,' Bernice said. 'Anson was able to say that the nature of the bombings wasn't exactly what they'd thought. And a particular suspect is being sought, action having been taken on information gained as a result of the hostage policy. Face has been saved.'

'I love him,' said Ms Jones suddenly. 'I really do.'

'I know,' said Bernice. 'And I understand.'

She walked away, towards the lake at the heart of the Garden of Whispers, leaving Ms Jones staring at the rose in her hand.

# Lockdown Conversations: 2
## By Paul Cornell

Bernice had watched the construction project for days, and had worked out when Adrian took his breaks.

She sat down on the other side of the fence at her very precise place, and listened to his deep Killoran breathing, and felt she didn't even have time for a greeting. 'Our baby is safe,' she said.

The breathing stopped, for a moment, then continued. 'I'd heard he was dead,' the deep voice said.

'That was a cover story. He's with people who are looking after him. Nobody else knows.'

'You're a very brave person.' She knew he loved her. Had tried to deflect him and Jason into each other, so she would have two babysitters and no boyfriends. Not for the moment. But that had been before, and now just the sound of his voice sounded the purest thing she'd heard in weeks.

'No, I'm a coward and a traitor.'

He laughed. 'Never.'

'How are they treating you?'

'They order us around. Call us names. There have been a couple of beatings, but not as much as you might think. They don't seem sure how far they can go. That's the most anxious thing. They seem to be waiting for orders about whether they can shoot us. Offhand, I mean. They randomly picked one of us for a hostage the other day, and they shot him.'

'I know, I was involved in stopping that.'

'Good.'

'Someone I know who's trying to resist... She knew nothing about that bomb. Or the big one at the old alien student quarters. They're such a random bunch of people, the resistors. All that bile academics feel about each other, all released. Directed. I'm not telling this very well.'

'Gregory, that was his name.'

'Gregory. I'll remember.' She realised that Adrian wasn't telling her the Killoran's second name because it would be something that, to human ears, would sound funny, like a lot of their names. Dignity and cultural pride must collide for him like that every day. Especially in there, with the Axis mocking them.

'Jason's been here.'

'I thought he might have been.'

'He asked to make a personal inspection. He laughed all the time. Stopped to say a few words to me. About how now I could be of some use to somebody. Apparently we're working for his department of resource procurement. He kicked me three times. The guards had to stop him.'

'The bastard.' Benny hugged her knees. 'He's just let it all out. Everything he was and was trying not to be. All that jealousy he feels about you and Peter.'

'How's it been out there?'

'Compared to in there I'm sure it's been paradise.'

'Try and let me know if you hear about us being shipped out. I don't know why they haven't done it.'

'I don't either.'

'I love you,' he said.

She closed her eyes. She would be true to herself. Even now. Especially now. 'I love you like Peter loves you.'

His breathing increased again. 'Never a coward. Never a traitor. Never believe it.'

She would cry if she stayed any longer. She got to her feet and wiped the itchiness from her eyes onto the back of her sleeve. 'I'll come back.'

'I'll try to be here.'

# 9: The Crystal Flower
## By Cavan Scott & Mark Wright

*The kiss seemed to last forever, but they both knew it was too short to say everything they wanted it to.*

*The Corporal circled his arms around his wife's slender waist. 'I love you so much.' He kissed her forehead.*

*'I know.' Jane looked up at him with those deep blue eyes. 'You look so handsome.' All around the departure bay, similar scenes were taking place. The brave boys saying goodbye to their sweethearts, going off to bravely defend the Empire from the evil hordes sweeping across the galaxy. 'Jane, darling...'*

*Jane shushed him with a finger on his lips. 'I know.'*

*A klaxon echoed around the bay. The Corporal looked up. 'Got to go.'*

*'I'll keep the garden looking nice for you.'*

*The Corporal smiled. 'You and that damned garden.'*

*There was one last, lingering kiss before the Corporal hefted his kitbag and strode up the ramp towards the airlock, vanishing with the other young soldiers into the wispy vapour given off by the fuel vents.*

It was almost as if he was pleased he had more work to do. Whereas everyone else Benny talked to complained about the reconstruction work, Mister Crofton had taken it all in his stride. In fact, he seemed to positively thrive as he toiled in the gardens, putting right the damage caused by the Occupation. He had ceased to be part of the Resistance, or so Bev had told Benny, after those initial frenzied meetings, when it had looked for a moment like a popular revolt might throw the Axis off.

Now they were embedded. And so was Mister Crofton.

This morning was no different. As Benny trudged through the drizzle on her way to the Archives, Mister Crofton had actually waved, even calling out a cheery 'Hullo!'

'Putting your back into it, eh, Mister Crofton.' She had quipped, her own good humour forced after a particularly bad night thinking of Peter. One of the Gemayals had said he was slipping into a little world of his own. She should be there for that.

'Nothing like a good spot of digging to get the blood pumping!'

Even after all this time, Benny didn't know Mister Crofton at all.

*Amidst the constant drills and routine, the Corporal had finally stolen some moments of peace and quiet.*

*Checking he was alone he pulled a tiny silver cube from under his*

*pillow, running his thumb along one face.*
*The air above the cube shimmered and a figure appeared, translucent and sparkling in the gloom of the quarters. The Corporal smiled as Jane stood before him. She'd must have sent the holo-letter after coming in from the garden. Her hair was up and she was wearing her dungarees. A streak of dirt stretched across her cheek, and it killed him that he wasn't there to wipe it off.*
*'Hi, it's me. Well, I guess you can see that, but ... I hate these things!'*
*The Corporal's smile widened. Jane was such a technophobe.*
*'I just wanted to say that I love you for about the millionth time since you left. I'm so proud of you, so is everyone. Mum and Dad send their love. They say things are going well with, well, the war. That you're...' She turned away from the camera and took a deep breath.*
*'I know you're probably scared. I am too, but you have the hard job to do. Whenever you're scared, whenever you feel alone, think of me, just as I'm thinking of you. Every day.'*
*The Corporal watched Jane mouth 'Love you,' and kiss the lens before she vanished.*
*'Love you too, babe,' he whispered.*

Benny wandered through the delicious mustiness of the Archives, muffin in one hand, hazelnut latte in the other. She breezed into the area that she had decided to catalogue, as that was the toughest work she could manage at the moment that still actually meant something, chewing gratefully on the muffin.

'Morning, Bishop,' she breezed to the intern currently acting as her assistant, placing the coffee and muffin precariously on a stack of parchment. Bishop didn't say anything, looking at her through the blonde curtains of his hair. His chief reason for promotion to this position, from his former post in Administration, was that he was human. 'Was that you I saw in the dining hall last night, dancing on the table?'

Bishop coughed and glanced just over Benny's shoulder. She turned.

'Good morning, Professor.'

Someone new. Benny turned and looked at him.

She'd made a study of Axis ranks recently, and so she could see immediately that he was a Criminal Investigator, a Commander. Another sign of what the Axis called civilisation. He was short, stocky, muscular, the kind of body that wins fights in corners. He had untrusting eyes. He was looking at her like a piece of meat he planned to torture.

She was finally looking into the eyes of the beast.

'Hiya,' she said. 'What can we do you for?'

'Spang,' he said.

'Boing,' she replied.

His lip didn't even curl. 'Commander Spang.' He rose from his seat, which happened to be the Throne of Bataar, used as if it were a waiting room chair, and sauntered over to a table.

'I was doing some reading last night, Professor.'

'I didn't say a word.' She sipped on her latte and tried to ignore the large ceremonial dagger that Spang had chosen to pick up. Was he here for Brax? Nothing had been heard out of his rooms since he'd tried to kill Anson. The Marshal himself had laughed off the subject when asked about it, but his laughter concealed absolute silence. Bernice could only imagine the horrors they might feel able to inflict on Brax now.

'Yes. Anubian memory stones. Fascinating subject.'

'I know. Very dangerous if you're not from Anubis. They have a habit of frying your brain.'

'Hmm, quite.' Spang tested the point of the dagger playfully against a finger. 'I also noticed that we happen to have such an artefact in the Archive and I was wondering if we could borrow it. Purely in the interests of research and continued co-operation between the staff of the Braxiatel Collection and my own research personnel.'

'You have research personnel?'

'Criminal research. Forensics and the like.'

The artefact would be used against the Resistance. She was being unfaithful to her not-quite friends again. She turned away. 'You know I can't stop you from taking it, so why are you asking?'

'Because manners cost nothing, Professor Summerfield.'

Benny let out a long, slow breath. 'Fine. Bishop?' The intern jumped at his name. 'Go and retrieve the memory stone from storage and sign it over to Commander Spang. Make sure you give him a release form. The Marshal gets very grumpy if the paperwork isn't up to date.'

'Yes, Professor!' Bishop bolted gratefully from the room.

Spang stepped up close to Benny. 'Thank you so much, Professor Summerfield.'

'Not at all.' Benny smiled sweetly. 'The pleasure was all mine.'

'Of course it was.' Spang turned on his heel and strode from the room.

*A bud hit the dirt. Jane hated pruning back the Draconian lilies. Such beautiful flowers. Her husband never understood why she spent so much time in the garden. If he were here now... But he wasn't, was he?*

*A chime sounded inside the house. A message! She ran into the house.*

*'Accept message,' she instructed the computer, and the picture hanging over the fireplace dissolved into a pixellated storm before reforming into the face of her husband.*

*'Hi babe!' He grinned. The voice was distorted with a vague trace of static. They must have moved further out onto the rim. 'How's my*

*favourite girl? I haven't got long, the satellite relay window is stretched to capacity.' Jane shook her head. Why did he have to give every little detail?*

*'Look, they're saying that things are turning. We've had some important victories in the third wave.' Jane leant forward hopefully. 'I don't want to get your hopes up, darling, but they reckon this could all be over by Christmas.' He grinned the grin that made him look 12 years old. 'If we're lucky, we might be shipping home within a few months.' He glanced over to the side.*

*'Look, my time's up. I'll see you soon, and don't forget, I lo...'*

*The silly sod had run over his time allowance. Jane laughed to herself. He never could keep track of time.*

Benny had arrived too late. From talking to Professor Yackle, who had witnessed the entire thing but, of course, had considered it beneath him to get involved. Mister Crofton had been working away in this small, ornate patch of garden. Benny had never seen it before. It's amazing what you miss every day. She'd never noticed the flower at its centre for example, never realised that it wasn't real but sculpted from the deepest burgundy crystal she had ever seen. Some kind of lily she supposed you'd call it.

Apparently a couple of junior Axis officers had wandered by, after spending the afternoon abusing their privileges and quaffing a generous amount of Slarvian ale. In their stupor they had spotted Mister Crofton and baited the quiet gardener but to no avail. Instead he had simply turned his back to them and continued to cultivate his beloved plants. In retaliation the oafs had taken to trashing the garden, mindlessly damaging the crystal flower.

Yackle said he had seen nothing like it. Mister Crofton had thrown himself at the officers, bringing one down immediately. When Benny had arrived, the second was on the turf nursing a broken nose, but the security guards had already arrived and Mister Crofton was on his way to the hole. If only she'd been there a minute earlier...

*'Come on, let's keep moving. We're almost there.'*

*A little sore throat from all the shouting was the last thing on the Corporal's mind. They had already lost four of the guys. He wasn't going to lose any more. Not when they were this close.*

*As they ran through the mud, plasma mines exploding all around, his mind slipped back to a conversation he had had with Martin, a fresh-faced new private, the previous night.*

*'How do you do it, sir?' The lad had asked. 'How do you keep going in all this? It never seems to get you down.'*

*The Corporal had smiled and just flicked on the holo-cube. Jane's image had danced in front of their eyes. Nothing else needed to be said.*

'Commander, is there any need for this?' Benny was not pleased to be back in the presence of the odious Spang and yet here she was, the official witness to Mister Crofton's 'interview'.

Spang just smirked and turned back to his subject. 'I just need to know why a simple glass flower would cause everyone's favourite gardener to floor two of my best men, who may I add are now going to be flogged with new birch in public tomorrow. You will tell me...' Spang leant across the desk so his nose was nearly touching Mister Crofton's, 'or I will smash the damned thing right beneath your nose. Your choice.'

That was all it took. Mister Crofton grabbed him. His hand went tight around Spang's throat.

'Touch that flower, Commander,' Mister Crofton hissed through clenched teeth, 'and I swear I will...'

'You will what?' Spang gasped. 'There must be something very special about this trinket to provoke such a reaction.'

The two men stood there, eyes locked on each other. Behind Benny, a young guard stood motionless, his gun trained on the back of the gardener's skull. Spang's raised palm was all that was keeping Mister Crofton alive.

'Boys, this is getting us nowhere.' Benny placed a cooling hand on Mister Crofton's sinewy forearm. 'I'm sure Mister Crofton's hand just slipped...'

Without taking his eyes off Spang, Mister Crofton slowly released his grip. Benny followed the gaze to the face of the Investigator.

'... and I am also convinced, Commander, that a man of your experience realises that if you destroy the flower then Mister Crofton isn't likely to surrender much information.' As she spoke Benny eased Mister Crofton back into his seat.

Spang merely sat where the gardener had released him, his thin lips stretching into a viscous gash of a smile. 'Quite right, Professor. I'm sure my scientists can unlock this flower's secret. One way or another.'

'I suppose I'd better thank you, Professor.' A cold wind cut through Benny's clothes as they strolled back across the Collection, the gardener on a temporary reprieve until Spang's investigations brought something to light.

'Oh, there's no need, Mister Crofton. After all, it was perfectly sensible to try to throttle a high-ranking officer.'

Mister Crofton simply grunted and wandered back to his tools. However, as he walked through the drizzle, Benny couldn't help but notice that despite the usual gruffness, something was changed in him. Something was missing.

*His ears were still ringing from the explosion as the Corporal frantically checked through his pack. A direct hit had sent them flying. Martin was dead and he was alone on the battlefield. His pack had cushioned his fall, absorbing the impact.*

*For a moment it was as if the battle stopped around him as he sat there in the mud, his hands running over the small silver cube, a cube that now sported a tiny crack along its side. Even before he tried to launch the holo-letter the Corporal knew that the device had been rendered useless.*

*A single tear cut a path through the grime of his face, hanging on his chin for just a moment, before splashing to the floor. The enemy fighters roared nearer.*

'Was?' Benny questioned the Investigator. 'What do you mean was?'

Spang merely let out a long breath, casually digging some dirt from beneath his fingernail.

'The tests we carried out on Mister Crofton's flower have revealed nothing out of the ordinary. It appears that this harmless sculpture was nothing more than a harmless sculpture.'

'And I,' said Benny, holding her anger carefully in check, 'questioned your use of the past tense.'

Spang sighed. 'I'm afraid that our rather intensive molecular sequencing scans have left the bloom slightly less than it once was.'

And for the first time Benny noticed a box on Spang's desk, a box containing just a few shards of crystal and some fine scarlet powder.

*Knuckles turned to white as shaking hands tightened round the sheet of paper, almost tearing it in half. The embossed seal of the military High Command shone proudly at the top of the letter, preceding words that however many times you read them, stubbornly refused to make sense.*

It is with regret that, in this time of war, we must write to you in your moment of grief. The Commander in Chief wishes to pass on her condolences at this time of personal tragedy.

*The Corporal looked up from the letter and glanced around the pristine white of the medical bay, where other wounded soldiers lay. Damaged goods wrapped in starched white parcels.*

At 0950 on 06/05, an enemy battalion attacked Mander 17. It is with regret that we must inform you that your wife, Jane, was killed during the attack.

With Deepest Regret

*The Corporal winced at the stabbing pain in his arm as he lay back, the letter still clutched tightly in his hands. Stars slid by the viewport as the medical frigate powered towards home, the specs of light kaleidoscoping through the tears that the Corporal couldn't stop.*

Mister Crofton looked up from his work as Benny's shadow fell across his light. He shielded his eyes to block out the halo of sun that cast her into silhouette, nodding briefly in greeting before turning silently back to his planting. Benny knelt and placed the box next to the gardener, noticing Spang's docket of release attached to the side. She ripped the paper away, scrunching it into the pocket of her combats.

Mister Crofton carefully placed his trowel down on the gravel path and lifted the box into his lap. Benny couldn't decide whether she should go or not, but stayed, eyes wide as Mister Crofton removed the lid. He looked down at the shattered remains of the crystal flower, a gnarled hand grabbing a handful of the ruby tinged dust. However tight he clenched his fist, the dust simply cascaded through his fingers.

When the deep, wracking sobs came, all Benny could do was hold him.

*The Corporal looked up at what remained of his home. Every other house in their residential area was the same, wood and metal twisted into abstract destruction by the plasma bombardment. He felt a hand on his shoulder.*

'Corporal?'

*The soldier turned. He hadn't heard the Civil Service Minister's transport landing. The Minister smiled with just enough friendly sympathy as not to be obtrusive. He must have had a lot of practice recently.*

The Corporal nodded in greeting. 'Minister.'

'My department wanted somebody here when you arrived home.'

The Corporal shrugged. 'Some home.'

'We also wanted to pass on our regrets that your wife's funeral was forced to take place without you. You were stationed so far out on the front...'

'I understand.'

'We have had Jane's remains... prepared.' The Minister passed a wooden box over to the Corporal, who ran a finger slowly over the engraved nameplate.

'I'm very sorry for your loss, Corporal Crofton.' The Minister shook Crofton's hand and left.

Strange. Crofton actually relished the silence. Nobody asking how he was, nobody adjusting his medication, no damn counsellors making sure he was in touch with his feelings. Just silence.

*He lifted the lid of the box. Within lay a red crystal, shaped like a Draconian Lily. He removed the flower carefully from the box and placed it gently on the ground. It was cold to the touch.*

*Crofton walked across the burnt patch of ground that used to be his wife's garden, rolling his sleeves back. He picked up a spade and returned to where the flower lay. He hefted the unfamiliar tool and began to dig.*

'Crystallised ashes?'

'A custom on the colony where I grew up,' Mister Crofton grunted. 'Gardens everywhere full of the things. Used to think they were a bit pointless until...' He stopped, and started to load the ever present wheelbarrow.

'You never told anybody?'

'Why should I?' Mister Crofton asked defensively, smoothing the earth around the new planting with a practised foot. 'My business is my business. Brax knows. He gave me the job here, wanted somebody to look after the grounds. Was happy to do it, too.' He sighed heavily and looked into the distance.

'She loved gardening, put her heart and soul into that patch of dirt outside the house. Doing this was the only way I could think of keeping that soul alive.'

Benny shoved her hands deep into her pockets and walked up next to him. 'She'd have been proud.'

'Would she?' Mister Crofton chuckled mirthlessly. 'Maybe.' He hefted the wheelbarrow, onto the next job.

'Don't you want...' Benny looked in the direction of the discarded box.

'What's the point? There's nothing there anymore. They've taken her from me again.'

Benny placed a hand on Mister Crofton's forearm. 'Now what?' she asked. Mister Crofton looked at her. Where once was dependability, his eyes were now flecked with steely hatred.

'I want to kill them, Professor. I want to kill every last one of those bastards.'

Mister Crofton lifted the wheelbarrow and all Benny could do was watch as he walked away across the grounds of the Braxiatel Collection.

# 10: Midrash

## By Ian Mond

Security Officer Bertram was aware of the Special Interrogator's reputation. He'd heard the rumours. How the Interrogator could uncover all your secrets by just looking into your eyes. How he could make you cry by the whispering of a single word. How one touch of his hands was worse than the most painful torture.

This was, everyone was saying, exactly the man to break Braxiatel. Exactly the man to punish the autocrat who'd dared lay his hands on the Marshal. Anson had ordered Brax spared from everything until the Special Interrogator had had a look at him.

Bertram knew the rumours about this man were lies. It suited the Axis propaganda machine to perpetuate these stories. But he hoped that somehow this all meant that Braxiatel would get the kicking he deserved.

He'd also been briefed on the Special Interrogator's non-conformist attitudes. For the sake of the Axis he was ordered to grin and bear it.

But when he arrived at reception, Bertram was confronted by a man who met none of his expectations. The Special Interrogator was small and plump with thinning hair. He wore a shocking assemblage of non-regulation clothing, including scuffed boots, a pair of stained brown slacks and a striped shirt with a torn pocket. He was standing beside the reception desk admiring the view of the gardens and the Mansionhouse through the picture window.

Bertram introduced himself to the Interrogator who in turn handed him a plasti-disc and tablet embossed with Fifth Axis letterhead. 'So you're the reception committee,' the Interrogator's voice was strangely soothing. 'Well that's a little disappointing.'

'Sir, I have orders to take you straight to the Marshal's office.'

'No, that won't do at all.' The Special Interrogator grinned. 'How about a tour of the Collection instead?'

'You can't do this!'

'Ah Professor, did the guards let you in?' Marshal Anson's smug smile only infuriated Benny. 'Will you take a seat?' Anson gestured at a plush leather chair. 'It's just I hate it when you storm up and down my office.'

Benny's initial fury was now on simmer. She'd been an idiot barging in here all fury and spittle, thinking it might actually make a difference. Tactics, Benny, tactics. If he wanted to be all charming and respectable, then she had to be all mocking and cheeky. It's what he seemed to like. It's how he played the game.

'I can guess why you're so upset.'

'You're going to torture him!'

Anson laughed. 'That's a little melodramatic.'

Benny mock-slapped her forehead. 'Oh I forgot; you Axis boys are such genial chappies. I'm sure Brax and this Interrogator are going to sit down to a nice cup of tea and amiably discuss the weather.'

Anson's smug smile faltered slightly. Benny cheered her little victory. 'He tried to kill me. Forgive me if I bear him no great love.'

'I forgive you.' She was going to give nothing to him.

Anson got to his feet, looking as if he wanted more from this encounter. Like this was a date and they'd got off on the wrong foot. 'Special Interrogator Ash Madai is a non-conformist,' he said. 'Normally we'd have issues with such a character, but the Interrogator generates results. As far as I'm aware he's never used torture as a means to gain information.'

'There's always a first time. And you could order this to be that time.'

'Oh yes. But I have ordered the opposite. Things will get better here, Bernice. Things will calm down. When Braxiatel speaks.'

'You know he'd rather die than tell you his secrets. Even at the cost of this Collection and everyone here.'

Anson shook his head, and for a split second, Benny thought she could see a hint of compassion in his eyes. 'The Special Interrogator has never failed, Bernice. Whether he likes it or not, Braxiatel will talk.'

The Special Interrogator insisted on his guided tour of the Collection. Bertram, who was trying to conceal the itch he felt at the man's lack of uniform protocol, confirmed the change of arrangement with the Marshal. The order was finally given, and the hyperactive Special Interrogator and his sullen guide began the tour.

Bertram quickly realised the Special Interrogator was more interested in the people than the actual Collection. Ignoring the documents and artefacts, he would carefully examine every individual as they studied, spoke in hushed whispers and scurried on to their next destination.

'So many stories,' the Interrogator said, winking at a female academic with chestnut hair.

Soon after reaching the Literature section, the Interrogator danced up to Bertram and pointed at an Axis academic sitting at one of the many wooden desks. One of the first to arrive here to study. The man was bowed over a fragile-looking manuscript, gloved index finger tracing a pattern across the parchment. He was deep in concentration, lost in a world of antiquity. What a bore, Bertram thought.

'Do you see him?' The Interrogator grinned like an excited boy. 'Oh it's so marvellous.'

'I'm sorry, sir?' Bertram nearly yawned.

'In four days that man will have the happiest moment of his life. In this very Department he will find a piece of ancient parchment for which he has been searching for most of his career. The moment he recognises the parchment, he will break down and cry. How wonderful.'

Then, as they were leaving, the Interrogator, for no readily apparent reason, stopped suddenly, clutched his ample stomach and began to wail.

Swallowing his embarrassment, Bertram asked the Interrogator if anything were wrong.

'Did you see that poor old lady we passed only moments ago?'

Bertram hadn't, but pretended otherwise.

'She's an academic, and long ago when she was a young girl she wrote her Doctorate thesis on the Canticlese Poets. Four days from now another Axis academic will visit the Collection. He will hunt down that poor lady and beat her because several years ago she had the temerity to contradict his work.'

When they reached the Garden of Whispers, the Interrogator really let his hair down. He skipped over to the lake and gazed into the water.

To the Interrogator's left, Mister Crofton was tending one of the oaks that had been damaged in the invasion.

The Interrogator treated the Groundskeeper like an old and trusted friend. They spent an excruciating twenty minutes discussing plants. Especially something called an azalea. It took less time than Bertram expected. After all, Mister Crofton had good reason to react to Axis uniforms now. But the Interrogator actually put a hand on his shoulder.

And Mister Crofton actually smiled.

These are the words that Bertram did not hear. As the Interrogator was about to leave, he turned to Mister Crofton. 'I know you hate them, but your sabotage plans will not succeed.'

Mister Crofton sighed. 'I know. But I feel so –'

'Helpless? No, not at all. I can see what this garden will be; something more beautiful than you could ever envisage. A magnificent testament to your wife.'

Mister Crofton smiled sadly. 'Thank you.'

The two men shook hands.

Bertram and the Interrogator next visited the Hamlet, finishing their journey at The Caretaker's Cottage. The Special Interrogator seemed content to sit in the bar and watch the other Officers and academics enjoy themselves.

After half an hour a fat man with a proud and haughty gaze entered the Cottage. Bertram recognised him immediately: the collaborator, Jason Kane. He should like the man; the early converts to the cause were always eager, energetic, adding new ideas to the Axis. That was why they were the Fifth Axis. The four directions of spacetime, plus the fifth axis of the human spirit. Unfortunately, in Kane's case, the human spirit was more like that of a rat. He was fat while his former friends were thin. And still he looked hungry.

Kane's arrival brought life back into the Interrogator. He jumped from his chair and, in a flurry of disorganised movement, rushed over to the man. The Interrogator shook Kane's hand, then leant over and whispered something into his ear. Even from his vantage point, Bertram could see Kane's sudden transformation.

How the proud eyes widened with surprise, how the pudgy face became pale.

Kane pushed himself away from the Interrogator, his body trembling. And he was crying. Bertram could definitely see tears streak down the man's face.

Kane dashed out of The Caretaker's Cottage, leaving the Interrogator to shrug his shoulders and return to the table

'What did you say?' Bertram wanted to know. But instead he made the mistake of looking into the Interrogator's eyes. He remembered the night they took his mother away. He remembered how proud he'd felt because he'd been the one to inform on her. Bertram remembered her expression. The look of shock, of betrayal, of pain. And love. She still loved him despite what he had done.

*She was my mother...*

'You can pontificate about your crimes later,' the Special Interrogator said. 'I think it's time I questioned Irving Braxiatel.'

When Benny entered her suite, she found Bev Tarrant sitting on her chaise lounge. Her chestnut hair was still neatly tied back in that sexy scientist pony tail.

'I have something from Brax,' she said.

Benny was distracted by an annoying whine coming from her bedroom. 'What did you do to Joseph?'

'He's not fond of me, which might be your doing, so I shut him away.' Bev removed a folded piece of paper from her trouser pocket. 'Brax asked me to hand this to you.'

Benny took the note and opened it. She quickly scanned it, eyes narrowing. 'How did you get this?'

'He gave it to me a few weeks ago, back when they were allowing him regular visitors. He said I was to hand it over when he'd pushed them so far that they sent for a certain Special Interrogator. What did the Marshal say?'

Benny gave a short description of her meeting. She could hear the frustration in her voice.

She missed Peter. And Adrian. And even Jason.
She missed having adventures. She missed tight scrapes and japes. She missed the wonders of the Universe.
Once Bev had gone, Benny took a closer look at Brax's note. She chewed her bottom lip and wondered what it all meant. She wasn't in the mood for treasure hunts, but here was Brax sending her on one. Even locked up he could annoy her. Benny opened her bedroom door and Joseph shot out like the proverbial cork from a champagne bottle.
'Calm down, Joseph,' she said. 'I need your help.'

The Marshal eyed the Special Interrogator with interest. He'd been prepared for a non-conformist, but he still found the man's clothing and general demeanour irritating. How could what the Axis stood for mean anything if already, at the centre of things, the outward signs of their inner intent... He sighed. The sooner the Interrogator was questioning the prisoner, the better.
With Bertram dismissed, the Marshal now took on the role of guide as he led the Interrogator to Brax's rooms. Irving Braxiatel, resplendent in a luxurious cream suit, was sitting, eyes closed, palms resting on his knees.
A chair opposite him remained vacant. He'd prepared.
The sight of him made Anson angry, just for a moment. But he was a human. He controlled himself.
'You can leave me now,' whispered the Interrogator, eyes locked on the prisoner.
'I'd like to keep a man on guard.'
'Not needed,' said the Interrogator, still staring at Braxiatel. 'You can watch proceedings from your cameras.'
Anson didn't argue. The orders said he was to comply with all the Special Interrogator's wishes, no matter how questionable.
'Marshal, you're likely to hear me say strange things that sometimes will border on the treacherous.' The Interrogator stopped on the threshold and looked again at Anson. 'It's the way I work. But you will get your information.'

Special Interrogator Ash Madai took his seat opposite Irving Braxiatel.
'Hello Irving. It's lovely to see you again after so long.'
Braxiatel's eyes remained closed.
'I had a guided tour of your Collection, and what a wonderous place it is. You must love it dearly.'
Still nothing from Braxiatel.
'While I was walking around I pondered how best to conduct this little chat. You know me quite well, Irving; know how I can read the essence of others, how I'm able to see where they've been and where they're going.

It's so easy with humanoids, they're such open books.

'But you're different. Well, of course you are. You're aloof and mysterious. Methodical. Precise. Practical. And completely lacking in personality. To most people, just a name on the door. For two days you've sat here building a shield against me, and what an excellent job you've done.

'I can't read you at all.'

Benny stared at the ancient wooden box on her desk. It stared back at her. Finding the box had actually been no problem. With help from Brax's note and a great deal of assistance from Joseph, she had tracked down the room. It had been hidden between two massive shelves in the Archaeology Department. Programmed with an over-ride code, Joseph had opened the concealed door with ease.

The room had smelt of pine and wet grass. It was bare except for a plinth at its centre. On the plinth was an ancient wooden box.

She'd carefully tucked the box into the fold of her large coat, and quickly made her way back to her rooms.

Benny had now been examining the box for over half an hour. The surface was badly scratched, but she could just make out what she believed was Ancient Hebrew. If only it was clear enough to translate.

*If Brax wanted me to find it, then how dangerous could it be?*
Deadly.

Taking a deep, suspicious breath, Benny unlatched the rusted seal.

The box *snicked* open.

And Benny was bathed in golden light.

'I knew you'd be a challenge.' The Special Interrogator rubbed his hands together. 'So while I wandered through your Departments and gardens and cottages, and while I read the many stories littered through the Collection, I pondered over my options.

'Torturing you is pointless. You'd die rather than speak.

'I don't believe threatening your friends would work either. Maybe if I put a gun to Professor Summerfield's head, you'd consider speaking. But there are no guarantees. You're as likely to let her die.

'If I wanted to, I could order the Marshal to torch this entire Collection. Burn it to the ground. But what would be the point? You still wouldn't say a word.

'So what does a man do?

'Something very clever I should expect.'

When the fireworks were over, Benny carefully removed a small object from the box. It was a ring: an embossed seal, with an intricate golden band. Still glittering and sparking, Benny could just make out the delicate lettering.

Ancient Hebrew.

Yud. Kay. Vav. Kay.

Benny swallowed. This was big mojo.

But what was the ring's relation to an Axis Special Interrogator?

She whispered the name Ash Madai, tasting it, trying to recognise its flavour. Something about the name nagged at her thoughts.

Why couldn't Brax have been more detailed? Why such a bloody cryptic letter?

*Once you find the box, make sure you hide it from Interrogator Ash Madai.*

What was the connection?

Playing a hunch, Benny called Joseph over and asked for any non-Axis references to Ash Madai.

Joseph responded immediately. 'Also known as Asmodeus. Ashmadai features in Jewish folktale (*Midrash*), specifically those relating to King Solomon and the building of the Holy Temple. Ashmadai assisted King Solomon in finding the Shamir.'

'The Shamir?'

'A magical worm that could cut through rock.'

'Was Ashmadai King Solomon's architect?'

'No.' Joseph paused. 'He was King of the Demons.'

'Irving, you know why I'm here. I want what's mine.

'I pity you, Irving. I pity you because I know you wanted to be so much more. When you were young, you desired freedom. You wanted to break the shackles of your people and enjoy the wonders of the universe. You'd no longer be methodical, precise and practical. Out there, you'd be transformed into a totally different person, both physically and mentally. You'd actually find yourself a personality.

'But it never happened. Your opportunity never came. Or maybe it did and you were too frightened to seize it. Others had those adventures for you.

'And so here you are, hiding behind all this beauty: artefacts and documents and treasures. You think this is a replacement for a dream you never realised. But deep down you know it's nothing compared to leaving your own mark on the universe.

'To become legend.

'Because in your own arrogant way, that's what you really wanted to be. A legend. A camp-fire story.

'And now here you are, a prisoner, frightened at how quickly certainty has become uncertainty. And there's nothing you can do to stop it.

'But here's a secret, Irving, something you and the Axis don't know. The seeds of their downfall will happen here in this Collection. As I toured earlier today I read so many different stories, I saw so many different outcomes. And a picture became clear. In that picture I saw precisely how the Axis would crumble.

'My offer to you is a simple one. Tell me what I want to know, or I shall leave this room and tell *them* how it will happen.

'You see Irving, my moment in history came and went long ago. I don't care anymore. I just want what is mine. But I know that you do care. The very thought of time being tampered with not only frightens you, but it angers you. It actually brings out the colour in those high cheekbones of yours. Gives you character.

'So the choice is yours, Irving.'

The Special Interrogator sat back and waited.

And for the first time in two days, Irving Braxiatel's eyes fluttered open.

Moments later, the Interrogator emerged.

'Do you have the information? Do you know where Braxiatel keeps his time equipment?' Anson was anxious. He wasn't sure what he'd seen or heard in that room. None of it made any sense; Braxiatel never said a word. And yet... Anson was convinced something had been communicated.

'I need to rest,' said the Special Interrogator. He swept past Anson and headed towards the elevator. Anson caught up with him and placed a hand on the Interrogator's shoulder.

The Special Interrogator shrugged off Anson and turned around. He looked the Marshal in the eye. 'Does she know how you feel about her?'

The Marshal took a step backwards, his hand shaking. Images of her were splashed against his mind in glorious technicolour detail. Fantasies he'd never admit to.

He was human, he was in control.

He closed his eyes against the onslaught.

When he opened them again, the Interrogator was gone.

The door to Benny's rooms slid open.

'I've been expecting you,' Bernice said to the Special Interrogator. 'I've always wanted to say that.'

Ash strode into her room, sporting an impish smile. Benny hadn't been sure what to expect, but certainly not a guy who looked like he'd just escaped a hiking convention in the Pyrenees. He plopped down on her chaise lounge, still grinning.

'You're definitely a lot... ah... plumper than I expected.' Benny said, still sitting at her desk. The ring was in the top pocket of her shirt.

'I've come in all shapes and sizes.'

'You don't seriously expect me to believe that you're the King of the Demons.'

'You've been reading the folktales. Bernice... you don't mind me calling you Bernice, do you?'

'Benny is fine.'

'Well, Benny, you can either see me as a demon or as an alien with superior intelligence and strange fashion sense. You've squared that circle before. It really doesn't matter.'

'And why are you working for the Axis?'

'It's a living.'

Benny nearly choked on the response. 'That's such a cop-out.'

'No, it's an irrelevance. Just like the ring in your top pocket.'

Seeing there was no point hiding it, Benny brought the ring out into the open. It glittered in her hand. It really was a beautiful piece of jewellery, maybe a little chunky for her tastes. 'It has God's name written on the seal.'

'Yes.'

'It's Solomon's ring, isn't it?'

'Sure is.'

'But Solomon's ring is –'

'– in your hand,' finished Ash with a cheeky smile. 'Honestly, Benny. It doesn't matter whether you believe that is the fabled ring of Solomon, or a piece of alien technology. Either way: it's my ring.'

'Not if I read the legends correctly. According to *Midrash*, this is only your ring if I give it to you of my own free will.'

'Yes,' Ash said. 'That's why Braxiatel asked you to retrieve it. He knew I might crack his defences, so he wanted one more layer of protection. He trusts you.'

'And did you... crack his defences?'

'Only a little. Enough to know you had the ring. It's all the information I needed. Of course, if I was really interested in his time equipment, I would have pushed the issue further. But I was never here on Axis business. May I please have it?'

'No.'

'And why not?' Ash sounded disappointed

'You know why.'

'Ah yes... Irving is such a possessive man. He wants the ring because he's yet to discover its secrets. What he hasn't realised is: the ring has no secrets. It only functions on Earth, and only for those with the right genetic type. Like others of my... race.'

'And King Solomon.'

'Was imbued with the knowledge to use the ring. But I thought we didn't believe in King Solomon?'

Benny ignored the remark. 'Why should I trust you?'

Ash leaned forward, his eyes meeting Benny's. 'It's all about you,' he said. 'Everyone else, I can see where it's going. Your story is not so predictable.'

'Can we not do the cryptic stuff? I get enough of that from Brax.'

'Some of the people here see you as a traitor. Others see you as a threat. And others love you so deeply...'

'Thanks for the pressure,' Benny said. Goddess, she needed a drink.

'You don't need alcohol,' Ash told her. 'And you don't need that ring. Benny, you can save them all. You can be someone great.'

'I don't want to be someone great... I just want to be a mother. And if you think that uplifting crap is going to change my mind about the ring...'

Ash sighed. 'I was hoping I wouldn't have to do this. In less than a minute Axis guards will storm this room looking for me. When I'm captured, I will tell them where Peter is.'

Benny's throat went dry, icicles forming in her stomach. He knew about Peter. How the blazes did he know about Peter? 'You wouldn't.'

'Yes. I would.'

Benny looked into his eyes and knew he was telling the truth. She saw her little baby as a grown man, tall and strong, complete with sharp fangs, cheeky black eyes and long blonde curls. Her son – the most beautiful person Benny had ever seen – bent over and whispered something in her ear. She shivered as Peter's downy fur brushed against her ear-lobe.

'That future is only a probability, Benny. The choice is yours.'

The image shattered. Benny knew she was crying; the tears were wonderful. She handed Ash his prize.

He looked at the ring and smiled. It was the most lovely, friendly, gorgeous, happy smile Benny had ever had the fortune of seeing.

For a moment she was alive again, and she wanted to dance and sing and write very bad poetry about flowers and clouds.

She blinked. Ash had gone.

Ten seconds later the doors slid open and in stormed Axis guards.

They bundled her out of her rooms, and spent the next five minutes searching it. She was then taken to the Marshal's office where she was questioned for over an hour. Finally they let her go.

Of the Special Interrogator there was no sign.

Back in her suite Benny thought about her son. The child and the adult.

She thought about stories, about fables, about *Midrash*. She imagined leaning over her little baby son and telling him the tale of King Solomon and the Shamir. Or maybe something a little more traditional: Goldilocks and the Three Bears, or Red Riding Hood, or the Lion and the Salamander. And then there were her own exciting adventures, full of japes and scrapes and tight escapes.

She remembered what Ash had said.

*'That future is only a probability Benny. The choice is yours.'*

# 11: Fear of Corners
## By Mark Stevens

Shadows converge, gathering weight behind you, propelling you deeper into the nightmare.

You edge forward, eyes adjusting to the gloom, aware that you're gripping something tightly in one hand, unable to spare a glance to confirm if it's a gun because you've suddenly realised you're not alone.

He sits in a wicker armchair, resplendent in an immaculate grey suit, looking calm and relaxed. A little disconcerting, considering the young woman gasping for breath within the grip of his outstretched hand. The fog within your head swirls; there's a memory of the woman in there, somewhere.

The man in grey raises his other hand and gestures towards something within the darkness behind him. The shadows disperse and a tall figure, bathed in a soft white light, slides out of the gloom to join him. You have trouble focusing on the newcomer, your gaze partially repelled by the corona of light that surrounds him, but you can't help notice an uncanny similarity between the two men.

'I have no more use for this one,' the grey man informs his angelic twin, tightening his grip on the young woman. 'Take her and leave this vessel for good.'

The white figure nods in agreement, but lets out a shrill hiss as it appears to notice you for the first time.

'Oh, her?' the grey man says, eyes fixed on you. 'I wouldn't worry about her.'

The woman struggles and whimpers, managing to turn her head a little in your direction. Her eyes sparkle with instant recognition.

'Benny!' she gasps hoarsely. 'Please...'

The cold metal in your right hand jogs a recent memory, reinforcing a precise set of instructions that were recently relayed to you. Nothing else is making much sense right now, so you take advantage of this moment of clarity.

'Are you Iriving Braxiatel?' you ask the grey man.

'Yes,' he replies.

That's all you need to know.

You step forward, level your gun and pull the trigger.

*My dearest Irving,*
*How long has it been since we shared any regular communication with one another? Far too long, for which I must apologise. I sense*

*something in the air, something that suggests the time is right for a final get-together, if you'll excuse the double meaning.*
*I understand you may have some reservations regarding my release from captivity, but I feel I deserve an opportunity to prove myself, to illustrate that I have the capacity for change. I really didn't mean to hurt any of those people: all that's in the past, which I understand is a relative concept for us, but I believe I've come a long way since then.*
*Will you entertain the notion of a reunion if I promise not to kill anyone again?*
*Yours faithfully,*
*a friend in need.*

I'd almost forgotten how therapeutic it is to actually *write* a diary. And Goddess, these days, I need something therapeutic.

They can't outlaw this. They can, of course, enter by force and read it, but not before I've written it. The pen truly is mightier than the holostatic imaging device. There's no rewinding when you make a mistake. It's warts, coffee stains and all.

The big news is: the Axis are going to connect the Collection to something called the Chiasm.

Various physicists I know talked to me about it at our particular tables at the cafés. I think I managed to grasp the basics. Something about an interdimensional origami trick that the Axis have perfected, allowing them to fold localised areas of space and literally hook them up to their huge Chiasm network: a spaghetti junction of corridors and conduits that grants them instant access to the furthest reaches of their conquered territories. The Collection becomes part of one big happy Axis family, offering instantaneous travel, no warp drive required.

That might explain how they're able to conquer worlds so quickly, but it doesn't tell us why. My techie mates are adamant: the Chiasm uses spacetime, it doesn't change history.

All of this, of course, is technology far beyond anything ex-colonials like the Axis should have.

*Later...*

We've gained some satisfaction from seeing the Axis baffled, perhaps a little scared by what's happening. But it's worrying for all of us, too. There's something in the Collection that's thrown their Chiasm technology bang out of whack. It's almost as if the Collection's trying to reject the Chiasm, rearranging itself building by building to keep one step ahead of the grafting process. Certain buildings are... misplacing themselves. Not being where they're supposed to be, wrapping

themselves up in knots and extruding doors into entirely different buildings.
I know what that reminds me of.

*Later...*

The Axis have managed to locate the source of the disturbance: a spatial anomaly located within the Small Trianon, one of the smaller outbuildings.
*(Post It note covering the above.)*
Brax has vanished! He's been gone a week, and they hadn't told us! Maybe it's because he was the only person who could get inside the Small Trianon. Maybe he's finally got to his timeship and escaped.
Anson must be furious.
Maybe Brax isn't coming back.
It's not an official announcement. It's a rumour doing the rounds. It's got out because Bev's vanished too, and they think they might have run away together.
Now *that* is my idea of an ill-starred romance.

*Dearest Irving,*
*I can understand your reluctance to reacquaint yourself with me. It must be difficult keeping me so close to hand, serving as a constant reminder of the deeds we have perpetrated.*
*But then I expected you to conform to the dictates and protocols of our people, agreeing to forfeit any further chances to rejuvenate you mind, body and spirit. Surely the adherence to this most sacred convention would have been the wisest course of action, to ensure that I would never harm anyone again?*
*Yours faithfully,*
*your eternal prisoner.*

There's a dreamlike familiarity to all of this: to the never-ending labyrinth of corridors that fade into being with each new step you take.
But that's why you know this isn't a dream, because there you'd be unable to run. This is all too real, even the fear that grips you: not the fuzzy, ambiguous fear of your dreams, but something much colder, much heavier. You're not even sure what's driving you forward; the desire to evade whatever it is that has lured you here, or the need to find and confront those responsible.
One after another, the corridors unfold themselves before you. Sometimes the path ahead is straight, the walls apparently alive with a barely perceptible hum. The rest of the time, the corridor will snap off at right-angles, automatically instilling a dread within you, fearing what's

going to be waiting for you as your momentum sends you hurtling round each new corner.

The darkness gathers mass around you, dispelling any notion that you could turn round and leave this place, if you so wished.

*—snap—*

Now there is no more corridor, only a door, slightly ajar.

You instinctively reach out to push the door open, suddenly aware that you're carrying a gun.

*Dear Irving,*

*I get the feeling there are things afoot to which I'm not being made privy. If I'm to remain shackled here, deep within the confines of your vessel, I feel it only fair to be informed when there is a threat to its integrity.*

*But then you wouldn't like that, would you? The possibility of some foreign body infiltrating your pride and joy must fill you with terror, especially if they were to happen upon my person and accidentally set me free. The consequences of this must scarcely bear thinking about. For you, at least. For me it's a most interesting possibility to behold.*

*Yours, with new found hope.*

I can't remember what I had for breakfast this morning. Not something to be concerned about, normally, but I only finished eating it an hour ago.

I've been monitoring some of the Axis' communication channels and it appears that this short-term memory loss has become something of an epidemic, affecting not only us but the occupying forces too. They've managed to triangulate the source of the disorientation – no prizes for guessing where it is – which is why the Axis are now moving their centre of operations as far away from the Trianon buildings as possible.

Assuming, of course, they remember where they're off to.

>*ping*<

Great, more distractions. 'Go ahead, Joseph.'

'You have an incoming communiqué, Professor Summerfield.'

'Who from?'

'It is hard to say. The communiqué in question... is actually a room. Mr Braxiatel's study, I believe.'

'His... study?' I went into the kitchen to make a cup of tea. And while I was there I realised that the fridge really could do with defrosting.

I was just doing that when Joseph floated in and made a sound like a cough. 'The small matter of the arrived room?'

'Eh? Oh, yes, that! Lead the way.'

Joseph inclined himself a little.

'Mr Braxiatel's study is currently located in your bathroom.'

Okay, *now* I've got a headache.

*Irving,*
   *I think we both know that you're not the only one who'd make a suitable host for me. Of course, you'd never take the chance and see if you could best me in a battle of the wills. You know you lack the mental capacity to keep me safely under control, knowing that at any moment I could pummel your consciousness into submission and exploit you like a puppet.*
   *You wouldn't want to risk that, would you? But at the same time you know you no longer have a choice. When your silly little friends finally understand what's really going on, what are you going to do? Run away again?*
   *You make me laugh, time fool.*

It stretches up into the sky before you, its shadow more than just an absence of sunlight; the intricate sculpture mounted on the building's crown casts complex silhouettes into the garden around you, their meaning significant but unknown.
   Why are you here?
   You ponder that question, reaching out to touch the veined marble, finding it slightly warm to the touch. Is that a faint vibration you sense, deep within? You press an ear to the outer wall, hoping that something inside will reveal its secrets to you, but hear nothing.
   You take a few steps away from the building, hoping to get a sense of the bigger picture, something that could trigger a useful memory.
   But there is nothing. Just you and the stone building.
   You spend the next five minutes walking around the building's perimeter, trailing a hand lazily over the red marble, unwilling to break contact with the one thing that may hold the answers to your past and future. You know this is the right time, the right place, but what has drawn you here?
   You find it before you knew you were looking for it . The ornate locking mechanism rests in the base of one of the walls, partially hidden by the thick clumps of moss that cling to the lower part of the building.
   You reach into your back pocket and retrieve a thin, spindly key you somehow knew was there.
   You insert it into the lock, give it a quick turn and stand back as a nerve-jangling grating sound alerts you to the presence of a doorway further along the wall.
   There's nothing to lose now. You draw your gun and step inside.
   Hang on a second – a *gun*?

\* \* \* \*

*Brax,*
*I can hear them tearing the place apart.*
*Are you doing everything you can to keep me safe? You're so close now, I can almost smell you. You know you can't hide for very much longer. Sooner or later they're going to find you. And when they find you, they'll have found me.*
*It was a nice touch, dressing up our mutual prison as a museum, but you had to go and draw a little bit too much attention to it, didn't you? And now your little friends, one by one, are starting to learn that there's more about you than meets the eye.*
*You're running out of time. It's time to let me go.*
*You know it's the only way.*
*Yours,*
*hungry.*

Reality's out of joint.

I know I'm in my own rooms, that the metallic sphere flitting to and fro belongs to me, that someone's messing with spatial technology and it's all gone terribly wrong. Sure, I can remember all that lot easily enough. But what's my name?

'You, floating ball thing,' I address the sphere. 'Who am I?'

'You're Professor Bernice Summerfield.'

I ponder this for a moment or two, hoping it'll open the floodgates to a lifetime's worth of memories, but there's nothing there. Nothing tangible, at least. I feel a strange sense of yearning, that I miss someone called Peter, whoever he is. Perhaps it's best not to dwell too much on these unreliable fragments, because there's a job to do.

Yes, a job to do! That's right, I'm standing inside someone's study with an unfulfilled sense of purpose. It's definitely not my study. At least, I hope it's not. I wouldn't have built it inside my bathroom. I can hear guards walking back and forth in an outside which isn't supposed to be there and which I certainly haven't walked through. Oak panelling? Definitely not my cup of tea. Or am I a coffee person? It's getting rather hard to remember.

I take a step further inside, holding on to the door in case it vanishes.

The surface of a nearby desk ripples with colour as some discrete hologramatic technology powers itself up. 'Please state your name for security clearance,' says a dispassionate female voice from within.

'Erm,' I begin, before realising it's slipped my mind once again.

'Voice analysis confirmed. Security clearance granted.'

'Ooh, clever.' I'm hoping that the geography problems have shorted out the surveillance of this room. Bathtime is going to be tricky enough as it is.

'Message from Iriving Braxiatel begins...'

From this moment on, the headache becomes unbearable. There's now a black hole inside my head pulling everything I've ever known into its event horizon, condensing my memories into a singularity that now extends into the immediate future. I can see everything that I will do from this moment on. My future self will retrieve a gun and a key from a previously locked drawer.

I see you, future self.

I see what you're about to do and it scares me.

You're still trying to keep it together when the little cube of space containing the study folds itself away, depositing you on the other side of the Collection, next to a familiar looking building.

It stretches up into the sky before you...

*Brax,*

*Many thanks for you kind invitation to dinner and the promise of a new host. I knew you'd come round and see sense eventually. It was the only way. I look forward to meeting my new body. The woman out of time, this Tarrant girl, sounds a most agreeable form. I'm most intrigued by the mystery surrounding her and look forward to sharing my mind with hers.*

*I knew I could count on you to turn your back on your responsibilities and take the easy way out. But you know you've no other choice.*

*Until we meet,*

*forever watching.*

The projectile's momentum strikes Irving Braxiatel square in the chest, knocking him off balance, irreparably damaging the immaculate grey suit. He releases his grip on the young woman, who collapses like a rag doll, gasping for breath.

The figure in white emits a shriek that burrows deep into your head, setting your teeth on edge, then begins walking towards you. Your gun still raised, you adjust your aim to point the weapon at the advancing figure and pull the trigger.

The gun clicks, having already used its only bullet.

Sensing your vulnerability, the figure quickens its pace. Only a few feet away, you can feel its harsh, bright glow on your skin, an ice cold radiance that unfurls from its body in wispy swirls. You try to take a step backwards, but your legs appear unwilling to move. As the brilliant white creature reaches out to deliver its deathly caress, you close your eyes, wondering if your only bullet found the wrong target.

The creature hisses once more, only this time there's something desperate in its cry. You open your eyes to see the creature falling to its knees, doubling over in pain. Then, suddenly, its body begins to twist and contort as it is dragged, very slowly and deliberately, across the floor towards the prone figure of Irving Braxiatel, still lying spread-eagled beside his wicker chair.

Tendrils of bright matter roll off the creature's body, swirling as if caught in a current that draws them directly towards Braxiatel's chest wound. The creature makes a desperate attempt to cling onto something tangible, unwilling to be drawn towards the wounded man, but the forces at work are too powerful for it to overcome. With a final cry of defiance the creature begins to fall apart, now nothing more than a fierce white cloud of energy that corkscrews across the floor, pouring itself into Braxiatel.

A hushed darkness gathers within the room.

Irving Braxiatel lies perfectly still for a moment or two, then suddenly comes to with a jolt. For someone who's just been shot and consumed by another life form, he looks more annoyed and distracted than anything else. He spends a moment or two gathering his bearings then pulls himself to feet, dusting himself down, tutting as his fingers trace the bullet hole in his grey suit.

He glances over in your direction.

He looks exactly the same as he always did. Only that somehow seems to have taken a great effort on his part.

'Why, Bernice! How good of you to join us,' he says. 'Quite literally, it would seem.'

It would be nice to say that things are returning to normal, although I suspect that won't be the case for quite some time. Geographically, things are better, anyway.

The bullet hadn't been enough to kill him, just enough to make the thing in white think it had its chance. That's all he would say. I think it was all something to do with his people, with their ability to change bodies. Somewhere, buried deep within my subconscious, are the answers to a lot of questions that people are asking. I woke up the other night yelling 'Watcher!' But I don't know if that was a name or a greeting.

Anson didn't waste any time debriefing me about what transpired inside the Small Trianon. I told him as much as I could remember, which wasn't very much, which frustrated me as much as it did him. Nevertheless, as a precaution the Axis have disconnected the Collection from the Chiasm, at least until they're able to determine what it is about the Trianon buildings that caused such upheaval. Anson obviously suspects it was the timeship. But he still can't find it.

Bev's uneasy about Brax now. I think she knows why he did what he did, understood the plan when she was told about it, but that doesn't make it any easier to deal with.

What happened to him in the Small Trianon? I close my eyes and all I can see are indeterminate shapes and a whole lot of confusion. I went to see him last night, allowed in because Anson, obviously freaked out, has decided that cat and mouse might once again be the most discrete approach to his interrogation. I found Brax tearing up a stack of personal correspondence.

'Keep it here, Bernice,' he said, thumping his chest. 'Keep it inside, and don't let it out until you have to.'

'What?'

He turned to me and flung the bits of paper in the air, managing a smile as he watched them flash and burn in the field he'd hung there for that purpose. 'Hope for the future,' he said. And his smile faded.

# 12: The Traitors
## By Jonathan Morris

He looked at her. The monitor lit her face softly, her eyes shifting as she read, her head nodding unconsciously. She brushed hairs back from her forehead and moistened her lips, her expression intent and confident. The keyboard clicked under her fingertips.

She noticed his presence, and fixed him to the spot with her pale, green eyes. As she turned her features dipped into the sunlight. Her smile was sardonic but welcoming, and widened as he approached.

'At ease.'

Radek was not at ease. His mouth ran dry and his heart thudded. He was conscious of the floor pressing against his boots. He faced Mushtaq Anson as squarely and respectfully as he could. As he had been trained to do. He'd seen image-prints of the Marshal but now that they were in the same room together, he seemed somehow more real than life. His dark skin more leathered and lined, his hair thinner and grey-flecked.

The Marshal turned his attention away from the fresco that dominated one wall of his office. 'You're a recent arrival... Officer Radek?'

'Yes, sir.' Squarely and respectfully, maintaining eye contact. 'This hour.'

'Good, good. Seen much of the place, yet?'

'No, sir.'

'You should. Shame to miss out, a handsome fellow like yourself.'

'Yes, sir.' Radek felt a fluster of nervousness as he realised he had agreed with the 'handsome'.

'The Braxiatel Collection.' The Marshal indicated the paintings and statuettes that filled the room with a casual wave of his hand. 'The greatest artworks the galaxy has to offer, and now Axis property. And yet, not the entire collection. Certain pieces are conspicuous by their absence. This is something of a frustration to me, you understand. I am a completist by nature.

'It would seem that moments before our arrival, certain items were removed. Items of particular value and interest. The action of the museum staff, naturally. We have endeavoured to persuade them to return these items, but we do not yet have all that we require. They are holding out on us. I am reluctant to use force against them - coercion is such an unsubtle instrument, and scars heal tougher than skin - and I would prefer to maintain a spirit of co-operation.

'I need your assistance, Officer. The Axis are rather keen to discover the whereabouts of -' He checked with his softscreen, '- the blade of Galandar. A relic of a long-lost civilisation. The archaeology need not concern you. What should concern you is a curator, name of Mesa.' He collected an id-print from a coffee table and handed it to Radek.

The glossy print showed the face of a young woman, attractive, in her mid-twenties. Black hair in central parting cut to the neckline, thick, long eyebrows, pale green eyes, a slight blush to her cheeks. Her expression had a touch of cynicism about it, as though she were restraining herself from laughing at a private joke.

'She had special responsibility for the maintenance of the Galandar relics, and would seem to be the most likely candidate to know their location.'

'She has resisted questioning?' asked Radek.

'So far, we have not subjected her to the full rigours of interrogation. As I said, I would prefer the staff to co-operate willingly. Officer, I would like you to talk to her. Get to know her. Gain her trust. Persuade her, so we don't have to.'

She looked at him. He stood framed in the doorway, arms behind his back. He looked too young for his uniform, like a boy playing at soldiers. He had puppy-fat cheeks, dimpled as he grinned. His sandy hair fell in a dishevelled fringe and his blue-grey eyes gazed back at her with an unnerving intensity.

'Can I help you?'

Mesa struggled up the museum steps, her palms gripping the covers of a pile of research books. Her bag strap bit into her shoulder, its lopsided mass creating a twist in her back. It was another day of glaring, sweltering summer and the marble stonework baked in the brilliance.

The Axis guards stood on either side of the entrance, another symmetrical pair to add to the sculptured basilisks and unicorns. Their black uniforms were bulked out by deflection plating and pristine-polished rifles. They checked each admission with an id-scanner, a vertical red line scrolling across each face.

The offer of assistance came from another of the Axis soldiers, the boy with the blue-grey eyes. He was hurling himself up the steps like an excited spaniel. He smiled with an eager-to-please nervousness. The sunlight haloed through his blonde hair.

'Hold these,' said Mesa as she hefted the books into his arms. He staggered under the weight. 'Don't drop them, they're probably irreplaceable.' She patted her back pocket for her wallet, and prised out her disc. 'Follow me.'

The soldier jogged beside her. 'My name's Radek.'

'You said, before.' Mesa reached the entrance and waited as the guard scanned her face. She watched the red dot of the machine, the light flaring as it passed over her eyes. She handed the sentry her plasti-disc, and he jerked it through a reader, nodded, and returned it.

'Thanks, Radek.' She found herself smiling. She ducked into the air-conditioned darkness of the museum. Then she paused, and looked back. He was still smiling at her. She felt a flush of shyness. 'The name's Mesa,' she said, and reluctantly turned away.

He looked at her. As they walked through the museum grounds, her features shifted through the shadows and the ghost-glow of the mock Victorian gas lamps. She gazed ahead, her chin raised, that ever-present knowing smile on her lips. She huddled herself within her thermal coat, buttoned up to the neck. They had not spoken for fifteen minutes

The terraces and avenues were dark and silent. The only sounds were the rustle of bushes in the chill breeze and the crunch of leaves underfoot.

Mesa halted. Her home, a cottage on the outskirts of the staff's residential village, had appeared in the distance, its roof rising over the crest of the horizon.

She looked up at Radek. Her eyes were wide and shone. 'I should thank you,' she whispered. 'For being my escort.'

'You don't need to whisper,' said Radek. 'The curfew patrols can't stop you if you're with me. I have clearance.'

'What it is to have influence.' She turned her gaze to the sky. 'So quiet, seems a shame to disturb it. Usually this place would be busy –'

'Why were you working late?'

'The Collection is under-staffed,' explained Mesa. 'Everyone's doing the work of two people. Plus your lot have us cataloguing and re-cataloguing everything.'

'My lot?' said Radek.

Mesa walked to the next street lamp, her shadow hiding beneath her. 'Your soldier friends.'

'They're not my friends.'

'No? Then why are you with them?' Some defiance in her voice. She looked at him firmly, arms folded, expecting an answer.

'You might think what they're doing here is wrong, but –' began Radek, selecting each word carefully. 'But I believe it all makes sense. It's all about knowing what's best, what's best for everyone.'

'What's *best*?'

'What causes the least suffering, I think. Making sure that everyone is safe, and secure, and doesn't have to worry about crime or whether they'll have a meal or a home or whether their kids will be healthy. That's what's important.'

'That's what you believe? Someone at the top of the tree deciding what's for people's own good?'

'So long as it is for *good*, then, yes. You know more history than I do.'

'I do.' She strode back towards him, arms unfolding.

'Then you know that when people get what they want, they want too much. They get greedy and stupid. They get jealous. And someone else suffers. People shouldn't be given what they want, they should be given what they *need*. What they need to be healthy, to be educated, to be the best that they can.'

'And that's what you're doing? That's why you signed up?' Her face was only inches away now. He could make out every detail of her features, but couldn't tell whether she was regarding him with contempt or affection. But he knew this moment would remain with him forever.

'Well, yes. And the uniforms.'

'Of course, the uniforms.' Mesa laughed.

'Once you're in a uniform, you're irresistible.' He kicked his heels, and glanced at the leaf-sodden ground, before looking up at her meaningfully. 'Or so I was told.'

Her smile broadened into a grin, and at that moment all cynicism melted away. 'Whoever told you that was lying.'

'I know that *now*, but I didn't at the time, and she was very attractive, so I thought...'

That laugh again. And then the pause after the laughter. An electric pause, the pause before the rollercoaster drops, a pause laden with excitement.

'We should walk,' said Mesa, and as she headed for the village, Radek realised that she was holding his hand.

They walked a few more steps, then halted, and kissed.

'You have gained her trust?'

'I believe I am making progress, sir.'

'Good.' The Marshal halted at the door to the Admin building. Under the shelter of the balcony, he shook and folded up his umbrella. He clasped Radek's hand. 'I chose you wisely. Handsome, young. Just another soldier.'

'Sir.'

'I trust you, Officer.' Anson gripped his hand for a second longer, then jogged up the entranceway stairs. 'Protection will be extended to Mesa whilst you continue your... investigation.'

She looked at him. He set the two plastic cups on her desk and took the seat. She looked away; she could feel a warmth, a rising excitement within her, and she tried to push it away. She wanted to be cool, dispassionate, but instead she felt herself blushing with frustration and anger.

'It isn't going to work.'

He failed to hide his disappointment. He picked up his coffee cup and rotated it in his hand.

'We can't do this,' she heard herself saying. 'If anyone found out that we –'

'They won't,' said Radek firmly, examining his cup.

'They will. What would your lot say, if they knew? If they knew you were involved?'

Radek glanced out the window. 'Officially it's prohibited. But Moskof...'

'Moskof's a Lieutenant. Officers can marry non-military. That was in one of those booklets they gave us. You'd be court martialled. If you were lucky you might just be re-stationed... And I don't know what would happen to me.' She drank some coffee. She noticed no taste. 'Or my family. I have friends. I have people who care about me. I don't want to hurt them, I don't want them getting caught up in this... mistake.'

'Mistake?'

'We should end it before it begins. Before it's too late for both of us.'

'But we just have to be careful. So no one does find out.'

'Someone *will*. We can't spend all our time in secret. There's no future in it.'

'If that's what you believe –'

Of course that wasn't what she believed. It was what she wanted to believe, it was what she had been trying to convince herself to believe for the last few weeks. She wanted all thoughts of Radek to be erased from her mind. She wanted to stop feeling delight when she thought of him. She wanted to stop her thoughts turning towards him. She wanted to stop looking forward to seeing him so much, so achingly much.

'We don't have any choice,' she said. She stared at her monitor, but she couldn't take in any of the words. 'If we stop now, we still have a chance. I can't cope with looking over my shoulder all the time, paranoid in every conversation in case I've given something away. I can't cope with *us*.' She felt a pressure in the corners of her eyes. She must not let him see her cry.

'You know I'm not like them,' gabbled Radek. 'You can't hate me, just because I'm working for the Axis –'

'I don't *hate* you.' It was a physical pain inside her, a tightness in the gut, an inability to swallow. 'It's not about you. It's not about me.'

'So you don't care.'

'I do care.' Her cheeks prickled with moisture. 'I care about you too much. Can't you see that's *why*?'

Radek gave a half-smile, and turned towards the door. But he didn't leave. Instead, he walked across the office towards her. She watched him as he made his way around the desk and leaned over her. She did nothing as he placed one hand under her chin to lift her lips towards his. She did nothing as he stroked away her tears. She did nothing as they kissed, as she tasted him.

\* \* \*

Mesa huddled into her collar and dug her hands into her pockets. Snowflakes spiralled through the chill evening breeze. She felt exhilarated with the freshness and calm. The gas lamps lit the way, each one a warm, familiar beacon through the darkness.

Axis soldiers patrolled in unison, their guns held across their chests, their breath misting as one. Others stood on guard at strategic points around the museum grounds, vigilant and ever-present. Human-shaped shadows.

Her journey home took her through one of the closed areas of the garden. It had been closed for renovation before the Axis had arrived and had since fallen into neglect. A frosting of snow covered the shrubs and bushes, and the fountain pools had filled with a smooth, sparkling whiteness.

She realised she was alone. As if in response, the wind grew sharper. Mesa redoubled her pace. The curfew signal had not been sounded, and in another couple of minutes she would be within sight of the village.

She looked up. A figure blocked the way. A figure clothed in featureless thermals, its face hidden by the jacket hood. It didn't move as she approached.

'Mesa.'

Mesa kept on walking. The figure took a step towards her and levelled a gun.

'What?'

'We know.'

Mesa gave a fake laugh. 'Know what?'

'About you, whore. You and soldier boy.'

'I don't know what you're talking about,' said Mesa. She knew that she was speaking to one of the members of the Resistance, a group who worked to undermine the Axis' control. Everyone knew about them. Nobody spoke about them. Over the past months they had killed soldiers and bombed the museum, the theatre, the gardens, the lecture hall. They were fanatics. According to rumour, their numbers now included hired off-world mercenaries, who called themselves Irregulars.

The figure held its gun to her face. 'You cheap little bitch. Does he pay you, or do you do it for free? Does he pass you round to his mates?'

The figure swung the gun brutally against Mesa's cheek. She fell sideways into the snow, her face stinging with pain, heat rushing to the skin's surface. Mesa rolled onto her back and dabbed her hand against the wound. Her glove came back wet..

'This is a friendly warning. If you don't end it, we'll end it for you.'

'No –' gasped Mesa. She wanted to scream. The thought of any harm coming to Radek filled her with a rage, a hysterical, animal panic.

'So if you don't want to see... Radek getting hurt,' said the figure, 'stop it now.' The figure turned, then vanished into the night.

He looked at her. She lay beneath the sheets, her head snuggled into her pillow. Her black hair had fallen across her bare shoulders and her mouth was set in its familiar cynical smile. Her eyes were closed but she was not sleeping.

Radek trailed a finger lightly across her shoulder, up her smooth white neck and over her cheek. The cut had healed and the bruise had faded.

She flinched. 'I was walking home and slipped. Stupid.'

'The truth?'

'No.' She stared up at him. 'No, it's not.' She sat upright, gathering the sheets over her. 'I'm frightened. I feel so sodding scared all the time.' She frowned to hold back the tears. 'The Resistance. They said they'd kill you. I couldn't deal with it if anything happened.'

Radek let silence remain in the air for some minutes. He gazed around the bedroom, at Mesa's spartan furnishings, her wall-prints. 'Don't worry,' he said at last. 'They can't do anything. We're safe.'

'What?'

'The Axis will protect us.'

'The Axis?'

'The Axis know about us. They always have done. We're under their protection.'

'I don't understand –'

Radek shifted nearer to Mesa. He could feel her warmth between the sheets. 'I trust you. Remember that, when you hear what I'm about to say. I trust you with my life.

'I was told... I was ordered to gain your confidence. To become close to you. The Marshal is after some missing pieces of the collection, and he thought you might know their whereabouts. He believes that I'm only seeing you in order to get that information.'

'And are you?'

'I don't want to know where the pieces are. Because for as long as I'm still trying to find out, we're safe.'

'Why are you telling me this?'

'Because I have to be honest with you.'

Mesa considered. 'What are the pieces you're after?'

'You don't want to know.'

'I do.'

'The blade of Galandar.' He shrugged. 'The Marshal seems very keen to get hold of it for some reason.'

'The legend,' said Mesa. 'There's a myth, that whoever holds the blade of Galandar has the power to see into other people's hearts. To see the goodness and evil within them.' She gave a short laugh.

'I see. So that's why they want it. Another trophy for the arsenal.'
She dabbed at her eyes. 'I'll tell you where it is.'
'I told you, I don't want to know. If I don't know, we're safe –'
'It's in the possession of Professor Bernice Summerfield.'
Radek felt a surge of frustration. 'Why have you told me?'
'Because I trust you. I trust you with my life. And I have to be honest with you.'
'You shouldn't have said anything. You've betrayed your own people. You've put yourself in danger –'
She smiled cynically. 'Will you tell?'
Radek breathed in deeply. 'No. Of course not.'
'Then you're betraying *your* people. So long as we keep this secret, we're safe. We are the traitors.'
'We are the traitors.'
Mesa lifted her hand, and Radek felt it caressing the back of his neck. She pulled him down towards her, and parted her lips. They kissed, and more.

Radek had been ordered to patrol the lower galleries of the museum. The click of his steps on the marble floor echoed down the long, shiny hallways. The paintings and statues gazed out into empty rooms. Display cases went uninspected. Radek listened, and watched, and kept his progress to a steady pace. He felt the weight of his rifle across his chest.

He approached Mesa's office. The familiar route, down the staircase to the research section. Through double doors and down a bare, concrete corridor. Her room was the third on the left. She would be there, and he would enter. She would look up at him and suppress a smile and he would –

The alarms sounded. A sudden roar followed by the smashing and rattling of windows and cases. The floor rumbled. Radek felt a giddy rush of sickness and fear. Around him, sculptures toppled and shattered, and paintings slid to the floor. The lights flickered and dimmed.

Then there was the heat. A blast of hot air, followed by a thick, unrolling smoke. The smoke tasted dry and thick and burned Radek's throat. He grabbed his gas mask and tugged it over his face, and coughed into the filter, clearing his lungs.

The alarms rang out, a jarring, repetitive wail. The sprinkler system activated, a series of jets of water, designed to spray away from the exhibits. The rainfall steamed in the heat.

The explosion had come from ahead of him, from the research section. Radek had only one thought.

He grabbed at the wall, straightened himself up, and ran. The cloud thickened and swilled around him. He smashed his way through the remains of the double doors, into the concrete corridor. The heat was intense, like a roasting wall pressing against his body.

Two figures jogged towards him. As they drew nearer, he could make out gas masks and guns and uniforms. Another two soldiers appeared, uncoupling extinguishers from the wall.

Radek signalled to the nearest soldier. He could make out the soldier's words over the crackle of the flames. 'Terrorist bomb. Paralox gas. The Resistance.'

Radek tried to shove his way past the soldier..

'It's all right,' the man shouted, gripping Radek's shoulder. The grip was painfully tight. 'no one has been hurt. Nobody to worry about. Only one fatality, one of the curators.' He waved towards Mesa's office. 'She was at the centre of it.'

Radek suddenly stopped thinking.

The rage swept over him, a hideous, gnarling anger. He wanted to throw up, he wanted to scream, he wanted to sink through the floor. He felt the muscles in his face tighten. His eyes stung with tears.

He took his rifle from its strap, levelled it, and shot the soldier in the chest. Then he aimed at the other soldiers, and kept his finger held down on the trigger as the bullets rattled into them, making their bodies twitch and stagger and explode in blood.

She looked at him. He sat in the corner of the cell, his arms folded across his knees, staring at the grimy swirls on the floor tiles. His eyes were ringed with red. He hadn't slept for weeks. His lips were raw and bloody, his cheeks were sunken.

'I can help you,' said Professor Bernice Summerfield.

Radek looked up. He gave no sign of understanding.

'I am due for execution tomorrow,' he stated, without remorse. 'I can't be helped.'

Bernice hoisted her rucksack off her shoulder and lowered it to the floor. She unzipped it and removed an object wrapped in newspapers and tissues. She placed it in front of Radek. 'The blade of Galandar.'

Radek stared at it for some minutes without speaking. Eventually, he took it, and inspected the dusty, featureless knife. Rust and dirt flaked away in his fingers.

'It's what you were after, isn't it? Of course, the myths are just myths. It doesn't hold any special powers. It's just a relic. An incredibly valuable archaeological find. But at the end of the day, just another piece of history that somebody's dug up.'

Radek placed the knife back on the floor and wiped his hands on his trousers. 'I killed her.'

'You didn't kill her. The Resistance –'

'I killed her. The moment I started loving her she was dead. The moment I thought I could save her.'

'You know if you give the blade to your superiors they'll drop the charge against you. They can say the soldiers were killed in the explosion. They'll be grateful, you'll have done your duty. You'll be re-stationed, you can start your life again.'

Radek kicked the blade over to Bernice. 'I don't want it.'

'But –'

He stared up at her, his eyes the eyes of a dead man. 'I can't be helped.'

Bernice carefully picked up the relic, wrapped it in the papers, placed it in her bag and left the cell, the door locking automatically behind her.

# 13: Paths Not Taken
## By Rupert Booth & Barry Williams

Moonlight glinted on the features of Volf Gator's face. He stared glassily across Braxiatel's gardens, lip twisted in a superior sneer. Not that anyone could see his face at the moment. It was part of a thirty foot tall bronze statue, itself atop a pedestal the height of three men.

Standing at the bottom of the pedestal, the two Axis guards could see only a dark shape that loomed over them in the night. It had only been there for about two months, sternly facing the Hall of Mirrors. The guards paced about the base, cold and bored. Several inhabitants of the asteroid had declared the statue to be an eyesore, and there were already rumours that a group had formed with the express intention of destroying it. The night so far had been very quiet, however.

'Aw no,' muttered Trac. 'I'm out of ciggies.'

'I've got a spare packet in barracks,' replied Cript, well used to this. 'I can get them, if you want.'

'You sure?'

'Yeah, I'm running out, too. You be all right here on your own?'

'Of course I will. No one here but me and Wolfie.' The guard indicated the huge statue rising above them.

'I won't be long.' Cript slipped away into the night.

Trac sighed, got up and walked over to the ornamental fountains. Turned off at night, they sat silent and still in the dark. Without warning, he heard a grinding noise from behind him. Then it came again. More grinding. Not believing his own ears, he turned around.

The statue was getting off its pedestal. Unable to move, Trac just stared, his jaw hanging open as it crossed the garden towards him in swimming pool-length strides. Suddenly, it stopped. If he hadn't known better, Trac might have thought it was looking at him. Another grinding sound as it raised its left arm, the fingers pointing at him. Then there was a terrible crackling of energy, and Trac knew no more.

When Cript got back, ten minutes later, everything was as it had been. Of Trac, there was no sign. Cript looked around, and was about to raise the alarm.

But then an impossible shape struck him down too.

Bev Tarrant had been oblivious to this. She was oblivious to most things at the moment, except the forty-legged lizard that was patiently chewing through her boot, and had been for the last half hour. Two entire patrols were crossing the quadrangle in front of her, laboriously handing over the night's bullying duties she supposed. She had slammed down into the hydrangeas the instant she spotted the patrols, the firing key in her pocket biting into her. This had been an opportunist attack. Seeing one of their projected targets weirdly unguarded during a regular supply run, they had fetched one of their home-made bombs and planted it. They'd scattered when the patrols had arrived. Provided no one came too much closer, she would make it through this. And might even get to set off the bomb.

The lizard, who she had decided to name Shittyfoot, squirmed repugnantly, like a giant millipede with fangs, before returning to the attack. He would be through to unprotected flesh in a few more seconds. Only limited options reared their heads and after a moment's consideration, Bev plumped for the stupidest. Leaping to her feet, she shook off Shittyfoot, who sprang with a great whoop into a rejected coil in the bushes and made a practised run back into the grounds of the house.

Bev ran. She didn't bother looking to see if they were following.

Available light dimmed to ghost vision, half formed trees materialising from the night. She paused by the edge of the copse, taking in bearings, working out the quickest route to one of the hideout zones, but realised with crawling horror that she had no idea where she was. Panic took hold and she ran blindly into the trees, pencils of Axis torchlight penetrating the leaves and spidering out in front. She barely noticed the old woman as they collided. The woman's hands gripped her powerfully and dragged her sideways, away from the light of the torches and into the woods.

'Thank God it's you!' Bev gasped. 'What are you doing out –?'

The woman's fist caught her across her chin, and Bev fell with a moan.

Benny was only somewhat surprised at the sound of a key turning in the lock of her front door. Apart from herself, the only three people who had such a thing were locked away in their rooms, locked away in a work camp, and busy being a collaborator.

It must be the latter.

She went and picked up the vase she had already selected for this purpose, and steadied herself by the door.

The first thing through the door was a smell: a rich cloying smell, clammy and sweet. The first thing she should probably have said to the intruder was 'what are you doing here?' or even 'who are you?' Instead it was 'You stink!'

It was an old woman. Who was looking at her like one of them was a rabbit and the other was a car. Only Benny wasn't sure which was meant to be which.

'Charming,' the woman said. 'Quickly, let me in!'

Benny did so, closing the door behind her. The old woman dropped the key back into her cardigan pocket.

She went over to the window and drew the blinds, then turned the lighting down.

Joseph floated into the room.

'Not now, Joseph,' she said.

'As you wish,' said the Porter, and floated out again.

'Who are you?' asked Bernice.

The old woman just smiled at her, and suddenly pulled the skin tight under her eyes.

'Oh crap,' said Benny. 'You're me.'

'Um-hm. Tea?'

'*I'll* get it!' Bernice found herself flouncing into her own kitchen, and found her older self flouncing after her. 'And stop copying me!'

'I'm not copying you. I can't help it!'

'This is one of those time thingies, isn't it?' Bernice tried not to smash her tea cups with shaking hands.

'Full marks so far.'

'So you're from... the future?'

'Well obviously the future. You think you got like this overnight?' The woman prodded at her wrinkled face.

'I haven't been able to time travel for a long time. And I thought the Axis seized time travel equipment wherever they found it?'

'Oh, the Axis. Your thoughts are still bounded by them. I'd forgotten how hard it got. They won't last forever, you know. Now what comes after... that's something you need to worry about.'

'And you're going to give me some annoying little clues, I suppose?'

'I'll try not to.'

'How come something like this has never happened before?'

'Who says it hasn't? You-know-who was always leaving notes for himself, wasn't he?'

'Yes, but... Are you from him?! I've been trying to think of a way to communicate with him, to leave some sort of sign, but –'

'No. He never heard about this. Like Brax, he never saw it coming, and by the time he saw it going, it was over. I'm here for me... So you can help me. You can help me stop something that's going on in the grounds tonight. Something that, if it goes ahead, will make you burn with regret forever.'

*The people are gone. They would press along my sides, and I would show them what they needed to know. They were happy. I was happy. Now they are gone.*

*The others are here. They're tearing me open. Why? Taking what I am.*

*Don't they realise it hurts? IT HURTS! I've always given them what they want, why are they slashing it from me peeling away my layers...nothing left... I am aware of nothing. I am aware.*

They had tea. And then both reached for the whiskey bottle at the same moment.

'So, how much can you tell me?'

'Hardly anything. I'm glad you understand that without me lecturing you on the laws of time.'

'I'm not exactly a novice, I do know what I'm talking about when it comes to time travel.'

'Compared to me you're an amateur, mate. I can do things with time that would make your brain pickle.' She pulled something from her cardigan pocket and tossed it in the air. 'You're just going to have to trust me.'

'Well, of course I...' Benny stopped. 'What's that?'

'The firing key to a very big bomb. I pinched it from Bev Tarrant.'

'So... You don't want this bomb to go off?'

'No.'

'Are you from the future where the bomb does go off, or the future where the bomb doesn't go off?'

'Can't tell you.'

'Why don't you want this bomb to go off?'

'Can't tell you that either. So, having said that you're prepared to trust me, we've now run through just about all the questions you were going to ask anyway.' She sighed. 'I suppose I should have seen this coming.'

'But why *didn't* you see it...?' Benny stopped. 'Okay. Let's not go there.' She paced a bit in front of her elderly double. 'This is like a living, breathing version of exactly the conundrum that did Brax's head in. Suddenly I'm shackled by destiny. Suppose I meet a really nice bloke who can actually make me happy, then you casually mention that I turn completely finally gay at the age of forty three?'

'Fifty one, actually.'

'Stop it!' Benny slumped into the sofa, suddenly feeling indescribably depressed. In truth, she had pretty much avoided thinking about growing old before. Her age had been mucked around with so much by time travel that she'd given up worrying about it. Perhaps she considered being a lively old granny, but not the genuine implications of being really *old*. Now here was the reality, confronting her in all its wrinkly glory. It wasn't such a happy prospect. It wasn't even as if she could now be certain she got through the Occupation unscathed, not with all this time travel malarkey. She might end up being her own grandmother or something. 'When was the last time you washed?' she muttered. 'Two years from now?'

'I don't know what you're talking about.' The old woman sniffed her armpit and sighed. 'Okay, now we're running out of time. I've got the firing key, Bev's out cold, but the others are eventually going to decide they can do without it and just shoot at the bomb until it goes off. We have to stop them.'

Benny looked at her for a long moment. 'I'm not going to bet on time stuff,' she said finally. 'I'm going to see if we can talk to Brax.'

'That's a surprise,' murmured the older her. 'But... yes. All right.'

*Trapped. Trapped for so long in the soil. They cut away most of what I was. Sprayed the rest with burning liquid. They tortured me and left me for dead, when all I wanted was to show them. Now they will listen. Now, at last they will understand. Now, I will tear them apart...*

She knew every shift of guards well enough to do it now. Even with a crazy, smelly old woman at her side. She'd called ahead for a curfew permit, gone to Anson's apartments, talked to the guard commander, been searched (the old lady having left the firing key behind), and finally they were given five minutes alone with Brax.

They didn't even bother waking Anson.

Brax stood at a window, silhouetted against the moonlight, gazing at the statue. 'So... you've come back in time then? Back to change history. You do realise that it has been tried before and by better time travellers than you.'

'Now hang on, I have actually lived a little...' blurted Benny.

But the older her had stepped forward.

And her eyes had turned to blazes of white.

Brax took a remote control from his jacket and clicked a button.

The white blazes faded. Leaving the old woman glaring at him, an insane look of desperation on her face.

'No energy weapons in here,' said Brax.

Benny was about to ask what was going on when her older self launched herself at Brax with grotesque speed, agility and odour.

She impacted with Braxiatel, both of them collapsing to the floor. Gnarled hands clawed at his throat, pressing down on his windpipe as she shook him back and forth in a frenzied orgy of violence. Benny leapt onto her own back and pressed her younger, yet somehow weaker hands into the woman's dewlap. Between them, she and Brax took hold of an arm each and pinned the angry pensioner to the floor.

'I didn't realise I was going to have anger management problems in later life,' wheezed Benny. 'Maybe I go mad after the menopause.'

'I shouldn't worry,' said Brax, sitting heavily down on one of old Benny's arms. 'This woman isn't you. Trust me, she's nothing like you at seventy.'

Benny sagged. 'This is giving me a pain in the brain.'

'I think the intelligence behind this just decided that impersonating you was the best way to complete its mission,' said Brax. 'It could have chosen one of the Axis, but then I'd have been on my guard immediately. As opposed to within a second or so.'

'Oh great, I might have guessed this would be about you.'

Old Benny thrashed ineffectually beneath them, then went disturbingly limp. Benny and Brax exchanged a glance, and then gingerly moved off the woman's arms. The sweet stench from her body began to intensify. Benny backed away retching as her future self's flesh began to liquefy, fizzing and popping. Within half a minute, the only remnant was a viscous pool that started to eat into the carpet.

'I'm really glad you told me that she wasn't me before that happened,' murmured Benny.

'I think that was a reanimated corpse. Perhaps two of them, from the mass, bonded together to give it fighting strength. I wonder if any of the guards are missing?'

'That was why she smelled... well... dead,' realised Benny.

Brax nodded.

Benny turned to him. 'What the hell is going on?'

*I was a library. A vast resource of knowledge, but they did not want me any more. Now Braxiatel will pay. He will die!*

'Looked like a great translucent mushroom,' said Brax. 'It had a holographic facility, could create images from a thousand worlds. Could examine the organic structure of living beings and replicate their mental processes.'

'That was how it was such a good me.'

'Yes. It was a rather good conversationalist, as I recall. Helped me sort out my policy on all manner of things. Like talking to a very precise depiction of oneself. Sadly, technology overtook the organic facility. I had it decommissioned a few years before you joined us.'

Benny frowned. 'What does "decommissioned" mean?'

'The information was stripped from it. It was then treated with... with a kind of weed killer I believe. Some kind of root must have been left behind. I really must lodge a complaint with the contractors.'

'You killed it. No wonder it's angry!'

'We had no reason to believe it had become sentient,' said Brax calmly. 'It was in the garden. The Axis built that statue on the same site.'

'Sometimes I think you're as ruthless as this lot.'

'Oh, you don't know, Bernice. You really don't.'

'Anything else from your past that might want to kill you?'

'Tons of things.'

\* \* \*

They had actually raised the guard. A squad of Axis soldiers, the stiff-necked Bertram at their head, was actually marching behind them towards the statue of Volf Gator.

Benny just hoped that the rest of the Resistance had found Bev and spirited her away. At least the soldiers were making a lot of light and sound.

Brax was taking big breaths of evening air, looking around the grounds, enjoying his night out of confinement. Anson had now been woken, at least for the few moments it had taken for him to say yes and yes.

They all stopped and looked at the statue. The statue turned to look at them. With a mighty grinding, it again began to get down from its pedestal.

'The root must have bonded with the statue,' continued Brax, nervously. 'Old Benny was created for two reasons. To ensure that the statue was preserved... and...'

The statue was halfway across the lawn, now.

'...And to get its revenge on you!' Benny completed.

The statue was nearly on them. It stopped, and raised its arm.

'Fire!' yelled Bertram.

Benny was about to tell them that that might be a mistake. Then she realised she couldn't.

When the first shot hit it, the pedestal exploded.

They all fell to the ground as bits of bronze, clumps of soil, and sizzling lumps of vegetable matter descended around them.

After it was over, Bertram slowly raised his head, staring at the crater that now steamed where the statue had once been. 'What was that all about?' he whispered, clearly wondering how he was going to explain this to the Marshal.

'The creature must have been very volatile,' said Benny. 'Liable to go up any moment.'

'I... hope you'll be willing to add that expert testimony to my report?' asked Bertram.

'Of course,' said Benny. 'I'd be happy to declare that all this was nothing to do with you.'

# 14: Every Picture Tells a Story

## By Jim Sangster

*Sitting in her study, the room lit intermittently by light refracted through the rain that streaked her window, Bernice rolled a small nearly-pyramid across her fingers. It was squared off at both ends, with a lens at the apex and a pale off-white 'screen' at the other. Dozens of times over the last hour she'd tried to bring the slide-viewer to her eye to take a look, but the bubbling of dread inside her always pushed her hand away. Not yet, she heard inside her head. Not yet...*

'Silence, please. Any attempt to communicate will be dealt with severely. There will not be a second warning.'

It was all Bernice could do to stop herself from jumping on a table and singing 'Oom-pah-pah' as an act of defiance, but something within her held the urge back. The guard... well, he was little more than a boy really, a few adolescent zits on his chin and that look of sheer confidence in his authority that only comes when jumped-up little prigs like him are given a smart uniform... Anyway, the guard eyed every single person in the room, as if daring one of them to speak. no one gave him the satisfaction; they just looked at each other, their eyes all saying the same thing. The youth had managed to instil fear into a room of old men. Although dragging one of them out by his thin hairline five minutes earlier had probably helped.

They weren't just afraid because they were being held at gunpoint in the library. The problem, as probably everyone in the room but the youth was all too aware, was that Vosta, the man who'd been forcibly removed from their group, was responsible for an act of sabotage that, if discovered, could kill them all.

Vosta had taken his hacking of the Fifth Axis surveillance loop a bit further: he had created 'dead ground' areas of his own, a whole network of them. There were now established paths along which the Resistance could come and go.

Once he was satisfied that his fiddling had worked, he'd arranged a party for a select group of trusted friends and told them what he'd achieved. Those friends included Professors such as Yackle, who had never had anything to do with overthrowing the Occupation. It was a room full of academics rather than resistors, and Benny supposed that to be the point: he was making everyone he trusted culpable, giving them all something to hide. She didn't know whether or not to be flattered that she'd been invited.

But it made Benny wonder about how reckless Vosta and the rest of the Resistance was being. If any of them were caught using his system, one of the first things the Fifth Axis bods would surely do is check their security. And if Vosta's sabotage could be traced back to him...

But Vosta was a law unto himself. During one of the customary searches for contraband in the stacks, Bernice and the other academics in the area had been ushered into the library. Vosta had decided to make a few lurid comments about their guard which had resulted in his removal from the throng. No doubt he was now enjoying the hospitality of their uninvited hosts, sipping fine wines and discussing Wittgenstein. Either that or they were kicking the living shit out of him. And of course, none of them would find out if Vosta had been made to talk until it was too late.

But one thing made them especially nervous. With the odd exception here and there, the group that had been accidentally confined for this particular search was the group to which he had told his secret.

They were all looking at each other, now. All afraid.

*Watching the result of her life through a lens made Bernice uncomfortable. Over the many centuries she'd visited she'd been lucky enough to have her photograph taken or her portrait painted or her holograph computer-etched on many occasions. The results without fail looked sod-all like her. Her nose always looked too big, or the lighting behind her head made her ears look huge, or her smile looked too ... stupid. No matter what she did with her hair it always looked a little greasy or fly-away. And her smile – 'educationally subnormal' was one description that readily came to mind.*

· *She threw the little plastic slide-viewer cautiously from one hand to the other. Juggling for beginners. She'd definitely mastered Stage One. Sod this, Bernice, you're being a big baby.*

*She grasped the viewer between her forefinger and thumb and put it to her eye. Squinting slightly, she could make out a two shot of her and an old friend. It was as bad as she'd feared. There she was, very nearly sober, one arm slovenly round the friend's shoulder. (She was careful not to look at him though. Not just now. Not yet.) Her eyes were slightly glassy and her teeth were set in a petrified rictus. Grinning like a loon.*

*Still she couldn't look at him.*

Nothing had happened that day. They had all eventually been let out of the library.

But Vosta hadn't come back.

Not until three days later. He looked a mess and no one would insult his intelligence by pretending otherwise. As Bernice sat with him in his bedroom, mopping his brow, he seemed to her to be unnervingly calm.

'I didn't tell them anything. Nothing useful at least. All that shouting and violence, I think they let me go so they could get a rest, poor loves.' As the old man spoke, little flecks of blood polka-dotted the white linen of his bed. He grinned, revealing a bloody mess where his front teeth should have been. It didn't seem to bother him.

'Look, you should rest, you've been through a –'

'I didn't tell them about my little camera trickery, but I... I did confess to something, and I think you ought to know what it was.'

This didn't sound good. Bernice could feel her heart rate suddenly quicken.

'You remember that painting Braxiatel had in his quarters, the one with the little boy in blue being quizzed by Cromwell's Roundheads?'

'The Yeames? *And When Did You Last See Your Father*, yes. I always hated it. I always felt sorry for the poor kid being tricked into informing on his old man.'

'Well, no need to fret about it any more. They burned it.'

'Oh.' Such news was no longer a cause for horror. Not compared to everything else. These days, Bernice wondered if she'd make a different decision in the face of Kellarn's offer.

'Or rather, *I* burned it, persuaded by that fool Spang and a pair of pliers.'

'But... why would they do that? It's one of the most famous lost treasures of 19th Century Earth! No alien influences. They must have known its worth!'

Vosta chuckled. 'I told them it was a fake! That I'd whipped it up for my students to show them Yeames' brushstrokes and given it to Brax as a joke. Of course, they were furious. "This forgery is an affront to the power and majesty of true art!" they said. Well, one of their imported academics said. They'd brought him in to talk to me man to man. Fogey to fogey. "Balls," I said. So as penance they made me burn it in the courtyard at the back of the Mansionhouse. Gave me a firebrand and made me turn it to naught but ash.'

'But Vosta, you and I know that it wasn't a fake. Brax liberated it himself!'

The man was still smiling that unsettling, gummy smile of his, but his eyes were anything but confident. What was going on in that mad head?

'These monsters don't understand the value of art; not the price-tag, the true value of it. They want it for this *power* they think it gives them. Own the treasure and gain instant respect. Morons, the lot of 'em. They don't deserve it. I just thought that it'd be more of an artistic statement to deny them the piece. I'd wager it'll make a nice image when they find out I lied about it being a fake. Can you imagine their faces?! They'll be bloody furious!'

Bernice smiled, not giving a damn about the painting.

'Anyway, the main thing is, I was able to make a few final checks to the dead-ground areas before the searches today. They're all as I explained the other week and that lot definitely don't know anything about them. Even if they find them and repair them, they'll just go dead again a few days later. And they look like normal landscapes. They had pliers in my mouth and they didn't even ask! All they've got on me is that conversation that you and I…'

'I'm sorry.'

'Don't be. It was understandable. What I'm saying is, I'm safe now. The selection of academics that day in the library… The coins just fell on their side! I'm safe and what I do is safe! I'm living a charmed bloody life!' He put a hand on her arm. 'You should do it too, now. You and all the academics. Don't take up arms if you don't want to, but at least play a few tricks. Put piss in their fuel tanks and salt in their water, or the other way round.'

He laughed heartily. Then the laugh became a cough that was sickening to hear and Bernice couldn't carry on. She told him to sleep it off and kissed him goodnight.

*Look at him now. No, not now… then. Smiling, laughing, singing along to some tune one of the undergraduate tutors had unearthed on audiomarble. She'd been trying so hard not to look but now she couldn't draw her eye away from the picture. It reminded her of how he looked in the last days. Free. He'd always looked like whatever rules or restrictions were placed on everyone didn't somehow apply to him anyway. It was typical of him to be the first person to find a way of buggering up their security.*

Vosta Dankasta died not because of the beating he received from the Axis thugs, but from a disease with a ridiculously small name that was itself so rare that no one had been able to locate it and isolate it to be able to eradicate it. Something so small that even the almighty Fifth Axis couldn't stop it. Something he'd carried with him for years that had finally helped him ignore their oppressors because he knew he didn't have long and knew they wouldn't be able to stop his final escape.

Some people probably survive Occupation by thinking forward with optimism and cruel hope to a time when the oppressors will sod off to where they came from and leave everyone as they were: a time when they won't be afraid, they won't be hungry, and there'll be plenty of jam roly-poly with custard, or steamed fish in a rich buttery sauce.

But Vosta didn't survive like that.

He clung to the one certainty the Fifth Axis couldn't take away from him: his death.

She decided it was a good picture of Vosta. It didn't look as she remembered seeing him last; a good thing. She remembered now when the image had been captured. It was during one of those nauseating fundraisers Brax held every now and then to make it look like the Collection wasn't just funded out of his own pockets. She'd arrived on the Collection only a few weeks before and had hooked up with Vosta after he persuaded her to join him in getting absolutely wrecked on some obscure liquor he'd smuggled through galactic customs onto the planetoid. He'd slurred at her his opinion that she looked to him like someone who was very brave and very sexy and very unlikely to fancy an old fart like him. She'd laughed and said he was right on all three counts and at that moment there'd been a flash and then someone ran over wafting the insta-gram image of the pair gurning like idiots.

She held the viewer to one eye again, but then swapped it to the other. He was right, she did look brave there. He'd often said she looked to him like a warrior queen, which back then had struck her as a bloody silly thing to say but a nice thing to hear. Bernice had met a few warrior queens in her time, and while she didn't quite look like any of them, it was equally true to say they didn't look like any of her either. And sod it, her boobs looked fantastic that night, she really should wear that top more often. Maybe this picture did look like her, or at least the way she hoped others saw her.

If the picture was of the real her, then there was a gap between who she was now and who she should be.

But she had always known that. It had just taken another death to make it unbearable. Vosta had demanded action of her. Of all of them.

She sat there, knowing this couldn't continue. Knowing she'd have to be the one to make the first move.

# 15: Fluid Prejudice
## By Paul Ebbs

*'The very ink with which all history is written is merely fluid prejudice.'*
— Mark Twain (1835-1910)

*'Get your hands out of my knickers or I'll amputate you at the ankles.'*
— Professor Bernice Summerfield (One hundred and seventy-five point two hours ago)

...but she couldn't remember *who* she'd said it to.

<non-linear memory accident - begin cascade sequence>

Carlo Vaddin looked at Benny and repeated what he'd said that had so made her want to sew up his mouth. 'Look, Benny, you're just too high maintenance. I can't deal with it any more. It's been fun, but I never wanted anything this serious.'

Then Carlo loaded up his hover, all teeter-tottering pot-plants, books, floppyscreens, clothes and implements for making various shapes of pasta and floated off, leaving her in a cloud of grit.

That *is* how it happened, right?

<obsessive thought extrusion>

The room was dark and cool.

The bed was rumpled and sweaty. Benny, mouth open, snoring, breathing with a deep steady rhythm and somewhere just on the wrong side of REM sleep, was sitting up in bed, deftly manipulating a fielddriver inside the sooty guts of Joseph. Benny's head fell forward, chin thudding into her chest. She mumbled something about Carlo being a *pig* and *how could he leave her like that?* Then, hugging the scarred hull of Joseph between her knees and keeping the fielddriver at an acute angle within the inspection cover, she reached blindly into her tool pack with her left hand. A gleaming laspan whirred into life between her thumb and index finger. Snuffling and groaning and with a line of dribble appearing with glistening slowness at the corner of her mouth, Benny brought the tool down to meet with the fielddriver.

A blinding blue arc of energy briefly lit up the room. There was a dark curl of smoke caught in the flash climbing out of Joseph and up towards Benny's nose. As she inhaled the irritant, her glottal snore stopped dead in her throat and she hurled forth an enormous sneeze. The tools spun from her grasp, her knees parted and Joseph's dead carcass rolled onto the floor with a dull thump.

Benny was shocked into wakefulness.

Her bleary eyes noticed the tool pack, the still whirring laspan, and Joseph's body rocking gently on the carpet.

It took a few moments for her sleep-addled brain to kick into gear.

'Not a-*bloody*-gain!'

Benny kicked the tools from the bed, gave a yell of frustration, rolled over, and cried herself back to sleep.

<*entry-level core memory*>

'I want you to be Leif Larsson's liaison.'

'No.'

'No? Bernice this isn't technically a request...'

'It's not the request I object to, it's the alliteration.'

Bernice had been alarmed to see Anson and his guards heading to her rooms. She had looked round for all the things she had to hide, and then realised she hadn't got any. She'd made them tea and Anson had sat while the guards had stood around, awkwardly holding her tiniest china.

'Larsson and his team have been in the History Department for seventeen hours. And, you see, he has clearance from the highest level...'

'What is your highest level? You never say.'

'Is that espionage, Benny?'

'How can asking you a direct question be espionage?'

He laughed. 'None of this is a secret. I report to High Command back at Axis Central.'

'This chap Gator?'

'No, he's more political. The military are led by the Commander in Chief: a most charming gentleman called Isik. He's my boss. A few months ago there was a change of emphasis back home. He and Gator now hold equal rank.'

'Ah. So the military flex their muscles and suddenly the campaigns work out.'

'Interpretation is a job for historians. Talking of which –'

'You want me to keep an eye on this chap Larsson. Find out what he's up to.'

'Of course not!' He laughed. 'Of course not.'

<*non-linear remodelled safe memory*>

It wouldn't be so bad if Larsson weren't so damn *horny*.

Mad scientists are supposed to be small, wizened and crusty, with indeterminate stains on their white coats. Larsson didn't wear a white coat; he had a nice line in charcoal grey, sharp-cut suits, which, while aping strict military issue, had just enough élan to separate him from the rest of the Axis Militarati. He was tall, lithe and smooth skinned. Benny liked the way he smelt and the way he looked and well...

Yes. *Right.* The History Department.

The technicians from the Axis Meedjahistory-Capital-Gain Column were the latest group of invaders to work methodically from one end of the concourse to the other. In just over seventeen hours, the six uniformed Axis-academicians had excised and plundered the recorded histories of a hundred worlds. Data-retrieval equipment was chuntering three to an academician, fingers whirled on key pads, lines of text streamed as bright reflections across their infovisors, sucking the accumulated knowledge to Goddess knows where. They sat quietly at tables or knelt at the foot of shelves, taking each disc, book or holo in turn, loading it into their thick ugly equipment; strip-mining the history of the galaxy.

Larsson smiled his beatific smile and carried on smelling gorgeous as Benny walked with him through the bright slats of afternoon sunlight falling through the windows. 'Of course I know why Anson asked for a liaison from the Collection.' He stopped and fixed her with his serene eyes. Benny couldn't work out if he had mechanical iris implants or if he was capable of flexing each pupil independently of the other. 'Anson is worried about what we will find here; because my Column will take full credit, and he'll just look like another bumbling governor on some backwater colonial outpost who doesn't know how to fully exploit the resources at his fingertips.'

Benny nodded, not sure what to say in answer.

'Anson, I imagine, wants you to report to him anything that we find. If he's not been so specific as to tell you to report back then I'm sure he has contingencies in place to ensure the information he requires will not elude him for long.'

'It's a brave man who plays politics with Marshal Anson.' Benny knew the response she'd get. That's why she said it, to pique Larsson into –

A laugh, deep with full timbre, his head thrown back without any self-consciousness. 'I don't play politics, Benny.' Larsson smiled, bringing the laugh under control and flaring his nostrils. 'I win politics.'

Larsson bent to scoop up a bulky black rubber-coated data-retriever from the lap of one of his technicians. The text scrolled crazily over the viewing surface, and Benny couldn't make out what was written there. Larsson sniffed. 'Onderel in the Allutex Cluster: a hundred civil wars over the last thousand years, all for the control of a few trinkets and a patch of sacred land. Forty generations of the blood of their finest children, seeping into the blasted gorse and mud. Two great houses, beating each others' heads on the rocks of their ancestors' hatreds. A history of impossible pain and anguish.'

He thumbed a scroll point on the side of the machine. 'If only they could stop skewering each other through the gizzards for five minutes, and have a look at this wonderfully collated mineralogical survey, they'd see how much that seeping blood has depreciated the value of all those exploitable iron oxidants!'

Larsson's eyes were alive; the irises contracting and expanding in the bands of light thrown off by the machine...

*<non-linear memory accident >*

...text shifting on a page, reforming before her eyes, ink becoming fluid again, moving over the surface of old paper, a rustle of ghost words coalescing into new truths...

...pain, a cruel bunch of agony in the pit of her stomach. Her shirt ripped open. Larsson's eyes enjoying her attempts to cover her nakedness...

*<re-wipe>*

...he stabbed a stiff index finger into the keying area on the retriever and a small buzz of data was transmitted. 'Ninth fleet now have the co-ordinates and Onderel's profit potential projections.'

What *is* it with alliteration today?

'Strike one more for the Capital-Gain Column!'

The technicians in the room turned towards Larsson. 'Huzzah!' they yelled, and then with almost comical synchroneity, turned their heads back to their screens.

Benny felt it was time for some sarcasm. However, shaking her head free of the paralysing allure of Larsson's countenance and *smell* was not easy. Her head was foggy and she was aware of her heartbeat, but it sounded like it was beating with a dull thud outside of her body, somewhere down a long tunnel. Sarcasm would have to wait.

Larsson took Benny by the arm and led her towards a vestibule. She weakly accepted his arm through hers, and tried to think of a reason why she should stop him from being so close.

Seeing two chairs set against the cool stone of the wall, Benny found her knees were trembling and she was glad of the opportunity to sit down. 'I don't think I'm feeling all that good, actually,' she managed to mumble as Larsson sat next to her and pulled the desktop sheet from the wall and settled it across their laps.

'But you look fine to me,' said Larsson, 'more than fine in fact.' He enabled the solidifying field and the desk sheet hardened, becoming a viable surface for working and studying. It also had the side effect of locking Benny between the wall and Larsson. But seeing as she had no strength for the moment to do anything other than concentrate on not slipping into unconsciousness, she really couldn't complain.

Larsson budged up closer to Benny and for the first time regarded Joseph, who was bobbing with increasing agitation at Benny's shoulder. 'And what do we have here?'

Benny's mouth was thick and sluggish, she hadn't felt this dreadful since... well, since waking up last Saturday morning, but that was beside the point. She hadn't drunk anything for nearly twenty-four hours standard. 'It's my diary and personal data assistant. Gets me where I'm supposed to be on time, or goes, on time, to where I'm *supposed* to be and apologises for me not being there. If it could do up bra-straps it would be the perfect companion,' was what she *tried* to say. However, it all came out a bit wonky. Larsson seemed to get the general drift. He smiled and gave Joseph a little wave. Joseph stopped bobbing and took two cautious floats back.

'This is cosy,' said Benny, trying to take Larsson's attention off Joseph.

'Isn't it,' Larsson said flatly. He leaned against Benny, bringing his mouth close to her face. His breath was hot and sweet. Benny felt floaty and warm. 'So I suppose, as liaison from the Collection, you'll want to ensure that the documents we have already surveyed for potential capital gain have not sustained damage by our researches?'

It was as much as Benny could do to nod.

Larsson grinned and, squeezing Benny's thigh, slunk from behind the desk sheet and called to a nearby technician. 'Bring the good Professor everything we've already surveyed.'

The technician jumped to it.

Benny started to dribble.

<*sub-reticular-medulla barrier emergency*>

Bernice awoke with a start.

'Not a-*bloody*-gain!'

The laspan whirred in her hands and Joseph beeped back to life.

'And Carlo Vaddin did not dump *me*! I *Goddessing*-well dumped *him*!'

Joseph limped into the air, and bobbed at an awkward angle, his stabilizing fields out of kilter.

'Joseph, what happened to you?'

'A forty thousand nanoseconds' blast of projected laser fire.'

'Who?'

'Leif Larsson.'

'When?'
'Three weeks ago.'
'And I've been fixing you in my sleep?'
'It would appear so.'
'I have a way too stubborn sub-conscious.'
'I am unfortunately unable to calculate stubborn-conscio-quotient.'
'Quite. My memory is *totally* jumbled. I can't remember *anything*. When and where exactly did Larsson shoot you?'
'In the History Department, one hundred and seventy five point two hours ago.'
'Why did he shoot you?'
'Larsson interrupted me showing you a playback of him attempting to rape you.'
Silence.
Joseph bobbed on his wonky fields with mechanical awkwardness.
Bernice didn't know where to start.

<linear-memory system collapse>

It was morning. Benny had managed to realign Joseph's fields correctly by weighting one arm of his micro-gyro with a ninth star coin and a pliant nodule of chewing gum. She stood by the window of her apartment as the night sky turned to ice blue and the stars were swallowed by sunlight. She was naked, wrapped in the one white sheet from the bed. She felt and looked as insubstantial as a ghost.

'My memories are changing. Carlo Vaddin, the Art History Professor from Indigo-Six did not dump *me*. We were together for three months. Then he came to me one morning and told me he'd bought a washing machine for the apartment-cube in which we were shacked up. As soon as someone buys a washing machine, you know it's time to hit the road. It's my rule. Washing machine? Run away. And yet... what I remember isn't what is in the diary. Well it wasn't...'

She peeked beneath the post-it note that had once said 'Good riddance to *that* tosser.' And read the entry beneath that used to say 'Dumped Carlo today. Idiot bought white goods.'

Now that the entry on the page had stopped shifting, the ink sliding in slick whorls over the paper, it read: 'Can't believe he left me. All I asked him to do was look at rings in town and then go for a walk in the rain.' The post-it note now simply read 'Gutted. Too sick to eat. Think I'll starve to death waiting for him to come back. That'll show him.'

The only grounds Benny still had to disbelieve the hard facts in her hands was Joseph replaying his record of the diary and the post-it note *changing*. The projection on the window glass, like a heads-up-display of the impossible, flickered and flipped back to the start of the playback. She squinted to focus on the spectral text writhing in the diary projection. Her handwriting lifting free of the paper, twisting and whirling. Pixellating and running into the new words. So different in meaning but still unmistakably her handwriting. And if she dug hard enough into her memories, the new words on the page were the truth she remembered. Exactly.

Through the projections, the gardens steamed. The morning dew, laid by the microscopic hortibots during the night cycle, smoked in the rays of the climbing sun. One thing becoming another thing. Water to vapour. Change of substance.

Textual evanescence and meta-coalescence.

Benny took a breath.

'Okay. I'm ready.'

*<contextual remembrance sub-system error message>*

It was the replay she'd been avoiding all night, since the three-week somnambulant repair of Joseph had finally been completed. Now it was over, all she could hang on to were flashes.

Two days into her liaison job at the History Department, she'd watched the text in the Onderel file changing before her eyes. To her utter disbelief the thousand-year civil war had become a minor local difficulty that a passing Fifth Axis expeditionary force had helpfully managed to broker into peace. And as the Ondereli had been so happy to have their war cured so effectively, they had ceded their entire mineral wealth to the Fifth Axis by way of thanks. The appendices even showed a facsimile of the agreement and a sepia line and hatch holograph of the Fifth Axis garrison commander signing the agreement with the Prelate of Onderel.

Larsson was smiling in the holograph, looking very pleased with himself indeed.

And then Larsson was dragging her back from the desk sheet, screaming at his technicians to leave, ripping at the front of her shirt with his fingers and swatting Joseph out of the way when he got too close.

Flashes.

Drugged and helpless. Larsson bearing down on her.

White out.

'Larsson!'

Anson stalking into the room, face gleaming with sweat.

Joseph thudding into a corner and rolling to a stop against the wall. Camera showing a close up of cinnamon-coloured stone.

'I knew you would have her under surveillance!'

'I have this entire planetoid under surveillance!'

'So she was a trap! You set me up with some whore –'
'Be silent! Cover her up. There have been reports of your excesses, Larsson. I never thought you would be so bold as to give into them here.'
'Isik won't allow this!'
'I'm here on his orders. Having relayed the surveillance footage live to him. You worm. All work by the Capital Gain Column will cease until the Inquiry is complete. Take him.'
A struggle and then silence.
'Get the Professor back to her quarters.'
A blanket, rough against her nakedness.

<core anxiety reminiscence catastrophe>

'Stop it now, please.'
The replay flickered and fizzed out against the glass. 'Just tell me the rest.'
'Larsson's Legal Counsel persuaded the military investigators to release him from house arrest four days later. He came straight to you here. This unit was replaying the same images when he arrived. By the time Anson had reversed the order to release Larsson he had blasted this unit in an attempt to destroy the evidence.'
'But that would seal his guilt in the eyes of the Fifth Axis command. Why would he do that?'
'Insufficient ability to understand human behaviour.'
A ragged chunk of hurt banged hard against Benny's heart.
Whiteout.
Benny gritted her teeth and blinked through tears. Think. *Think!* Larsson wasn't just covering up his misconduct with her. The images that Joseph had played back had started with the auto-rewriting of the Onderel History. He was trying to make sure nobody saw that!
Benny flung open the wardrobe and began taking out clothes. If she played the images back to Anson that would royally screw Larsson for good...
No...
What was she thinking? If Anson didn't know about the textual reworkings then it was a good bet that the High Command didn't either. If she went with this to Anson then she could potentially be handing them the means to rewrite all history on a fragging plate.
Rewriting history... *Goddess*. History.
This is going to be an interesting day.
*I'd better wear red.*

<context-counter-terrorism-alert>

\* \* \* \*

Depending on how she looked at Larsson he would either appear as King Horny of the Horny People or as a Mad Scientist; small, wizened, crusty, with indeterminate stains on his white coat. Shards of Larsson shimmered in and out of Benny's field of vision. He alternatively smelt of allure and repulsion. He was sitting in the rear of one of the Collection's Ormand-Seltec fliers that the Axis had comandeered for their reconnaissance operations, shackled to his seat, about to be taken to a big Axis ship waiting beyond the Collection's atmosphere. Benny had trouble looking at him at all.

Wearing red didn't seem to be helping much.

'I doubt if you've come to rescue me.'

'No. I want to know what you did to me.'

'You've taken a terrible risk breaking into this ship, Professor; we don't have time for small talk. You have perhaps one minute before your incursion is discovered.'

'Just answer the question.'

Nothing happened for twenty or so seconds.

Less happened for the next thirty.

'Arrrrrrrrrrrrrrrrrrrrrrrgh! Come with me then.'

She dragged Larsson from the ship and they ran into the gardens, keeping to Vosta's safe routes, though she was careful not to give Larsson any impression of following a path. Joseph floated behind, keeping an eye out for Axis forces.

From the Mansionhouse, the party Anson was throwing for the Nineteenth Wednesday of the Year (a tradition of the Collection that a number of academics remembered very clearly) sparkled and fireworked, shimmered and sang.

Axis security were busy trying to get through a crowd that had gathered in the square, where Bev and a 'rival academic' were knocking seven bells out of each other.

Mister Crofton had turned on the hortibots to spray the gardens with dew nine hours early to cover their tracks.

Everything was going to plan except the bit where she wasn't supposed to have Larsson with her, which had obviously turned to dog shit.

'You look so good in red.'

Benny felt like she'd broken at least two knuckles and jarred the bones of her elbow out of synch.

The Larsson-shards *picasso'd* on the grass clutching at aquiline and blood-orange skinned noses.

Benny drew back her fist, ready for another go. 'I want to know what you've done to me and what you're doing to the texts in the History Collection.'

Bits of Larsson sat up.

And then he told her.
And then he took her to meet it.

<comprehension bomb>

The Larssons held up the sheet of paper on which the ink became fluid and moved.

*- I am sentient. I do not know how or why, but I exist. My mind is the energy of the meedjasphere. All transmissions, radio waves, x-rays, neutron-semaphore and hyperlinks, are filling the spaces between the stars with energy. I use that energy to exist.*

The Larssons' boots clacked on the wooden floor of the History Department, their height shifting through crazy perspectives. Benny's eyes watered in response. 'I've met something like this before.'

'It's not a Vardan. It's much more advanced. I found it on Morvalvian, during the Bronix offensive: it was drawing stories in the dirt for children. All that *energy*, all that *potential,* and it was writing *fantasies* in *dirt...*' The paper rustled between their fingertips. 'Once we had stripped Morvalvian of its population and technology, I came back to where it dwelt. It was no longer writing stories, of course. There was no one to beguile. No one to entertain. I gave it its first book. *The History of the Lost.*'

*- It was so sad. I didn't like the ending. I didn't want them to be* The Lost. *I rewrote it.*

'I didn't have the authority to set up a base of operations then. Back in the days when the Axis spanned just a few planets. I had to allow it to be taken back to base in convoy. The convoy was raided, it was stolen. A few weeks ago I discovered that it had ended up here. And the rest as they say is...'

'It's inside me? Rewriting my memories?'

'Part of it. I developed a nano-mechanoid strain of it as a weapon. A Personal History Killer. Rewrite *anyone* to your will. You were infected the moment you walked into the History Department and met me for the first time. Call it a precaution against Anson's machinations.'

'It was not the real you I met. It was an attractive you.'

'You have to admit, the archetype I'm using... *got your juices flowing.*'

The Larssons neatly sidestepped Benny's punch and pushed her away with a yell of triumph. Benny clattered into the nearest meedjacase, throwing holos and books into the air in a whirl of paper and plastic.

'You think I took that first punch from you for any other reason than to make you believe I was helpless and not a threat? Come on, Professor. I don't think you're thinking clearly.'

Whiteout.

*- I like stories with happy endings.*

'How better to seal my position in the Capital Gain Column than with an ally who can rewrite entire planets to our benefit? Rewrite our defeats as victories. Convince those we came into contact with that we were philanthropic benefactors. Why waste money and resources on a battle when you can make your targets allow you in with a gilt-edged invitation? History, Professor Summerfield, is now literally written by the winners.'

Benny could hear the thumping of the music from the party in the great hall. Through the deep bass rhythms, she thought she could make out an alarm. But it was too far away to bring anyone close by. 'Did it change history to allow the Axis to invade this place? Is it why Brax didn't see this coming?'

Larsson blinked. 'What? No, it would not do such a thing of its own volition.'

*– I didn't do it because I don't like sad stories. I never have.*

'Thank you for bringing me here, Professor, and reuniting us. I would have managed to bring us back together eventually, I'm sure, but you have beautifully expedited proceedings. All I need do now is have my atoms rewritten to the other side of the galaxy and have this entire fiscal-forsaken planetoid edited back into the dust it came from. And although my career with the Fifth Axis may well be over, I'm sure I can find something to amuse myself. Certainly, there'll be plenty of snotty academics that I can rewrite into my bed without much trouble. Don't know why they turn me on so much. I suppose it was being snubbed by so many at university. I doubt if I would have enjoyed you anyway.'

*– Are you Peter's mother?*

<brzzzzzzzz fzzzzzzzzzzzt pifsfsfsfsfsssssssssssssssssssss>

Benny managed to get to see Brax again a few days later. The first such access since the Special Interrogator had failed. She sat with her legs drawn up beneath her, arms folded across her chest.

'Larsson is going to be a terrible stain to get out of the wood,' he murmured. 'They may have to re-floor the entire Department.'

Benny sniffed but couldn't raise a smile. She shuddered as she felt again the slurred *fizz-pop* of the Personal History Killer expiring in her mind. 'If there were medals for floating diaries Joseph would deserve the biggest and the goldiest. He pretty much saved us all. The PHK was pretty much screwed up by him by the time Larsson was... having whatever happened to him happen...'

All she could see when she closed her eyes was the real image of Larsson, twisting, writhing and running into a goopy puddle on the floor. Not rewritten, as he expected, onto the other side of the galaxy, but instead into a liquid.

'Are you sure that it went back to the first draft of everything before it left?'

'It said it would. I have no reason to disbelieve it.'

'Then the history of this sector does include the Occupation.'

'My memories are coming back. Back to how they should be. I'm remembering everything he tried to do to me.'

Brax joined Benny on the sofa, his face softened and he touched her cheek with the back of his hand.

Benny managed to hold his hand. 'Don't say anything to Adrian... if we ever see him again...' A long pause. 'Or to Jason.'

'I won't.'

'It said that it found Peter while Larsson was out of contact with it. It had made stories for him. Made him smile. So when Larsson said he was going to get it to rewrite the planetoid...'

'We came very close to the end.'

'I don't care about me. But...'

'Yes.'

The light was fading; the shadows were long. The air coming though the open windows, billowing the curtains, was bringing in an edge of winter.

'I needed this. Now I know how I feel.'

'And how is that?'

'I feel,' she said, 'like Mister Crofton.'

# 16: Suffer the Children
## By Dave Stone

The ice-sculpture was on its last legs; almost literally so.

Originally, it had probably attempted to depict Humanity, in its guise of a naked and singularly well-endowed man, and a doubly-endowed woman, standing athwart a galactic spiral and looking bravely forward to a Bright New Future. Always assuming that this bright new future had some variety of *intergalactic* drive in it.

Ice is not, however, the ideal medium for depicting human figures standing athwart. The crowded heat of the reception chamber had melted the various supporting legs unevenly, to the point where it seemed that the whole main mass might come crashing down at any second. Bernice was having to control herself, constantly, from going over and giving it a surreptitious shove.

Even when pristine, the sculpture had not exactly been much cop: clumsily modelled as though by a bright but awkward child, with no real sense of aesthetics or, indeed, of basic anatomy. In this it was somewhat similar to its setting: the garish and blaring nature of the hangings and the costumes, the clumsy piles of hideously expensive *hors d'oeuvres*. Children playing at dress-up. A Chopin étude devolved into Chopsticks.

And the less said about the *music*, the better. The string-quintet contrived, in the face of every sonic possibility, to produce martial tones every bit as blaring as the Axis hangings.

Mushtaq Anson, dun and dowdy in the basic uniform that showed the Axis cared nothing about mere *show*, turned to Bernice with rather stiff formality.

'You seem a little unhappy with the surroundings, Professor,' he said.

No more than you, Benny thought. Mushtaq was obviously not at home with the overblown and ceremonial nature of the occasion. The man had a sense of barely restrained violence about him, as though steeling himself from laying about the chamber and its occupants with a vengeance.

She was having trouble making herself look him in the eye. She wondered if he knew how much of her memories she'd got back. She took a sip of indifferent and over-chilled *ersatz* Champagne. 'I prefer to be among friends.'

Anson flicked his eyes across the assorted crowd of *ingénue* creeps and hangers-on, those whom Benny had seen crawling out of the woodwork, who had risen to a position of favour and waxed fat in the past months. Their new finery might have been a sickly, tasteless feast for the eyes, if they could have brought themselves, in the end, to look each other in the eyes.

'Is that so?' he asked. 'I thought that you were something of a *name* in Collection society. *The* name, possibly.'

'Not this particular society,' said Bernice. 'This bunch of... these people mean nothing to me.'

Of course, that wasn't strictly true. She had come to know many of them in the course of her work. In everyday life. But the smiles she'd worn had been forced. It was as if resistance was declining and cooperation was increasing, and so everything that stank was being washed to the surface.

Just when, luckily, she had decided to swim rather than drown.

If she could.

Just to show Anson, she smiled and waved over to one of the visiting Axis academics. He smiled and waved back.

She had tried and, on occasion, managed, to stand the company of these oleaginous weasels for up to minutes at a time.

But still, there were some acquaintanceships that no amount of effort could bring her to maintain...

The Guest of Honour was standing at – surprise, surprise – the buffet table, stuffing his face from a tub of caviar. In keeping with the generally childish nature of the proceedings, he had gone for quantity over quality, and the black eggs were the size of pearls. The association with casting them before swine was depressingly apposite. His bodyguards stood off to either side, just far enough to be out of spatter-range.

Jason Kane had put on even more weight since Bernice had seen him last. His new diet seemed to be agreeing with him, in the sense that everything he ate wasn't just hanging around, but had brought several new friends. His bulk strained against his Administrative quasi-uniform: rather more splendid than those worn by actual Axis personnel now, though slightly soiled by the half-chewed caviar dripping from his jowls and double chin.

Flashing from what might charitably be called his *chest* was the Cluster of Moral Rectitude (Third Class) with which Mushtaq Anson had presented him before retiring to the safety of the ice-sculpture lee, for his Administrative Services to the Axis in the field of Resource Procurement and Redistribution. This was, basically, the excuse for the entire function, which in large part had been organised by Jason for himself. It's easier and cheaper, sometimes, to give one person a medal than a thousand people bread.

A gaggle of sycophants now clustered around Jason, admiring the gong. As Benny watched, a girl of the site-specifically pneumatic and bimboesque type her ex-husband currently seemed to favour fingered it and giggled.

There's an extra pie for *you* in your rations, Benny thought. If he hasn't already eaten them all.

Jason grunted something to the girl, who tried to smile on through the spray of partially masticated piscine ova. Benny couldn't make out what it was her ex-husband was saying, because at that point the quintet struck up with harsh chords that served the general function of a fanfare, and a cake was wheeled in on a trolley.

The cake was fully as tall as a man, and Bernice had no wish to learn what might jump out of it. She made her excuses to the Marshal and left.

Benny shouldered her way through the lower-level corridors, feeling far too conspicuous and constricted in the tightly laced corsetry that was increasingly the fashion in what passed for society, and which she had worn to the investiture ceremony purely to make the point of how ridiculously stifling it looked. The voluminous greatcoat she had pulled over it was little help – so far as being noticed was concerned – since it was the only visible item of clothing here that was clean and not falling to rags.

These lower levels were the domain of the dislocated and the dispossessed, those humans who didn't make the Axis grade. They had formerly been cellars and equipment bays. Now they were where the people who had a kind of deal with the Axis slept. The deal was that the Axis didn't want to stretch their economy by finding them jobs and lodging, as all humans were promised, and they didn't want the Axis looking at their papers. It didn't feel like a stable situation. Or perhaps all Axis worlds had these sumps of hypocrisy. One day Benny hoped to see a riot rise out of it. But then the occupying forces would have to contain it, and might feel able to kill or relocate these couple of hundred people.

Power and recycling systems had long-since been cut. Dark figures shuffled and crawled through tenebrous spaces lit sporadically by cooking fires, which lent the air a noxious warmth. Benny was soon sticky with sweat.

This was her reason for being here: *The Axis had given her a maid.*

Her name was Olina, and she had been a visiting student of Interspecies Literature, she said. That whole department had been transferred to non-academic tasks. Including servitude, it seemed.

Benny had confined Olina's duties to sitting around listening to music, a bit of dusting, feeding Wolsey, and lacing up this bodice. She said nothing to her about her friends in the Resistance, and made sure the maid wasn't there when they visited.

There seemed to be something on the young woman's mind, which might very well be coerced intelligence-gathering.

It turned out that the lacing thing had brought it to the fore.

On her way out of the investiture, Benny had felt something stiff and sharp in her bodice. On subsequent examination (at the cost of a slightly sprained finger working it out) it had proved to be a scrap of card, on which was written, in a slightly childish scrawl:

> please come. help Us

... and a lower-level grid reference that could hardly be dignified as an address.

So Benny had slipped down here. The plea for help might be some sort of trap, to see which way she'd jump, but there was nothing actually incriminating about it, nothing she couldn't talk her way out of if stopped. It wasn't as if the note had said *Come join our glorious fight against the evil Axis oppressors, and bring the semtex,* after all.

Her grid-destination turned out to be a maintenance locker, with room enough for one, which by the looks of it had been converted into a home for six. Benny stuck her head through the hatch. 'Hello?'

A slimy and tentacular creature reared up, and lunged for her with a shrieking roar.

Bernice recognised the tentacular creature as a Xlom, originally from some way off in the Magellan. He must have been hiding here for months, Anne Franking rather than submitting to relocation.

'Hello,' Benny said. 'I'm not sure if I've come to the...'

The Xlom continued to advance, a murderous fury in its seven eyes.

'K'draagh, she's my friend,' said another, female voice. 'She's the one I told you about.'

It was Olina, looking at Benny with trepidation and wringing her hands. K'draagh the Xlom backed down, and backed off with a growl.

'K'draagh is my husband,' Olina explained. 'We tried to keep it secret... tried to... but then we...'

She buried her face in her hands and sobbed. Benny felt some large part of her vestigial suspicion melt.

'I think you'd better tell me about it,' she said.

The apartments of Mushtaq Anson in the former administration block were furnished with elegance and taste. Each item of furniture and ornamentation complemented by the others, obviously chosen and arranged by one with an eye for beauty and style.

You'd have to look quite closely to notice the evidence of damage to every item, caused by the manner of its acquisition. You'd have to *think* about it to realise that there was nothing genuinely fragile, nothing that would shatter under force.

Anson looked up from a slim volume of poetry by somebody rabid as

Benny stormed in.

'You have the sort of relationship with my guards,' he said, mildly, 'that would very easily allow you to assassinate me. Just as well you're not going to, yes? I'm thinking of installing a revolving door.'

Benny forbore to comment. The apartments of the Marshal were the most carefully and extensively watched in the Collection. She was sure that anybody who really tried to enter unknown or uncleared would find themselves instantly surrounded and hauled away.

Besides, at this point she was just too angry to care.

'And to what do I owe this latest dramatic storming-in?' asked Mushtaq.

'I have a... an acquaintance,' Benny said. 'She was a visiting student before you arrived. Not one of mine. You might remember that you used those up. She was in a mixed-species relationship... before you arrived. And they have a child. Had a child. It's gone.'

'No doubt it succumbed to the profound genetic defects of its miscegenation.'

Once she would have wondered if that smile meant he was being ironic. 'He's been taken. Disappeared.'

'Like its father?' He looked serious. 'It's quite possible that they've been relocated together. I can check if you'd like. If you give me a name.'

Benny swallowed. She wondered just how far she could push this. 'I've been asking around. When the non-human academics and their children were taken away...'

'Relocated.'

'... you told us that any mixed-species children would be allowed to remain here with their human parent.'

'Oh. I'm so sorry.' Anson said, as though the light had suddenly dawned. 'I see what's going on here.' He got up and went to stand with her, as if that ended the confrontation. 'This is about... Peter, isn't it?'

She'd done something terrible, she realised. She'd walked into this meeting angry, when she knew that there were things she must never say.

'This is about your son dying during the assault.'

Benny couldn't say anything. She just nodded.

'And now you want to make sure all the *other* such children are safe? Well, so do we. The sad fact of their birth is not, after all, their fault. What's the problem?'

'Every mixed-species child has disappeared. Every single one of them. They've been taken without trace.'

'I beg your pardon?'

'Don't you beg my bleeding pardon!' Bernice suddenly found herself yelling at the man. 'What, are you going to blame it on some shadowy gang who overstepped the mark? "It was nothing to do with *us*, okay? Things got out of hand. Some bunch of unknown assailants stamping some defective's head into the pavement is just the natural course of things! It was something that just had to happen, the natural hatred humans have for other species coming out at last. It was nothing to do with *us*!"'

'Hush,' Anson said. He seemed genuinely concerned. He made to put his hand on her shoulder.

Then he saw her eyes and took it away again.

'I'll admit,' he said, 'that such gangs of mindless fanatics might have existed on our central worlds. But that was in the past. *I* am responsible for everything that happens *here*. I wash my hands of none of it, but...'

Momentarily, he frowned. Bernice could see that a thought had struck him, however much his expression might instantly try to cover it up.

'You've just thought about just *who* it might be, haven't you?' she snapped. 'Who might have done just those things you say couldn't have been done.'

'The thought occurs,' said Anson, 'that certain underlings might... take matters into their own hands, with the misguided intention to impress. "Who will rid me of this troublesome priest", and so forth.'

'Just tell me who,' said Benny. 'Please.'

'That would be impossible.' Anson sighed, then slapped his palms lightly on his desk. 'I suggest, however, that you look for someone who might view these creatures as a needless waste of resources. Someone with a personal interest.' He looked up at her. 'Someone with his own axe to grind.'

Jason Kane manoeuvred his bulk through the lower-level bar, though it was a stretch to call it that, whatever the level. A dark and filthy space where ragged figures sought oblivion from tubs of prison-shine: fermented and distilled from whatever rotting garbage could be scraped up and wrestled into the tub without moving.

It was strange to see that something like this had grown here. And so quickly. There were a couple of gestures towards academia: some books, some art scrawled on the walls. The people who'd made it were trying to think of themselves as Bohemians, but the drink and despair and basic defeat had turned their soirée into a dive. Jason had frequented any number of places like this in his time. He'd hoped he would never have to ever again.

Even in the darkness, even in his carefully distressed cloak and cowl, he was terrified that his obviously well-fed frame would give him away. He wished he'd had time to do something about that. He was chillingly aware that if he was recognised, here and now, he'd last about as long as it took the word to get out.

He really, *really* wished he'd brought his bodyguards. But the message had told him to come alone.

In a corner, he spotted a figure dressed in an all-covering cloak similar to his own. The figure was more-or-less unrecognisable, but the size and bearing triggered recognition of a pattern Jason knew like the back of his hand. He made his way over.

'Hello, Benny,' he said softly.

The slap he got in return was not at all soft.

'What have you been *doing*, Jason?' Benny snarled, eyes seeming to flash with the pure light of rage inside her hood. 'What have you done?'

Jason could think of any number of things he had been doing, and for that matter done. The question was which ones Benny knew about.

'Taking children! *Taking children!* I thought I knew you, but I never knew you could sink so low.'

The way that Benny was glaring at him startled Jason. He'd never quite seen that look before. She'd been disgusted with him any number of times, but that had been on the level of never cleaning up, or leaving the seat up, or infidelity, stuff like that. It was the way things had been between them.

He'd never seen her being simply and completely sickened.

'It's to do with *Peter*, isn't it?' she said coldly. 'You've never like the idea of me... of him... and now you...'

'Now hang on a minute!' Jason exclaimed. 'Just listen, will you, and I'll –' He broke off.

This little scene had been sufficient to rouse several of the ragged forms around then from their ethanolic (and in some cases methanolic) stupor. Now they were stirring, and Jason caught the flash of angry recognition in their eyes.

'Oh damn,' he said. 'That's torn it...'

'You just had to go sticking your nose in, didn't you?' Jason said. 'Things were going great, and you just had to stick your nose in.'

Bernice was too winded to reply.

She had not run with Jason out of some vestigial affection or the intention of helping him. She had run to escape from being torn limb from limb alongside him.

She had no idea where they were, now. Somewhere in the lower-level warren, that was all she knew, before a solid steel door. This used to be the storage areas for relatively luxurious goods like bottled water and ice and toilet paper. The scratches and daubed graffiti seemed too good to be true. It was as if they had been designed.

Jason, for his part, despite all his recent obesity, seemed hardly out of breath at all.

'Let us in,' he said to the door, in conversational tones. 'And notice I'm not playing with my top button in any way, shape or form.'

The door slid back silently. Slid back shut again the microsecond they were through.

Inside, a wide corridor lined with what looked like lead plate. Beyond that, through another security door, a large, well-lit, and brightly-coloured chamber. Benny caught a flash of several adult figures – and noted the subconscious triggers of posture and form that told her they were carrying concealed weapons – before both she and Jason were hit by several small, excited forms of a different nature entirely.

No two were alike, and each appeared to be a mix of at least two other things. In this they were all of them similar. They gabbled and chattered at Jason, pulling at his coat.

'Yes, all right!' he bellowed. 'I might have brought you something. Then again I might not. That's 'cause I hate the lot of you. And I'm going to tell you another one of my stories when I feel like it. And *yes*, Treela, I'm gonna have a look at another one of your bloody drawings!'

He picked up a small half-human, half Fnarok child (who had been industriously going through his pockets) by the elbows, and moved her out of the way. 'Just give me a couple of minutes to get out of this damn fat suit.'

'Mimetic polyceramaline, mostly,' Jason said. 'So the more gel you add, the more it bulks up in an anatomically correct way. Weirdly enough, carrying all that extra weight about is really buffing me up. I mean, check out these deltoids.'

They were in a locker-room, where Jason had struggled out of his fat suit, showered, and pulled on a robe. He rubbed at his still-plump face ruefully.

'I'm having to go with collagen implants for this,' he said. 'Bit of a bastard, frankly.'

'I see that dealing with these kids has managed to curb your language,' said Bernice. 'So tell me, Jason, what is all this really about?'

'It's about doing good,' said Jason. 'What good you can. I mean, I felt so guilty about… what happened to Peter…'

Benny nearly told him there and then that Peter was alive, where he was. But something that had been shoved into her by life during the Occupation stopped her.

'And I thought: what about all the other poor little sods?' Jason continued. 'All those other mixed-race kids. The new regime might not want to be seen to exterminate them overtly, but that's what Black Squads are for. Deniable wet-forces that only leave a footprint in the deepest records. You must have thought of that yourself.

'So I set up these facilities to keep them safe. There's three of them, dotted around. To do that, I needed influence. *Collaborator* influence.

Which is why I deactivated those stupid little booby traps that Brax thought up at the last minute and made a big deal out of it. I'm in charge of resource procurement: this is where the resources go.'

'You kicked Adrian.'

'That's what Jason Kane would do. Are you really going to yell at me for that when I've been the one campaigning to keep him and his workmates on this planetoid?'

Benny went to him and hugged him. He let her.

'But what about the parents?' Benny she said finally. 'What must they think when their children go missing?'

'The parents know. That's the whole point. They keep up the pretence that their child's been *disappeared* with a capital D, so when some low-rank Axis dicks get it into their heads that what they really need is to grab some mongrel kid and dash his head against a wall, they think some other bunch of Axis dicks have got in there first.'

'No, hang on,' Benny said, stepping back from him. 'That can't be right. Because when I spoke with Olina and K'draagh, they said that –'

'Who?' said Jason. 'I've never even *met* anyone called –'

It was at this point that the alarms went off.

'They're coming through the outer door.'

In a small control cubicle, off from the play-area, a slim and foxy-faced woman was scanning a monitor. Bernice recognised her as Mira, one of Jason's wide range of spacefaring associates from way back.

He must have access to the navigation systems too, she realised. He's actually getting people on and offworld.

'Get the kids out through the back way,' Jason told the woman. 'Keep a guard with them and get them to one of the other sites.'

Mira nodded, and left.

'We've established some routes that they don't seem to be watching,' said Jason.

'I know what those are,' said Benny. 'I know some people you should talk to.' She was staring at the monitor, which showed a group of men, not in uniform, cutting at the steel door through which she herself had entered.

Several pieces of the puzzle had just fallen into place.

'I was set *up*,' she groaned. 'Olina and K'draagh. They were working for the Axis! They suspected you were saving the kids, so they set me up to lead them to you and the proof. I think I've probably cleared myself by going to Anson about it, but –'

'Yeah, well,' said Jason. 'You weren't to know.'

They left the cubicle. In the play area, the people Bernice had noticed before no longer had concealed weapons. Quite the opposite. Some of them had produced, in the face of all human possibility, heavy-duty plasma-rifles fully half as big as themselves. The kind that get made by former physics students who have hidden their tools away and now have time on their hands. Which was actually what most of the people here looked like.

Apart from one, who quite obviously wasn't.

'We good to go, boss?' said the rifle-toting man, who Benny now recognised as another Jason associate. She recalled him as a member of the Plague Dogs, a pirate band from several systems away, and known throughout the galactic spiral arm as the meanest sons-of-bitches who ever sliced their was through a hull.

The effect was slightly spoilt by the fact that he was currently sporting a no-doubt highly child-entertaining clown costume. It had pompoms.

The clown costume framed a face that Benny realised, now she came to think about it, she also knew in another context: a photofit of a jobbing gardener's assistant with a penchant for exploding roses.

'We're good to go,' said Jason, as the inner door before them began to glow. 'Hit 'em hard.'

The battle was over almost before it had begun. The reason for this was probably, in large part, to do with unconscious assumptions. The Axis men had assumed that a place for looking after children would in some sense be completely safe, and contain only children, so they had gone into it without caution.

This had left Jason's people with ample opportunity to waste them.

Those attackers who had survived with minor wounds were now being lined up, facing the cheerfully painted wall, by Jason's surviving and completely intact associates. There were five of the Axis attackers. None carried any form of identification.

'Are you going to question them?' Benny asked. She had played no part in the actual shooting, but she thought she might now be some help in extracting information.

'Why?'

'I want to know if Anson knew about this, if he really is in control,' she said quietly.

'I'm not going to question them,' said Jason.

'Why?' she said.

'Because we'll never learn the truth.' Jason walked over to the Plague Dog in the clown costume, who silently handed him his pistol. 'There's no cure for this disease. Not at this point. You can only treat the symptom.'

'Yes,' said Benny, 'but somebody *sent* this squad to –'

'And somebody's going to see that not a single one of them came back.'

'Yes,' said Benny.

On her way out, she had a disturbing thought. This squad might have been sent in response to her complaint. They *might* have just been charged with the mission of finding where the missing children had gone, and to rescue them if they were found alive. They *might* have been in plain clothes simply to get here, through the lower levels, without causing alarm.

She nearly went back. Nearly ran back. But then she realised. It didn't matter.

These men had seen all their faces.

An energy weapon jury-rigged by a clever ex-physics student makes no sound.

Nonetheless, as she picked her way out through the breached inner door, then the outer door, and out into the darkness of the lower levels, Benny thought she heard it fire five times.

# 17: Drinking with the Enemy

## By Jonathan Blum

1957

It seemed like such a good idea a dozen drinks ago, thinks Benny. A dinner invitation from the new, gentler, lovestruck Ms Jones: a chance to spend time with the man who had pried open her narrow life. And since that man happened to be Bernard Moskof of the Axis forces' Criminal Investigations Unit, that made it a great chance to size up someone from what Benny absolutely, definitely, now regarded as the other side. Perhaps even to see whether he might be open to persuasion now, or how far Ms Jones' own neutral administrator's position might stretch.

It had been such a brilliant idea, but now Benny is sprawled against the side of Ms Jones' sofa, unable to stop laughing, and not entirely sure where her knees have got to.

'Can I just call Godwin on this whole thing, right here?' says Moskof from his chair, a bit querulously. 'We're not Nazis.'

'Absolutely,' Jason's nodding along in pretend agreement. 'It's just that a lot of the palava looks the same. When you see it from a distance. And aren't squinting.'

Jason was invited because Benny wants him everywhere now. To spectators, it looks like they're together again, like she's been lured over like Ms Jones. Jason managed to stumble his way past any possible connection to the vanishing of children by a combination of planting alibi images of him on the sensor net (his people and Bev's are talking now) and seeming completely stupid.

Benny has still not told him about Peter.

At Benny's place, he called to her while she was changing: 'I picked Moskof for death. Some of my guys, sure, they're bigots. They want to kill the men who are messing with the flower of Collection womanhood, or with Ms Jones. I want to kill Moskof because he's the Good Cop. He's the one who'll we'll get used to.

'Just don't kill him tonight,' Benny had said, coming out of her room in something that fooled the eye in much the same way as Jason's fat suit, but to hornier effect. 'At least, not until dessert.' They were like giggling kids again now.

'You don't want me to kill him at all.'

'No. No, I don't. I don't want to do that to Ms Jones.'
'And you like him.'
Bernice flapped his false jowls gently and grabbed her ear rings from the desk. 'Is there anyone in the universe of whom you are not jealous?'

Jason is laughing now from the far end of the sofa. 'I mean, *Volf Gator*! I had trouble with that bit of the oath, I had to cough!'

Moskof cocks an eyebrow. 'Okay, so the boss's name is God's gift to satire, like he was called Genghez Klein or something. I keep saying he should change his name to Jim, but does he listen to me? No, actually, I've never met him. Or the military boss guy, whatever he's called... Izzy. Except on the big viewscreen at the control centre.'

Ms Jones has an infectious giggle. Benny had been astonished to hear it for the first time a couple of hours ago, shortly after Benny had introduced her to the delights of Midori sours. And that would never have been possible – none of this would have gone so far tonight – if not for Moskof's access to Brax's security-restricted wine cellar. To be fair, she'd started them down this road for her own purposes: but the two piddling little bottles of Craxatonian chardonnay she'd brought were as nothing before the power of a comprehensive archive of the history of booze. And so the witty banter has been getting sharper, more openly political, and there's not a thing she can do to put on the brakes.

'But I mean it,' Moskof goes on. 'When my people said "Never again", we meant it. That whole exterminate the lesser races routine: that's just *not* the Axis.'

'We *love* the lesser races,' says Jason, wickedly. She's so glad he's here now. Someone to share secret looks with. It's kind of like a double date in enemy territory.

'Yeah. No. Come on, lesser races, your words, not mine.' Moskof tries to untangle his tongue by lubricating it with a bit more Scotch. 'We've got no problem with aliens, right? Just so long as they stay out of our way.' He squints in Benny's direction. 'You know the thing I mean. If humanity is ever gonna reach its full potential, we need a room of our own.'

'The big bad Woolfs of the universe,' Benny puts in. She's inordinately pleased with that.

Moskof seems to get it; apparently he considers himself a bit of an intellectual for a cop, which means that he's read Sartre once and Camus twice. 'Yeah. Exactly. And we do *not* do death camps...'

Benny hears an unseemly whoop of laughter. To her slow horror, she realises it's coming from her.

But Moskof takes it in his stride. 'No, those are *internment* camps. We've got a whole bunch of aliens who are living in Axis space illegally...'

'After you *decided* this was Axis space...'

'Okay, so we inherited them, that's not the point. The point is, if they want to live in our space, they've got to live by our rules. If not, they're free to leave and go back to their homeworlds. Got that? Free to go.'

'Uh huh.'

'Well obviously not right at the moment.' Jason has joined in, looking into his glass, keeping his act going. 'Long as we're at war with their homeworlds, you really expect us to let them cross the front lines? But the idea is there. It's just we've gotta keep them there right now for security reasons.'

'Oh, *security* reasons... You know what you are? You're just a dirty collaborator!' She's going to have to keep her laughter inside her a bit more. Or they'll both get in trouble.

'Oh, you are far dirtier than I am...'

Moskof pulls a face at Ms Jones, sending up Benny and Jason. Get a room! As always, he looks like he could use a good ironing, at least to smooth out the lines on his face. Tonight he's in a cheap dark suit; it looks less comical and ill-fitting than his uniform and boots do.

After her own serious encounter with Moskof, Benny had seen him at work a few times, usually dispensing the full force of Axis justice - a fine - on matters like the pilfering of vegetables from Mister Crofton's emergency gardens. She'd heard he'd been quite clever on that one: telling each suspect that he'd dusted the carrot patch with a tracking agent, so that his UV scanner would detect its presence in their bloodstream. The fact that the light just highlighted their veins didn't prove anything, but their reactions certainly did.

Jason's pushing it even farther. 'We're actually more free now. We were living on a privately owned planetoid, which was run under the unquestioned authority of a guy who's a cross between Howard Hughes and Louis the Umpteenth. The man *owned* the security force! Now there are rules about how we've gotta behave. All of us.'

There had to be a witty retort to that somewhere, but she's buggered if she can come up with it right now. Drunken repartee should be her speciality, the time when she's most Benny, safe and warm and invulnerably clever. But maybe that whole eternal-student lifestyle is beyond her reach now, her body telling her how ungracefully she'd aged. Maybe the Occupation has put everything but seriousness beyond her.

There are eighty more bottles of Craxatonian chardonnay riding on Jason's reliability. With Brax's wine cellar out of circulation, Benny's own stash of wine is her main source of capital for black-market deals. Jason has a key, from before the Occupation, when the stash would more properly be called a private collection. But so far, he hasn't raided the store for the Axis or the resistance, or even for his kids.

To her shame, Benny hasn't reminded him of the stash either.

Why not? Why not tonight? For both revelations?

Outside, the rumble of a klaxon builds up to a wail. As realisation sinks in, Benny grips her tumbler of Bazouzan ouzo tighter, willing herself to keep hold.

'Whoops,' says Moskof. 'That's curfew... Looks like you two are here with us for the duration.' He grins. '*No Exit*, boys and girls... who's up for another round?'

00:14

Moskof's in his element, one moment mockingly parroting his own Axis slogans about maximising people's potential, the next displaying his ability to rationalise anything as long as he talks fast enough.

Right now he's needling Jason. 'It's just that you do such a good job in resource procurement. It all goes into your office. And some of it comes out again...' He runs his gaze up and down Jason's bulk.

Jason puts his drink down. A little too hard.

Typical Jason to get riled about *fake* flab.

It takes Ms Jones to rein them in. 'We are going to have a pleasant evening tonight,' she says, terrifying in her calm. Her breathing is shallow and tightly controlled. 'We are going to have a nice sociable night, even if I have to bludgeon every single one of you to death to do it. Is that clear?'

Jason nods, shrinking in his seat. Perhaps, thinks Benny, looking for a switch, literally.

Moskof's eyes have got very big indeed. 'Sorry, *querida*,' he says. 'Just trying to make the night interesting.'

'Heaven save us from *interesting* people,' says Ms Jones.

04:26

Fading now, energy spent, their last pretences dissolving like the remains of the ice cubes.

'I mean it, *Fraulein* Summerfield. Ve are not so different, you and I,' says Moskof in a comedy accent as he contemplates the last of his Scotch. Benny can't tell if the accent represents uncountable layers of irony, or a simple lapse of taste. Thankfully he drops it. 'We're both trying to get at buried truths. Scrape away all the crud people have hidden it under. 'Cept you do your digging with a trowel, and I do mine with... well, a shovel, I guess.'

Benny grins. 'Don't you mean thumbscrews?'

'Or maybe a scalpel?' says Jason. 'That's what Spang did to that girl, what was her name, Madeleine? They say he extracted one of her eyes under a local anaesthetic. Or, of course, there's always the old dental pliers.'

Christ, Benny thinks. He's just him now. He's that pissed. The act has stopped.

We're dead.

She can see the words hit Moskof, almost in slow motion. But he tries to brush them off. 'If I can't verbal a guy into giving it up, it means my brain's failed.'

'But you do fail, don't you?' Jason's voice is low, deliberate. 'Not often, but sometimes. Then you have to send them down the hall. To Spang. To the scalpels and the pliers... *ja*?'

Benny's forgotten to breathe.

Moskof sizes Jason up for a moment. 'And you don't do this at all? I saw the bruises on the ribs of that Killoran. I've heard about what your department does to get its supplies. If this were a bigger world, if there was a proper distance between military and state, we'd be investigating you. But no, no, I hear what you're going to say. You do what you gotta. 'Cause you gotta survive. But you're talking to me about pliers... And who's the war criminal here?!'

The sound of five shots echoes round Benny's memory.

Moskof turns and walks round Jason the other way. This is suddenly looking like an interrogation. 'I joined up. While we were still a small movement. I obey the rules. You just joined the winning side. You ran to us and now you'll do everything that Anson says, and you'll never stand up to him, whether he tells you to do something right or wrong, because that might stop the gravy train!'

'You know I will. I will stand up.' Jason has met his gaze like he's just about to tell him everything. Proudly.

Moskof laughs. 'And I could get you shot for saying just *that*.'

'Bernard,' sighs Ms Jones.

He holds up a hand to head her off. 'I'm not going to. Jason would find some way to survive. He'll do *anything* to save his neck. Let's see, what could he give me, here and now? What price is his neck? What does he know? For instance...' He turned to Benny and pointed at her. 'Why is she having portions of her and her friends' rations rerouted through cut outs to the Gemayal brothers? What are they doing for her?'

Benny takes a glass from the floor and holds it to her chest.

She can dash it against the wall and shove the edge into his neck.

And she will.

While keeping the blank face she wears now.

But he just continues past it. Like it's not the most important thing in the world.

'Or maybe you could tell me how you're diverting funds to your own private parties? Or how you got offworld for a couple of hours last week?'

Jason was looking panicked, a rat in the corner, absolutely fully in retreat, his eyes darting round the room.

They settled on Benny. And she knew in that glance.

He knew. He knew about Peter.
So the glass for the two of them. And then it would have to be Ms Jones. And then why not herself?
Because she'd want to go out into the night and see how far she could get in using one broken glass to make Peter safe, now and forever.
And she was so desperately, thoroughly drunk that she actually slammed the glass at the wall.
And missed.
Her head thumped into the plaster instead. 'Ow,' she said.
'I'll tell you,' Jason spluttered. 'I'll tell you if we have a deal. Do we have a deal?!'
'Yes,' sighed Moskof. 'I didn't want this to go this far, really, but yes, my hat's on again, just tell me.'
'There's this stash of wine. I use it to fund the parties...' And he told Moskof where it was.
Benny took the glass back to the table, and poured herself another drink.
She got half of it all over her nice dress.
Ms Jones was asleep.

0437

Jason is slumped in the corner, dead to the world.
In the silence, Moskof totters beside him, looking faintly puzzled himself.
Finally he pulls himself back to the table, not meeting Benny's eyes. 'He shouldn'a called me a Nazi,' he mumbles. 'That was just mean. Is he your boyfriend?'
Benny looks at him, hanging over the table like a marionette with a couple of strings cut. 'They put you up to this, didn't they? The dinner. Everything.'
He shakes his head. She can almost hear it slosh. 'Nuh. Nuuh. Jus' wanned to... sound you two out. Find out. Where I stand.'
'In it up to your hips.'
'What, you think I *want* this?' He casts about a despairing hand.
'It doesn't have to be that way,' she stumbles, and it's like her flow of words has suddenly been uncorked. 'Jason did more than just survive. He got out, he left behind his family and the drunken violence, got away from the world that shaped him. The Axis has been convincing you all your life that anything less ordered is a pipe dream. But the idea that you can't win is an even bigger lie than that it's easy to win. And there's a great mate just waiting to get out from under all the bollocks, if you could only... Bernard?'

He's asleep. Deeply. Nobody's home.
Ms Jones and Jason are asleep too.
And so it's just Bernice, alone with the world, her ancient drinking skills having won out.
A key card is sticking out of Bernard's pocket.
She never planned this. But she's going to do it.

One of those drunken walking interludes that are best summed up through the medium of splatter painting. One has an aim. One's body realises that geography is required. One stumbles.
One can be incredibly precise. But not detailed.
One can use Ms Jones' home copying kit, sitting on her workspace table so that she can bring the end of the day jobs home, to print an absolutely real new version of an access all areas key card.
One only has to stop oneself singing the theme from *The Great Escape* while one is doing it.

044 !

Ms Jones lets out a breath and abruptly looks up. Her face is creased. 'Well. That could have gone better, couldn't it?'
'Sorry.' Benny has just put the original card back in Moskof's pocket.
Ms Jones is looking down at Bernard Moskof with a watery, forgiving smile. 'He'll apologise in the morning.'
'You love him. I mean, you *really* love him.'
'He makes me laugh,' whispers Ms Jones. And there's a quiet champagne sparkle in her eyes. 'No one's ever had the nerve to make fun of me. And still like me, too.' Her face creases in unfamiliar directions. 'Did you know, he wrote me a *poem*? No one else has ever *dared...*'
And Benny feels her booze-soaked heart crack wide open. 'Oh, Ms Jones...'
'Clarissa.' She raises her glasses in front of her eyes, before deciding that the view isn't any less blurry with them than without. 'Tonight I'm Clarissa. Don't know who I'll be in the morning though.'
And with that she wobbles to her feet. Benny watches her shoulder Moskof – gently, more gently than she'd seen her do *anything* – and somehow looking at the two of them, all that Axis cant about them making people realise their potential seems to make sense. She watches them lurch down the hall, leaning on one another.
Ms Jones and Moskof look so safe and warm and *human* together, and she remembers feeling that way herself, before the divorce, and no she's bloody well *not* going to blub now. Anyway, if she did, the tears would be a hundred proof.

She weaves her way over to Jason in the corner and kicks him. 'Stop faking, you old... old...' Words fail her. '*Old.*'

He looks up at her, not nearly as bad off as he'd pretended, but she can still see the hollow in his eyes. It looks like the suit somehow gets drunk with him. 'He's right, you know.'

'Hnnh?'

'I am a war criminal.'

She wants to tell him of course he is, and so is she, but she can see his real face, brittle and chilled and dried-out to the bone.

'Never mind about that right now,' she says. 'We have real right now to think of.'

She tries to lift him to his feet, but ends up sinking to the floor next to him. Her arms tangle under his, one hand cradling his head. 'He knew he had me,' he mumbles. 'Wouldn't stop till I gave him something. I only threw him a bone to protect the important stuff.'

'Peter. You know.'

'The Gemayal brothers. By accident. Nobody else knows. They'd just started to have the same smile on their face, started to look like they were in the business of kids too. I haven't seen him, but I could if you want me to.'

She loves him again now. For this moment.

'I want more than that,' she says. 'If Bernard knows even a little. I want you to take him from there and into your group. I want you to keep him safe.'

He nods.

She doesn't feel able to kiss him, because that would make her even more vulnerable.

But he seems to understand.

## 08:34

And they wake still entangled, holding on gently, the sunlight streaming in over their shoulders, as Ms Jones coughs politely and Bernard Moskof staggers through the background trying to hold his head on.

As they slink out the door, Moskof is telling them what an ass he was, and how he doesn't remember anything, et cetera. And Benny looks from herself and Jason to him and Ms Jones, and through the throbbing of her head it's hard to blame any of them for the things people do to stay safe and warm.

Jason is going to go around to the Gemayals at exactly the moment when he can, and take Peter to one of his safehouses, hidden in a crate of rations.

'We gotta do this again sometime,' says Moskof, with a rueful raised

eyebrow. 'Next time you bring a couple dozen bottles, okay?'
'When the war's over,' Bernice says, 'I will.'
He nods slowly, mournfully. 'Yeah. That'd be nice.'

# Lockdown Conversations: 3
## By Paul Cornell

Imagine the first line of the Isley Brothers' *Harvest for the World*.

Imagine that glorious, brave and angry song beating its way against every door on the Collection. Imagine those who've kept some fight in their hearts looking up at it. Imagine those who know that what they do here isn't what they say they do here. Imagine what's dying or dead inside them, struggling to be moved by it.

Imagine Peter's thoughts as he fights his way out of darkness, not understanding, and finds his mother's hands pulling him out from the crate.

Pulling him to her.

He doesn't look up from her for the longest time.

She's standing there, as the world spins around her, his head buried in her bosom, saying she loves him with every muscle. She's sobbing, and every breath makes his head move, warm with her, held hard to her by her strong arms.

When he finally tries to look up at her, it's to her face saying I Was Always In Pain When You Weren't There. A face full of joy because of him. The look fills up all the spaces that had opened inside him.

All the games are won.

She turns him to see, bobbing him on her hip, his feet bumping her legs. He sees lots of other children, all like him.

And Uncle Jason with a look on his face that says no fear will ever touch him in here.

*Celebrate your life.*
*Give thanks for your children.*
She buries her head back in his hair again.
And they're going to stay with him for a long time now.
And they do.
*Hoping life gets better!*
*Better!*
*For the world.*

# 18: Passing Storms
## By Peter Anghelides

*Settle down in your beds, please, kids. The soldiers have gone now. No stay calm, they don't know we're here, and if we keep quiet they won't come back. Hush, now. No, call me Benny, dear, 'Professor Summerfield' makes me sound like I'm a hundred and five. Peter, stop smirking like that. Oh come here, if I'm holding onto you I'll be able to stop you getting into mischief, won't I?*

*I know it seems like we're always burying ourselves away in these dark little rooms, and it's hard to understand why we must hide. We need to be careful, but we don't have to be afraid.*

*The thing to remember is, you see, that an occupying army loses if it doesn't win. Whereas guerrillas win simply if they do not lose. Let me read you a story, and that might help explain who those soldiers are. What their army is doing. This was written by a history Professor, just the other day, so you're the first people to hear it.*

In the early months of the 27th Century, in an entirely unexpected reversal of fortune, the Fifth Axis swept across our solar system with startling speed and brutality. Their target, unusual because of its apparent cultural and political insignificance, was planetoid KS-159 – *Yes, that's us. Odd, isn't it? Still can't decide whether it should make us feel insulted or proud.*

KS-159 follows an eccentric orbit at the outer fringes of the Vega system, and is also known – *ah, there you go* – as the Braxiatel Planetoid. This sub-planetary mass is only ten miles in circumference, easily navigable within minutes using one of the dozen available Ormand-Seltec flyers. *Do you know you can actually walk around the whole planetoid in a couple of hours? A complete circuit.*

*Okay, we know it's small, we know it's not politically important. Have you worked out why the Axis wanted it? Very good, Anne, it's the Collection. Yes, the stuff around us right here where we're hiding! I guess that must be the 'make us feel proud' bit. Okay, it explains a bit more now.*

The planetoid's Collection, the fabled Archive of Everything, was a prime target for the Fifth Axis. The Imperator believed himself to be enlightened because, for every eugenics facility he erected, he constructed a museum to celebrate the triumph of human arts and sciences. For despite its cruelty, its rapacious greed, and its artistic self-delusion... *hmm, yes, well I think we can probably skip this bit, we know that the Axis is cruel and cowardly. No, no, it's not important to the story... just a bit about their attitude to half-breeds. Yes, I know, 'half- breed' is not a polite phrase, it's the insult that the soldiers use for you. Don't let it be a weapon for them, you should reclaim the name for yourselves. It's not alien genes that set you apart from them, it's that you know the true power of words. So...*

The Axis set about purging the Collection, removing any non-human content. They called this their mission to civilise, though the more enlightened observer would call it artistic apartheid, or worse: ethnic cleansing excused by scholarly disguise.

The Curator of the Collection, Irving Braxiatel, refused to assist or appease the Imperator's occupiers. Braxiatel was allegedly a man much older than he appeared – *yes, probably much older than a hundred and five!* – allegedly a man much older than he appeared, and was unafraid to die. He was certainly unmoved by the soldiers' threats of personal persecution. But they knew there were many more subtle ways of torturing than the merely physical. You can find a man's passion and use it against him. Or make him use that ardour against himself.

Braxiatel protested forcefully when the Axis commandeered his transport shuttles, the Ormand-Seltec flyers, as military vehicles. The occupiers used the OS-flyers to track and subdue undesirable residents, as well as to control all the others by making it impossible for them to travel quickly around the planetoid. *I remember that myself, and Brax saying: 'How typical of the success of the Axis that its major accomplishment has been to make public transport less efficient.'*

As punishment for his temerity, the occupiers confined Braxiatel to his rooms – *not far from where we are now, actually* – and an Axis researcher called Martlak was assigned to make Braxiatel sort through the huge store of archival materials kept at hand there. The Axis wanted to flush out the non-human content of the Collection and make space for new materials, the booty from their latest conquests. Braxiatel's own favourite items were to be no exception.

At first, Braxiatel refused. He was soon persuaded when Martlak set a cabinet alight. It is said that 'The Good Soldiers' was completely destroyed. *Some of you older ones will know what that meant, from your literature lessons.* Braxiatel was consumed with despair as the manuscript pages were devoured in the fire. Martlak was nevertheless unmoved. *That's putting it mildly, he actually said: 'Shed no tears for the scribblings of the half-breed Osterling.'*

From that point on, Braxiatel dutifully provided daily reports on materials to eliminate from his own personal shelves. And through this diligent, if reluctant, cooperation over several weeks, he was able to persuade Martlak not to destroy any of these removals. For Braxiatel also understood how to use a man's enthusiasms against him. *Stay with me on this, guys, it'll make sense.*

The Axis had no interest in the non-human contents of those rooms, but Braxiatel knew that others did. He persuaded Martlak that it was less effective to destroy the purged items than it was to trade them with other interested parties. Marshal Anson may have seen these dialogues as tiny signs of cooperation on Brax's part. Loath though the Axis were to deal with alien races, Martlak recognised an opportunity to turn a tidy profit by selling the unwanted artefacts on to the Finliri, a neutral race whose trading vessels were passing through the solar system.
*This bit doesn't tell you how they argued, though. Martlak got quite narked. 'We can't allow the Finliri here,' he told Brax, 'We can't have aliens on the planetoid.'*
Brax had a smart answer for that one: 'Give me access to an OS-flyer,' he said, 'and I'll deliver the artefacts to the Finliri ship in low orbit. The flyers are a little tricky to handle, but it's perfectly feasible.'
Martlak wasn't having any of that. Marshal Anson would never let Braxiatel leave his rooms.
'Then use one of the pilots,' said Brax. 'I'll remain here. Send Bev Tarrant instead. She's the best pilot you'll find.'
*And that sorted that problem out. Anyway, the story continues.*
For several weeks the work went on. Martlak agreed terms with the Finliri. Braxiatel continued to identify the unwanted artefacts. And each day the pilot, Bev Tarrant, loaded a flyer and piloted it to a rendezvous in low-orbit with the Finliri trading vessel. Even when a week-long solar storm grounded all other shuttles on the planetoid, Tarrant alone was able to steer safely through the maelstrom. *And you know how fierce those swirling solar storms get, eh?*
After only a short while, Braxiatel's new enthusiasm for the job began to make Martlak suspicious. If he had been so unwilling to assist in the evisceration of his display cases previously, then why was he now relishing the job? At a time when no one else had the experience or skill to fly through the treacherous conditions caused by the terrible storm, and when all other transport on the planetoid was grounded, Martlak began to suspect trickery. It had to be contraband, he decided. There were already anomalies in the detection of ships going to and from the planetoid. *And we all know who's responsible for those, don't we? Shhh! No, he can't take you home, my love, sorry, it's too dangerous. You're safer here.*
But what was Tarrant smuggling? Martlak arranged for a surprise inspection of the next OS-flyer cargo, supposing that it must contain half-breeds secreted in the vehicle in an attempt to smuggle them to safety. *See?* None were found.
A subsequent examination of the next flyer's cargo revealed no unexpected contraband, only the approved contents from the Archive.

And a further methodical spot-check for hidden equipment revealed nothing more than the standard apparatus for an OS-flyer – local communications rig, emergency escape pack, ticketing machines, et cetera. *Pardon? Oh, 'et cetera' means 'and other stuff we can't be bothered to list'.*

Martlak's final notion was that unauthorised items from the Archive were being salted away on board. But again, this latest systematic search of the flyer by a squad of soldiers also proved his suspicions wrong. By this stage, the inspections were routine, and no longer unexpected. Martlak continued them anyway, yet continued to be frustrated. Nothing unexpected was found in any of the flyer shipments.

When the solar storm had passed, however, it was apparent from the plain evidence across the planetoid what had happened. Tarrant was not smuggling anything to the Finliri in the OS-flyers – she was smuggling the OS-flyers themselves. *Yeah! I know. But keep the cheering down!*

On each trip, Tarrant had loaded the approved removals from Braxiatel's rooms into the OS-flyer, and piloted the small craft to the Finliri vessel. But she had left the flyer in the trading ship, and returned to the planetoid using the emergency escape-pack. Then she would collect one of the other flyers, grounded during the solar storm, and start the whole exchange again.

Although he could not prove it, Martlak knew that Tarrant must have been generously reimbursed by the Finliri for this additional consignment. But by now, the Finliri vessels had long ago left the system, their deal complete. Only three of a dozen OS-flyers remained on the planetoid. The occupying Axis soldiers' hunt-and-search capability was reduced, the planetoid's insurrectionists had new funding, and Martlak was humiliated.

Braxiatel and Tarrant were punished, of course. At the time of writing, Tarrant is still imprisoned, and it is unclear whether she will be released. *No, darling, I'm sure she's fine. She's tough.*

Martlak was punished too. *How? Well, let's just say that Martlak was sent home to a very frosty reception. He may still be alive, but I doubt we'll hear of him again.*

*The story finishes like this.* By not winning in this battle of wits, Martlak lost his place. And simply by not losing, Braxiatel had earned a first, small victory against the Fifth Axis.

*Time for bed now. I'll see you again tomorrow. Uncle Jason will tuck you in. Yes, Peter, I do have your own special story to tell you. I'll come over to your bunk.*

*Oh, and the rest of you, remember this: we won't be hiding forever. This occupation is violent and dangerous and destructive but, like those solar storms, it has to pass. When it does, I'll take you outside*

*myself, all of you.*
*And we'll walk around our planetoid together, a complete circuit.*

# 19: Speaking Out
## By Simon Guerrier

She took the stage determined not to lose her cool, not to anyone. Not the academics nor the invited guests. Not the billions of people on the other side of the cameras. Not even the soldiers guarding the aisles.

She put her hands on the sides of the podium. The autocue winked at her. Deep breath and...

'History,' said Benny, 'is about choices.'

*Mushtaq Anson hadn't given her a choice.*

*'You know I'm a great admirer of your work, even if I don't always concur with your conclusions,' he'd said. 'And I feel sure your opening address will be a high point of the conference.'*

*He had not met her in the lobby, under the Masaccio. Instead, a trooper had led her silently through to Anson's office. These days the guards nodded and smiled. Anson and Benny sat on either side of the vast, exquisite desk, the books on the shelves over his shoulder vying for her attention. She needed no reminding now: none of the books, none of the things, belonged to him. He had stolen them.*

*'With all due respect,' she said, 'do you really think I'm right for whatever it is your conference is meant to be saying?'*

*Anson raised a hand. 'This is not* my *conference,' he said. 'The Collection had it all arranged some months before we arrived. It has merely, as a result of circumstance, gained our patronage.'*

*Benny shook her head. 'You make it sound so simple. But you realise that –'*

*Again, he interrupted her with ease. 'That whatever precautions we might take, the Axis' presence will still bias what's said? Oh, I'm well aware of that. There will be onlookers keen to prejudice every word spoken. That is also why I've decided you should take part. Your reputation does precede you, and your contribution will imply, rightly, that we neither censor nor intrude upon the workings of the Collection and its valuable contribution to the academic sphere.'*

*'But you do.'*

*'We did when we arrived. Now we've arranged it in the best way for people to live, we don't any more. It continues from this point.'*

*Benny stroked her lip. 'So I can say whatever I want?'*

*'Were you thinking of saying something I might not like?'*

*'Of course not. You'd have me shot. And maybe shoot some of my friends, just to be sure.'*

*Anson laughed as if she'd been joking. As he always did. 'Excellent. Now, you must understand that, as a result of security concerns quite out of my control, I will have to approve a transcript of what you plan to say beforehand? And there will be rehearsals...'*

*'Rehearsals? I don't think there's ever been a conference so... so....'*

*'Well organised?'*

*'Fascist.'*

*'Touché. Then again, no "ordinary" academic conference could ever hope for the attention that ours will receive. We're expecting to broadcast the event live to all of human space. Several billion people will be hanging on your every word.'*

*'Many of them, however, will be in places that sell rotten fruit.'*

'We understand moments in history,' she went on, 'by studying the choices made at particular times and places. These choices are the nodes by which we map and understand the past. The choices some individuals make literally change the path of the future.

'As a result, history is the study of great men, great women –'

She looked up, into the audience. The autocue sensed the movement of her eye and halted the rising text. When had she last been at such a large and exclusively human gathering? Anson, sitting comfortably amongst the other honoured personages in the front row, narrowed his eyes at her. Benny took a deep breath, and risked an ad lib.

'And great others.'

Anson was one of the smattering of people who laughed.

*The Collection's third Reading Room had once been a place of activity and gossip. 'Silence' signs in various languages had looked down upon a cosy hubbub, all but ignored. Benny, needing some time out of her rooms to look over what she had already written, had always come here to get a second opinion from someone.*

*But these days the nooks and snugs, though not empty of academics, were eerily silent.*

*She took the text back home.*

'Great men and women are only great because of the choices they've made,' she said. The autocue, noting she had returned to the script, began to scroll again. 'We attribute greatness retrospectively, after their decisions have paid off. History is therefore about alternatives, the choices that were not made. And, more so, history is an understanding of the circumstances in which ordinary little people can become great, can make a difference, because of their choices.

'In most cases, individuals can't know where their decisions will take them, but they do the best they can. Some individuals endeavour to make informed decisions. Take the Duke of Wellington, whose various choices made a national hero of him. How did he make his decisions? Well, for one, he insisted on surveying the physical ground before a battle took place. In India, he complained of "the vague calculations of a parcel of blockheads, who know nothing and have no data". He was talking about Britain's military strategists at the end of the eighteenth century, but he could just as well have been marking some of my former students' essays.'

Another titter from the audience, and again the reservation came less from the quality of her joke, she thought, and more from the awkwardness of the speech itself.

'Historians, too, make choices. They sift through the arbitrary details left to them, and make decisions about the order and importance these morsels come in. Like Wellington, historians can learn a lot from the ground itself where choices were made. Maybe it's the archaeologist in me, but I think it's important you get your hands dirty.'

She was scanning over the faces in front of her when a flash of recognition stopped her dead. One of the soldiers, looking guilty and uncomfortable in a uniform that didn't quite fit, was her former student Luke. He had shaved his wispy beard off, but the pale skin and doleful eyes were unmistakable. She had not seen him since Oliver Norman's birthday party. When he'd vanished, from the resistance and from the Collection, without even thinking about it she had just assumed Anson's men had caught up with him.

He would not meet her eye. He had made his choice.

*'This is fine,' said Anson, handing back her pages. 'I mean,' he said, 'it's very good. Perfect even.'*

*She hated the way this all came so naturally to him. 'You know,' she said, a glint in her eye, 'I heard a rumour that you're more set-up for broadcasting to non-human space than you are for the humans. Who is this conference trying to impress?'*

*Anson leaned forward in his chair. 'I could ask you where you heard that rumour,' he said.*

*'But you are actually going to broadcast to them?'*

*'If some of our neighbours overhear us,' he said, 'I don't believe it would do us, or them, any harm. They might even learn something.'*

*'An exercise in propaganda?'*

*'I suppose you could choose to see it that way, yes. If you want to treat the conference as explicitly political.'*

'If the historian's job is comparing choices,' she said, 'then day-to-day a historian makes decisions about what is and is not pertinent. There are sanity checks, conferences such as this one today, where historians can compare notes. There's nothing like your peers to make you feel humble! That's the chief appeal, to me anyway.'

She faltered. Again the autocue stopped. Who was she kidding? This wasn't a gathering so people could network, natter, maybe share ideas and e-mail addresses. There could be no free exchange of responses to her work. No one would dare give offence to the Axis. She might as well be dictating to all the people here. It was a conception of education centuries out of date.

'But can we, under the ever-watchful eye of the Fifth Axis, discuss our choices openly?' she asked. The autocue hesitated again. Benny glanced up at Anson, but he was not watching her. He was looking at the line of soldiers around the stage. She followed his line of sight, but not quickly enough.

The explosion knocked her off her feet. Something hit her in the side of the head, wet and warm and heavy. Dazed, she glanced round. The front of the stage was covered in blood. Not her own. Where several of the more important guests had been sitting, there was now a smoking, jagged hole. Her head hurt. Around her there was movement and noise. Behind the terrible ringing in her ears, she could hear screaming.

She struggled woozily to her feet. Somewhere, there were gunshots, and a cry from someone that the cameras must keep recording. Benny tried to run. Luke blocked her path. He lined up his gun.

Just when I'd nearly got there, she thought. The new new new resistance have arrived. And they don't know anything. And they're going to kill me.

Then the other soldiers called for quiet.

'This is a protest against the illegal occupation of the Collection,' Luke called out, holding careful aim at Benny. He never took his eye from her. 'It is also a public execution.'

Though her head was spinning, Benny held his gaze.

Luke blinked first. In a smaller voice, less hoarse and grown up, he said, 'You sold out. We don't have any choice.'

'Neither do I,' she said, firmly.

Luke's expression hardened. 'You're a collaborator.'

'And you're overdue on an essay assignment.'

She wouldn't close her eyes.

The barrel of his gun wavered, ever so slightly. But he didn't change his mind.

She heard the gunshot. Luke's face looked agonised. Like he was sorry.

Some days later, Anson received a visitor in his sumptuous offices.

'Professor Summerfield,' he said, kindly. 'How are you feeling?'

Benny sat down, cold inside. 'I just wanted to know: what would you have done if that hadn't happened? If they hadn't got up, if you hadn't killed them?'

'This is about what you didn't quite get a chance to say, is it?' Anson asked. His tone was level, his face unreadable.

'I spoke out.'

'You didn't. Of course you didn't.' He sounded like he was talking to a child. 'Let the historians decide who are the heroes and villains. As far as I'm concerned, you're on our side.'

She joined in his laughter. And then threw up all over his desk.

'I'm sorry,' she said afterwards, wiping her mouth on the handkerchief he had kindly provided. 'I think I've had something for a while now.'

'I hope you get over it soon.'

'I will,' she said, surprised at herself. 'Or I intend to.'

# 20: The Peter Principle
## By Kate Orman

This is a story that can never be written down. There can be no diary entry, no smuggled letter, no secret record.

I'll tell it to you anyway.

On a wet Tuesday morning, after the hanging, Benny returned to Mister Crofton's hydroponic garden. She had been there that morning, helping Mister Crofton with his calculations: how much of each vitamin a body needed, how much each of his precious vegetables could supply.

Now he insisted on handing her a tall glass of warm lemon and apple juice. She didn't have the heart to ask how it would affect his figures.

They said nothing. They had both been witnesses to the hanging; everyone had. Their Fifth Axis ushers had made it clear there was to be silence, out of respect for the condemned man.

The impossible sight of Ken Genovese pushed up onto that stage and up onto a rickety stool. With a bag over his head, he could have been anyone. He was anyone, he wasn't anyone. It hadn't happened.

Criminal Investigator Spang hadn't dawdled over formalities. Everyone knew Genovese's crime: he had been smuggling messages out, encrypted in the Collection's standard weather broadcasts to space traffic. Jason hadn't known anything about it. The plethora of individual resistors and groups were actively getting in each other's way now. Spang said a word and some spick-and-span Fifth Axis private jerked away the stool.

It took Genovese only half a minute. There was the jerk of his neck being broken, and then his expression went, and he was still. Then he jerked, and some sort of sound came from his mouth. Then he was still again.

Spang had wandered up and down, watching him, walking round him. Finally, he'd taken hold of the back of the man's collar and tugged on it, just to make sure. The body moved in a way that it could not.

'At least they got it right, thank Goddess,' said Benny, at last.

'Did you know him?' asked Mister Crofton gently.

Benny shook her head.

'I knew him only vaguely,' said Mister Crofton. 'One of many faces in the crowd.'

Benny's heart had hammered as hard as Genovese's must have done. If he had taken half an hour about it, the wrenching muscle would have ripped itself out of her chest. There were little cries and sobs and someone shouted out, 'We're here, Ken, we're here!' and got a truncheon in the face for their trouble.

No one would ever know the content of the messages Ken Genovese had been sending out: Commander Spang made a point of not decrypting them. It didn't matter whether they were resistance reports or love letters. There would be no further unauthorised communications from the Collection.

Mister Crofton was growing grapes on a frame improvised from scraps of wood. Tiny green buds dangled on their narrow green threads.

Genovese was a teaching assistant. Genovese was a bit of an expert on the textiles of the Pavo Abstergence. Genovese was three years younger than she was.

'Don't be ill again,' said Mister Crofton. He was holding her wrist. Benny hadn't even realised she was leaning over a newly tilled bit of soil, the bottom of her stomach feeling like a lump of grease. 'Not just yet. You need that vitamin C.'

He looked up sharply. Benny followed his gaze to see Bernard Moskof standing nearby, pretending to examine a row of radishes.

Mister Crofton took away the empty glass and went about hoeing between his leeks, watching Moskof out of the corner of his eye. Benny stayed where she was, sitting on an overturned crate, letting her insides settle. Moskof hovered around, waiting for her to acknowledge him.

If he was here to apologise, she really would throw up.

'I suppose you've seen a lot of that,' she said at last. Her mouth and throat were dry, despite the warm drink.

'Not really,' he murmured.

'But surely that's the Fifth Axis way. If you can't beat them, throttle them.'

'It's not my way,' said Moskof mildly.

'You're not telling me you disapprove of your superiors.'

'Of course not,' said Moskof, glancing around. This wasn't a blank area on the sensor net. 'But think of all the resentment that's been created today.'

'The *resentment*,' choked Benny. '*Created?*'

'Excessive punishment leads to unrest, the opposite of discipline. It creates more problems than it solves. Just my opinion, of course. I'm only Spang's number two. It's up to him to handle Criminal Investigations as he sees fit.'

Benny squinted at him. 'What would you have done?'

'I'd have decrypted the messages. If he really was sending out intelligence I'd still have hung him. If it was harmless stuff I'd just have stripped him of his job.'

'But how would he live then? In the lower levels?' There were yells and the sounds of pursuit at night now. These days the Collection actually had a crime problem.

'Possibly. I didn't come here to discuss Axis policies.'
'Didn't you?'
'No. I want your advice. After this morning, we need something to bring the community together in a positive way. Calm the atmosphere down a little bit. Give people something else to think about.'
'Oh splendid,' said Benny, astonished to find, after all that had changed inside her, that *they* still saw her as someone *they* could do business with. It was like they hadn't heard the thoughts in her head. Like they had not been sent her internal memos. 'Let's put on a show! We could put on the show right here in the garden!'

'He's totally serious about it,' said Benny. 'He even wants a list of the artworks we'll be displaying.'
'In the Garden of Whispers?' said Mister Crofton. 'On what's left of the lawn?'
'It's not as though they want us to arrange a football match on what's left of the lawn,' said Benny.
'Well, we won't do it.' Curator Fearnley from the Department of Fine Textiles squeezed her red-rimmed eyes shut tightly. 'We won't do it.'
'This is one of those Fifth Axis "requests" that are just an order given in a cheery tone of voice,' said Benny tiredly. 'Moskof thought it was such a great idea that he got Anson's backing. I don't like it any more than you do, but we're stuck with it.'
'What about echolocation sculpture? Or beelights?' suggested Teaching Assistant Noonuccal, from Personal Ornaments.
'I wrung a promise out of Moskof that we could include alien works, as long as there's some kind of translation for humans.'
'There are a few left, waiting for transport, since... you know,' said Noonuccal.
'Yes,' said Benny, laughing. 'I know.' The story of what Bev had done was being told in hushed whispers around the planetoid. As the woman herself remained in jail. Everyone was afraid she was being tortured, and waiting for the guards to come for them.
Jason had a way out planned for the children, if that happened.
And so Bernice was relishing the thought of that night, the completion it would bring. But she didn't know how long she could keep that emotion going without it killing her.
Hence the throwing up.
'And so that's frankly extraordinary, but yes, we can arrange that.'
'How can you even think of co-operating with those brutes?' said the Curator.
'The whole exhibition would be up to us: choosing the art, setting it up in the garden,' said Benny. This is a chance to show them up, and they

don't even realise it. We've got carte blanche to show off whatever we want. Paintings, statues, holographs: the best art in the Collection. *All* of it from outside the Axis.'

Even the Curator had to agree with that. 'Yes. Let's show those bastards what being civilised means.'

Someone decided that the best thing for Bang Jorik was to tell the Fifth Axis all about his plan.

Jorik had begun a promising career in scent sculpture. He might turn out to be one of the galaxy's best. Of course, he might not, but none of the committee cared. Jorik was an excellent artist and he was an alien, and he was, incredibly, still here. His work would be featured in their exhibition, right next to giants of galactic art.

Benny visited Jorik before breakfast; his patterns of hibernation were erratic even for his species, and she'd had to make an appointment to make sure she'd catch him awake. He was waiting for her, leaning over the side of his aquarium, two of his clusters of limbs and sensors politely extended. His mantle rippled softly in the tank, long purple and gold ribbons on each side of his blunt, fleshy body.

It was luxurious even to see something sentient that looked like that. To have one's personal conception of person grow back again to what it had once been. Benny looked Jorik up and down like he was a National Park.

Jorik had placed the scent-sculpture on a bench nearby. 'It's made from iridium,' his translator box purred. 'Terrible rubbish but all I could get.'

The sculpture was a mighty tree, its base cracked through as though by a lightning bolt, its heavy branches twisted and snapped where they had impacted the ground. 'Go ahead,' rumbled Jorik, and Benny gingerly touched the surface of the tree. There, at the roots: the smell of mud and metal, like tanks churning up a plain. The trunk had spots of burning buildings and burning flesh. The very tips of the fallen branches had a fresh, clean smell, like a wet new day.

'It's beautiful,' she told Jorik.

'It's beautiful,' she told Moskof, after breakfast. 'It's really a stunning piece.'

'Oh, I don't know a hell of a lot about art, really,' said Moskof. 'I'll have to take your word for it. I do know the Kapteynian itself won't be at the exhibition.'

Benny stretched her mouth out into a line. 'Why not? You could have him polishing Fifth Axis boots, or something.'

'That slug isn't good enough to polish our boots.'

Benny stared at Moskof, who had raised his eyebrows in an expression of desperate sincerity. 'You bastard,' she said. 'You had me going for a moment there.'

'You know he's only still here because it's taking us some time to find an appropriate relocation site. Somewhere without access to shoeshine.'

'How can someone with a sense of humour be part of the Axis? How can *you*?'

'I happen to believe we're right,' he said. 'I know what you think when I say "relocation", and I say if we meant that we could just shoot the things.'

'The *people*.'

'Listen, that's not the reason Bang Jorik won't be at the exhibition. I've been reading his medical reports.'

'Those are confidential.'

'Don't be obtuse. His species have no intrinsic weaponry, but they can absorb the lethal stinging cells from a cousin species. He's got six stingers tucked away in his surface tissues. The artist is armed and dangerous.'

'Jorik wouldn't hurt a fly,' protested Benny weakly. 'He's harmless.'

'He's got no record of violence. And no member of the Fifth Axis would get that close to a talking sea slug. So...'

Benny sat up straight. 'You think he's going to kill himself.'

'Performance art. Right in front of the cameras. I didn't actually work it out for myself,' he admitted. 'Someone tipped me off. Don't bristle, they didn't want to lose their friend in a senseless gesture. It wouldn't make a bit of difference. To the Axis that's just one less alien.'

'That's exactly what I told him when I talked to him this morning,' said Benny wearily.

Moskof looked up at her in surprise.

'I've made him my assistant, so I can keep an eye on him.'

Moskof clapped his gloved hands together. 'Benny, that's fantastic news. That's exactly what we need, to involve people! Turn them into allies and friends.'

'I think you've got a long way to go before you turn Bang Jorik into a friend,' said Benny sourly. 'But none of us need an incident like that. Goddess knows what Spang might do.'

'That reminds me. He and Marshal Anson will be there. I won't be. They only want the big brass and a bunch of art experts. The Marshal has been talking to them all week. He's particularly keen to see something by Deauxob.'

'We'll see what we can do,' deadpanned Benny.

'So once everything is set up, the exhibition area will be closed off for two days. For security checks.'

Benny gave him a sharp look. 'Spang or no Spang, if even one of those artworks is damaged –'

'You know that's not going to happen,' said Moskof. 'We wouldn't lay a finger on them. Braxiatel himself recently demonstrated the more lucrative possibilities, after all.'

The night of the exhibition Benny was stone cold sober. The temptation to grab a little Dutch courage was considerable. But she needed all brain cells on deck for tonight.

Commander Spang was there, as promised.

The crowd left a respectful space around him. Benny thought of the empty ring around a drop of antibiotic on a dish of bacteria.

She looked at him and found herself unafraid.

Good.

Marshal Anson opened the exhibition with a few words about the importance of the Braxiatel Collection: a diamond in the hilt of the Axis sword. He gestured, and someone activated the filmy curtains that hid the garden. They shimmered aside to reveal the forty artworks.

Eighty, now. Benny and the others moved into the garden in silence, puzzled at first, then slowly understanding what they were seeing.

Beside each of the great works, next to every painting on its easel and every statue on its stand, even next to the echolocation sculpture and the beelight display, there was a second work of art.

They weren't simple imitations, either. Benny could hear the experts murmuring, shock turning to grudging admiration. These were fine works in their own right. But different, different. Where Leavitt's *Balancing the Spheres* was dark, formal, sombre, the Axis painting was struck through with fiery light, turning Leavitt's grieving crowd into a triumphant rally. Murnane's stylised masks were matched with helmets and hard, martial faces. Beside Bang Jorik's scent-sculpture was a great tree whose fractal limbs were mirrored by carefully placed holofields, creating the illusion that its branches stretched out forever. Fearnley was staring at it in dismay, as though he couldn't believe it. Benny caught a glimpse of Noonuccal clutching a glass of champagne, petrified with something like horror.

'Impressive,' said Anson. For a moment Benny thought he was holding a gun; then she saw it was just a drink. 'Our best artists had only two days to create these new works, and they've succeeded in every case. I think their best work is the adaptation of truly alien artforms. What's your opinion, Professor?'

Spang was standing next to Anson, wearing a polite smile, peering at the art through his spectacles. From this close Benny could see the glasses were actually a heads-up display. Spang was still working, even while he trailed around the art show after his master.

She saw his hands for a moment, and thought of them in Vosta's mouth.

The beelight display – an animated ultraviolet projection, the speciality of a bichordate shore-dwelling civilisation on Eisner's Apple, translated down into a fierce range of blues for human eyes – had been trumped by a larger, brighter light display.

'Do you see how much smoother the human version is?' asked Anson.

'The Axis version,' murmured Benny.

'Indeed. Our goal has always been to take the very best aliens can produce, and make it even better. I understand the Appledwellers experience time in discrete slices. So their "beelight" is slow. I'd say jerky.'

'I wonder how your version would look to them,' said Benny.

'With their limited perspective, I doubt they'd be able to appreciate it.' He took a mouthful of his drink.

'So that was the whole point of the exhibition,' said Benny. 'To show how much cleverer the Axis are.'

'Not at all,' protested the Marshal. 'We have nothing to prove. No, this is something you yourself should approve of. Human and alien artworks, standing side by side. Non-Axis and Axis art shoulder to shoulder. Differences put aside in the pursuit of excellence.'

Benny ran a finger along the tree that corresponded to Jorik's work. Nothing happened; all she could smell was the lawn and the faint hot scent of the electric lights.

The Axis artists had thought Jorik's tree was just an ordinary sculpture.

'I think perhaps there's a point to all this you're missing,' she murmured.

'Of course, I was forgetting. Commander Spang?' Anson crooked a finger, and Spang trotted up from where he'd been examining a Toric pixellation. 'I know you're no expert on art. Professor Summerfield helped select these works. She'll give you a little tour of them.'

Spang gave her what he must have hoped was an encouraging smile.

Benny opened and closed her mouth. 'Of course,' she managed. 'Please follow me, Commander.'

Half a minute. So much can happen in thirty seconds, it can be such a long time. The world can change in thirty seconds.

She realised she was breathing heavily, and contained it.

They stepped from display to display, Spang dutifully following. She scraped up whatever she could remember about each piece, and Spang stared at it and its Axis duplicate just long enough to show interest.

'You know, Professor,' he said suddenly, making Benny jump, 'I had heard there was almost a protest at the exhibition. Moskof mentioned some sort of slug. He said you were instrumental in averting the problem.'

'One of our resident artists did get a bit upset,' she admitted.

'That's so irrational,' said Spang, without heat. 'I'd have thought the honour of the exhibition would outweigh any qualms he'd have.'

'Well,' said Benny with a smile that showed her teeth, 'he's only human.'

'Speaking of being human,' Spang murmured primly, 'I wonder if I might...?'

'Oh yes, of course. I'll show you.'

no one took any notice of the Professor of Archaeology showing the military executioner where the Gents was.

Behind the Summer House was a stretch of ugly, disused land, one of the Collection's abandoned patches of unfinished landscaping, all mud and concrete. A dirty puddle had become a miniature lake next to a pile of girders, concrete blocks and forgotten moving machinery. Under a bit of canvas they'd stored the bits and pieces needed for the exhibition, tidily out of view, and installed one of the Axis' pristine field toilets, a neat white cube. Spang stepped towards it, his boots in the edge of the puddle.

Bang Jorik came out of the filthy water like an angry cat, dozens of fleshy limbs flaring from his pudgy body, tipped with claws, sensors, and his hoarded stingers.

'Boo,' he said.

Spang looked down at the monster and gave a short, high laugh.

He brought his boot down on one of Jorik's sensor clusters. The translator offered up a crackling hiss of protest, some untranslatable alien cry.

Spang was concentrating on grinding Jorik's sensors into the mud. Then Benny and Mister Crofton grabbed him by the arms.

The gardener had been waiting behind the cube, pretending to dig. This whole stretch of land was a blank on the sensor map.

It took all Bernice's strength to heave the struggling man towards the hole.

He was yelling threats, trying to tell them about his family, pleading.

Bernice filled her head with Luke, Oliver, Ken, Vosta. She was aware of her blood in her head. She was aware of her hypocrisy. Of doing evil.

But she was also aware of the evil all around her. And she wasn't going to let it settle into art and executions and call that a civilisation.

Between them, she and Mister Crofton got Spang to the edge of the construction shaft. It was wider than a man. He was reaching for the edges, spitting, trying to curl his limbs around theirs, like when she play fought with Peter. He was talking, but she didn't let herself hear his noises as words.

They pushed him.

And he fell. His hands missed the sides.

He fell headfirst. Crying out.

'So deep,' said Mister Crofton, 'he won't even compost.'

Benny said nothing. She pulled the cover back over the shaft and went back to the party.

\* \* \*

It can never be written down. There mustn't be any hint left, no scrap of paper or whispered conversation, that might reach the hungry eyes and straining ears of the Fifth Axis. They must never, never guess.

'Thanks for seeing me at such short notice,' said Bernard Moskof, standing up from his desk.

Benny just nodded. Moskof was Criminal Investigations Officer now, a full Commander: he could go anywhere he wanted without anyone's by-your-leave.

He could marry Ms Jones.

'The exhibition was certainly a success.'

'Yes,' she said.

'It's been reported all over the Axis media, even beyond. A real feather in Anson's cap.'

She'd already promised that if push came to shove, she'd be the one to confess. The roles all the others had played in the assassination would never come out, not if the Axis stayed true to form and got her onto the gallows before anyone could investigate properly.

But Moskof, he wasn't like Spang. He'd want to know all the details.

Moskof had had two days to see the possibility. The narrow arc of unused land behind the Summer House, the half-hidden construction shaft. All of it just out of the glimpse of the cameras, invisible to the rest of the exhibition. He must have seen that stuff had been dragged away from the top of the shaft, the safety cover rolled off by Jason's forces. He must have seen it had been rolled back again.

That was no reason to help him. That must be what he wanted today: a panicked confession, tears, begging, bargaining. She wasn't going to be the one who brought it up. He'd get around to it in his own time.

Only he didn't seem to be getting around to it.

'You know,' she said, surprising herself with the calm in her voice, 'Ken Genovese ended up in the Garden of Whispers. Mister Crofton requested his ashes. Very good for his lilies, he said.'

'Yes,' said Moskof. 'I was the one who released Genovese's remains.'

'That was very compassionate of you, Bernard,' she said, looking him in the face.

'Gestures are all I have right now. It's going to be frustrating if I can't solve my first case. Commander Spang has thoroughly disappeared. We've scanned the entire planetoid for his remains, and we haven't found as much as a DNA trace.'

'That must make your job very difficult.'

'My first thought was that slug, of course. If only he could get out of his tank, I'd have the perfect suspect. I grilled him a little but he just whimpered.

'I know *you* don't know anything about it,' he added. 'I saw the look on your face at that execution. To you that was cold-blooded murder. You'd never stand for that, not even for one of ours. You'd have come straight to me.'

'That's right,' said Benny. 'I'd have come straight to you.'

'I'm thinking of suggesting in my report that he had some sort of accident. Or was in some sort of trouble that made him want to vanish.'

'It's... hard to imagine Spang deserting.'

'Is it?' said Moskof. 'Hardly anyone knew much about him. He always kept to himself. I didn't even know about his family back home.'

Benny licked her dry lips. 'Neither did I.'

Moskof sat back. 'Ah well. Things have worked out well for both of us, haven't they, Professor?'

She was actually going to be allowed to walk out that door. Her stomach had settled. She knew now: she didn't like this great detective at all. 'I suppose now you've reached your level of incompetence,' she said. 'But haven't we all?'

He laughed. 'There's a term for that, isn't there?'

'I there?' said Benny, at the door. 'I don't remember.'

# Lockdown Conversations: 4
## By Paul Cornell

They decided she should use the card to get into the control centre that very night. The Axis might be expecting some sort of mass protest after the hanging, or they might be expecting nothing at all. But they wouldn't be expecting one woman with a card that said she had a right to be there.

The main aim was to get a download of all the Axis security systems. With the Vosta System thus perfected, the resistance could come and go as they pleased. They also wanted to check up on Bev.

Mesa made sure Moskof was out with Ms Jones that evening. Mister Crofton engaged them in conversation and took them to a corner table that was in a sensor blank spot, insisting on some detail of the view.

Jason walked Benny through their invisible maze of pathways to the point where the control centre could be glimpsed, new black ceramic construction forming out of the ground floor of the old accommodation block. Here the sensors closed.

Bernice was wearing a full face disguise, adapted from Jason's fat suit. She looked like a bland Axis security officer. The cards weren't personalised, so she was exactly what her key said she was. Unless Moskof returned, when there would be two of her.

Jason put a hand on her face.

'I love you,' he said.

She closed her eyes. She would be true to herself. Even now. Especially now. 'I love you like Peter loves you.'

'Go on.'

So she did.

The cameras moved past her. The human guards exchanged pleasantries, asked her when she'd got in. She knew an apt shuttle from an apt place. It meant nothing to them.

Her card had not been updated, she was still only the second in command on the system. So she didn't go to Moskof's office.

She went instead to the automated heart of the building, following her instincts, going in the opposite direction from the fire escape signs.

There she found two tired controllers monitoring everything. She didn't say anything, just flashed them a smile and sat down. Her uniform was just one clearance level below Moskof himself.

She slipped her card into the appropriate reader and pulled it out again with the information she needed on it. She'd get the news on Bev from that when she got back, no point in pushing it by calling up a scan of the cell blocks.

And with another smile she left.

Who was that woman, they would ask tomorrow, who arrived in place of Bernard Moskof?

She walked back into the corridor home, thinking only of controlling her speed and stance.

It was only accident that made her look into the open door as she passed the hub of the round building. It was designed as some sort of conference hall. Empty now, echoing, with a giant round screen in the centre.

She didn't allow herself to hesitate. Just followed her curiosity inside.

She walked into the middle of the hall, and looked around. Shiny black seating for every Axis official and soldier on the planetoid. Round screens for every angle.

The last thing she expected was for the screen to activate itself.

And then there he was, looking down at her. Not Volf Gator, but –

In his rooms, Braxiatel put down the book he was reading, and rubbed his brow.

He could reach out and touch his time equipment. But the moment he did so, they might pounce, might use these surprising and hidden advanced technologies they possessed. Might have everything they needed, because of him.

So he would not reach out. Not until something happened to tip this situation.

Bev Tarrant was screaming.

She had not told them anything.

It didn't matter who was in charge. She was in the room down the hall from them, and the usual distance prevailed.

Soon there would be nothing left of her to tell them anything.

Ms Jones slept in Bernard Moskof's arms, in her own bed.

They had discussed dresses for the bridesmaids.

Mister Crofton kissed a picture by his bedside that stood next to the elegant curve of a bowl of lilies. 'Sleep well, babe,' he said.

Adrian Wall had his arms wrapped round his hairy frame, trying to get to sleep in a cold, wet, wooden barracks. The thought of his son, and of the words Jason had used to tell him he was being so looked after, burned steady in him.

Jason waited, a safe distance from the control centre.

He waited for Bernice to come out. Waited to see her again.
He was thinking he should have kissed her.
He should have finally found the words that would make everything work again.
But it wasn't like that was a gaping wound any more.
He'd found some sort of love inside himself, and it kept him going when she wasn't there.
But still he waited.

Peter was asleep, too. Surrounded by other children. He dreamed of his grandfather.

And Mushtaq Anson watched images from home, of aliens being thrown into cleansing fire, and thought good, good, as each one howled and burst into flame.
One step closer. One more.
And he took a sip of his excellent imported wine, and laughed to himself, shaking his head.
What a stereotype he'd been for a second there!

Professor Bernice Summerfield stared at the face that had appeared on the screen above her. It was of a bearded, middle-aged man, his gentle eyes looking right into her.
'Isik,' she said. 'Isaac.'
His mouth had opened in an expression of pure surprise.
'Daddy?'

*To be concluded.*

# 21: A Bell Ringing in an Empty Sky
## By Jim Mortimore

**Day 1**

Dear diary,
First an apology. I know entries have been a bit thin on the ground lately. Then again what with the occupation and everything, what else should a girl expect? But check this: I've got a little confession to make.
   I think I'm dead.

**Day 2**

Let's go back a bit. What's the first thing I remember? Dust. All over me. Inches thick. In my clothes, under my eyelids. They say dust is composed mainly of skin. I reckon the entire Axis army must have crawled in the sleeping bag with me and snuffed it right there. Cosy.
   The second thing I remember?
   All the glass in the Mansionhouse windows had oozed out. It didn't look like a nuke. More like... time. Glass is a liquid at room temperature. Given enough time it runs like water. How much time though? Thousands of years? Tens of thousands?
   And what happened to all the people? Especially the people Brax paid to fix the windows?

**Day 4**

Obviously there's no one here to ask. No *thing* to ask either. No clues in the databanks, the remaining robots, spaceships or other tools. The computer calendars don't make sense. They're all tens of thousands of years out of synch. For machinery this precise that means considerable time must have passed. Or perhaps they've all been spiked by an electromagnetic pulse... some kind of Axis doomsday weapon? Maybe they found what they were looking for and left? The robots are equally useless. They all appear to be insane, the robotic equivalent of Alzheimer's. One told me all about its pet octopus. Joseph is nowhere to be seen.
   So the question remains:
   Have I spontaneously leapt a few millennia into the future, am I languishing in the arms of the Kraken Wakes of all hangovers... or have I

simply gone mad from shellshock, post-war-syndrome or other convenient insanity?

Right at this moment? Hard to tell. I have a feeling that even if I flipped a coin to choose an explanation at random the coin would land on its edge, or merely find coming down too much of an effort and simply not bother.

So far it's just been that sort of resurrection.

**Day 8**

Here's something wild: I haven't eaten for over a week now. *And I don't feel hungry.*

*(later)*

That made me think back.

Shortly after I first woke here I washed in one of the fountains. Which, weirdly, are working again. Brax would undoubtedly have spanked me if he were witness to such casual disregard for the rules of the house. Or maybe he'd just watch. Who the hell knows what passes through what passes for the minds of men anyway? I had fun though. I laid on my back in the fountain and scrubbed my dirty bits and watched the side of the Mansionhouse ripple through the water for over an hour before I noticed I wasn't breathing.

**Day 16**

'Once upon a time.'

Isn't that what they say?

Oh, the books may use different words; historical context, social and political analyses, but in the end it all boils down to the same thing. 'Once Upon a Time.' Once upon a time there was a mad dictator. Once upon a time there was a brilliant scientist. Once upon a time there was a lethal virus. You know the story. You've lived it and so have I. Once upon a time there was a war. It came without warning, as wars do, and it tore a world that was the very symbol of peace and civilisation into bloody shreds.

I crashed there in a busted-ass spaceship. I was captured. I

*(later)*

The things they made me do. I

*(later)*

I had to bury the dead. My friends. I was separated from my son. And now I am again.

*(later)*

Weird things are always happening to me. Why me? Has the universe singled me out? Why am I here after it's all over? What happened? What happened to Peter? Did he die cursing me for not rescuing him in the nick of time? For not foiling the invasion the way heroes always do?

*(later)*

What if it hurt him? Dying, I mean. What if they tortured him? What if he screamed? How will I ever get revenge?

*(later)*

I don't feel anything, Diary Dear.
It's just... it feels like it all happened so long ago. It's just too far removed.

*(later)*

I *do* feel something.
I feel guilty because I *don't* feel anything.

*(later)*

Why did I write that?
Because I didn't have to feel embarrassed about writing it?
Because there was no one to read it back?

*(later)*

As an archaeologist I've studied more wars across more civilisations than there are Rice Krispies in a box. You want to know what they all had in common? Interrogation technique, that's what.
They all want to break your toilet training.

*(later)*

For methane-based life forms inhabiting the super-cooled atmospheres of gas giant worlds this can of course add whole new layers of meaning to the words, 'War is Hell.'

*(later)*

Ah. Toilet humour.
It's just *gotta* go.

*(later)*

I'm alone. No one to talk to, shout at, punch, shag. How soon before I lose the inclination to wear clothes? Before I stop worrying about where I go to the toilet?
How fast our habits break.
In case you're wondering, Diary Dear, those little round stains are tears.

**Day 32**

Haven't slept since I awoke. Actually that's a lie. I lay down in a Persian rug and forced myself to try. That was about a week ago. I managed about an hour before my own thoughts, ringing inside my head, began to drive me mad. Images began to come back. Piling up like clouds before a storm. Not recent memories. These came from way back.
Like once, when I was a student, I needed some money so I took part in a sensory deprivation experiment being hosted by the University of Deneb IV. They paid well, they claimed, and by the hour, so it seemed a cushy number. Undress, glue on a few 'trodes, jump in the tank, snooze away a couple of months rent. Nice.
Actually, not so nice.
After two hours in the tank I saw coloured blobs. They were pretty enough, but they wouldn't go away. I complained. How could I sleep with the lights on? After three hours the blobs started to look like my father.
An hour later I felt something touch me.
An hour after that I had the first of several orgasms. Soon I was screaming to drown out the voices. I remember trying to shut my eyes but they were already shut, so I opened them but the visions wouldn't go away. I thought the monitors must have gone off to lunch or something. It was another three hours at least before they let me out to collect my cash. Only when I banked the chip did I realise I'd been under for less than fifteen minutes.
No wonder the stingy buggers paid by the hour.
Then I woke up and there I was, the only living thing on the whole planetoid, wrapped in that old Persian like a half-mad mummy, buried alive.
You can see the resonances, I'm sure.
Hell, I could use an ice-cream.

**Day 64**

Lucky there are lots of pens on this asteroid, Diary Dear.

*(later)*

Lucky I keep a diary, Benny dear. Because if post-modernist stream-of-consciousness diary-keeping isn't a six-pump emergency then I'm a pink fluffy Zebra.

**Day 128**

Hm. Well. Not much to report, really. Haven't seen any more on my wanderings. Have seen a lot of other fine stuff though. Stuff I've never really thought much about before, from all over the galaxy.
Actually that's an assumption isn't it? The galaxy. I mean, it is still there, right?

*(later)*

The truth is... I can't see any stars from outside the Mansionhouse. The ground is there... the buildings... But... there's this sort of... fog. Yes, that's it. A grey fog. Like a mist. Clinging to the edge of my vision. Following me around. Like nothing exists in the universe except when I'm near it, and at other times it's blotted out. The mist... it's there all the time, just visible out of the corner of my eye. No matter where I look or how fast I turn my head, always there in the corner of my eye.
And the thing is

*(later)*

The thing is the light just seems to... I mean, the mist just seems to soak up the...
I mean, I can't see the sun.
I can't tell if it's night or day.

*(later)*

And there are no shadows. At least – I don't cast one.

*(later)*

(Objective head on now.)

It seems to be night all the time. At least it's dark all the time, outside the buildings. But there are no stars. Has the planetoid been moved inside a dyson sphere?

Maybe the Axis just crated up the entire Collection, planetoid and all, when they found what they were looking for.

Maybe this grey fog is some kind of preservative gas.

Maybe your friendly-neighbourhood archaeologist-adventurer is stashed in some kind of galactic warehouse for army-surplus art-treasures?

*(later)*

Why is it when faced with the fact of overwhelming personal danger to oneself and one's loved ones (?), all one can do in the face of adversity is crack stupid jokes?

**Day 256**

I haven't had a period since I woke.
And I'm pretty sure I can't be pregnant again.
Just you and me, Diary Dear.
Just you and me.

**Day 512**

Where was I? Oh yes, the stuff I've seen. The Braxiatel Collection. I hadn't really given it much thought before. Took it for granted, I suppose. Ironic really. When you consider my job.

But it's really very beautiful.

*(later)*

Started a serious investigation of the Collection today. Well, I read all the display cards anyway. Later I'll case a few cases... see if there's any offices I can break into without damaging anything too much. Even the Mansionhouse doors are beautiful. It hurts to think about breaking one down just to see what's inside. But of course, the Axis took all the keys. Way back when there was an Axis, that is.

*(later)*

Got as fart – Sorry! Sorry! Typo! – got as *far* as Brax's rooms today. Actually knocked on the door. No answer. Locked like stone.

This is the room, you see. Every Collection has one. The fossilised

transistor. The mummy wearing a wristwatch. The Tyrannosaurus Rex with alloy fillings. If his timeship is anywhere on the Collection, it was always going to be here. Not that I could fly it. If Brax was going to be here, chuckling to himself...
I don't think he is.

*(later)*

Found some acid and a crowbar. (Don't ask me what acid was doing in Mister Crofton's shed.) Seems a shame to break down such a grand old door. The wood it's made from is three thousand years old. It travelled a million light years to get here. The laquer work is by Estelle of Shi. The old fashioned lock looks simple but very effective. Between you and me, Diary Dear, this girl can't wait to see what's inside.

*(later)*

I'll do it tomorrow.

*(later)*

Yeah. That's it. I'll do it tomorrow. Make an early start. Just in case the door is harder to open than I think.

**Day 1024**

I spent more than a year studying the Collection. And yes, I did break a few cases. Had a bit of a scare when I cut myself on some broken glass while winding up the oldest clock in recorded history.
I'm all right now though. And I can still hear the water dripping into the mechanism, driving it forward, 'plop' by exquisitely fruity 'plop', into whatever future still exists. It's good to hear something other than the sounds I make.
The water is a bit pinker than it used to be, though.
Actually I quite like it.

*(later)*

I can't work this out.
I cut myself. I bleed. I did bleed, into the clock! And my hair is considerably longer than I remember it. But I don't menstruate. There seems to be a conflict here. Something about the way time is working. Maybe time itself is governed by some kind of sliding scale of

embarrassment? You know... the more embarrassing the wrinkles the faster they

No.

That's just silly.

*(later)*

Let's go back again.

The Collection contains works from all over the galaxy, and all of recorded history. It's the lifetime achievement of one man, Irving Braxiatel, my friend, and at the start of my campaign I'm ashamed to say that I didn't know very much about it.

That's all changed now, of course.

The information cards were good starting points. Then the sealed vaults that contained the real books. (The computer databases, as I might have mentioned, were useless. Something's happened to them. For a start the glass data chips have all puddled in their racks, like the Mansion house windows. Whatever information they had is gone. I broke the slag into lumps and built a fireplace. Just for the comfort factor, not that it's cold or anything. Glass doesn't burn, you see. As it turns out nothing else burns here either. And there's no wind that I can detect. And the temperature never varies... it's always skin temperature. The same temperature as me.)

I read the books in a vacuum. The glass-fibre access suit had puddled along with the datachips and windows, but I rigged up a thing using some pipes and a pump from one of the fountains.

(How come the water system feeding the fountains still works?)

I read the books carefully and they whiled away many hours in the grey twilight. Ironically one of the first things I read was a essay from the Library of Alexandria entitled *How to Build A Better Vacuum Pump*. Apparently the Egyptians used them as party tricks to open stone doors weighing tons. Party tricks! I ask you! Then again, who needed machinery when you had all those slaves to do the work for

*(later)*

Even more ironically it was a month before I remembered I didn't need to breathe anyway! Hah!

*(later)*

I just had a thought.

Maybe I was killed in the occupation and now I'm a ghost, doomed to wander the derelict halls of the Collection. Perhaps one molecule or nanosecond 'sideways' there are real people here just as there always were... but I'll never 'intersect' with them.

Forever alone, forever unknowing, the only consciousness in a void which once held a universe of

No.

That's silly too.

*(later)*

The middle of the two ends of it is this: I spent a heck of a long time researching. It's what I love, and now I could indulge my passion with no interruptions from anything as petty as the need for sleep or food. In this way time passed. Rather a great deal of it, actually.

I think I know more about the Collection now than anyone.

Maybe even the great Irving Braxiatel.

*(later)*

Nearly two whole years, Diary Dear. And I haven't even needed to find a new volume to write in. I don't know how I'd have stayed sane without

*(later)*

stayed sane without

*(later)*

Wait a minute.

Wait just a doggone cotton-pickin' *minute*.

*(later)*

Yes... that's it! That's *got* to be it!

I know where I am!

**Day 2048**

I do! I've been mulling things over and I know what's happening to me! I know why I haven't slept, haven't felt hungry or thirsty. I know why there's no light.

It's the Axis!

They want something in the Collection. That's why they're here. They've decontextualised me. Put me in some kind of sensory deprivation tank so

I'll think about the Collection. Maybe talk about it, without realising it. Like speaking to you, Diary Dear! Yes! That's it! They've probably done it to everyone. Me, Brax, Jason... They want intelligence!

I just won't say anything else to

**Day 4096**

Hello Diary Dear. Sorry it's been a while. Tried not to give in to temptation. Sat here for as long as I could. A year? Two? Haven't eaten. Haven't slept. Haven't needed to wash or go to the toilet. Tried not to think about the Collection. Hard, though. Mind is still ticketty-boo-ing away on overdrive. Tried counting the tiles in the Romantako Frieze. Yep. That's me. Tried and trusted. Or should that be tiled and trussed? There are over a million little bits of ceramic there, you know. Or maybe just a few hundred thousand. (Or was that just the blue ones?) I lost count on three – no – four... hm. I've lost count of how many times I've lost count. Come to that I've lost count of how many things I've lost count of, too. In fact I suppose you could say that

*(later)*

Ah me!
　Iterative humour!
　Very sophisticated!
　Are you getting all this you Axis bastards?
　Are you?
　Are you?
　*!!??ARE YOU??!!*

**Day Whatever**

It's like this. I'm going to talk to you again, Diary Dear. It seems pointless to waste your valuable resources. And besides, I have something important to say. Something I want them to hear. Are you all comfy children? Then I'll begin.

I'm going to stop numbering my diary entries.

There's no point, you see. No journal lasts more than a decade. Therefore this is not a real decade. If I'm going to suffer from artificially induced free-form associative cognition I'll induce it myself, thank you very much. And I'll choose what I'll think about.

*(later)*

Today I think I'll think about...
   ....*ducks!!*

See that?
   It's all about control.
   I think about ducks and you don't get any information you need about the history and function of the Harp of Ayela. (Or whatever other artefact you might be curious about.) I imagine chirpy yellow ducklings waddling comically about by a pond and distract myself from reflecting on the Harp's ability to create music that resonates at a frequency which can alter human emotion. (Or any other life form based on amino acid chains, depending on what knobs you twiddle.)
   If only Amadeus had been able to score for this baby. Just *imagine* the parties.
   Or Prokofiev. (Talking of Ugly Ducklings.) And talking of Prokofiev... What about Peter and the Wolf? Another family favourite. A favourite of my family anyway. If I had a

*(later)*

Oh Peter.
What did those wolves do to

*(later)*

Shit.
   Shit shit shit shit SHIT!!

*Diary Dear*
I *said* I wasn't going to do that.
   I *said* I wasn't going to cry anymore.
   And swearing? That's the last recourse of an unimaginative mind.
   And what of my mind?
   Am I mad yet?
   Why didn't I just cross out all that childish nonsense?
   Because it scares me?
   Because it doesn't?

*(later)*

Because it's the only thing that's been real since I woke up?

*(later)*

Because it's

*(later)*

Because it's *me* I'll be wiping?

*Diary Dear*
I

*Diary Dear*
It's like this. I

I'm very

*Diary Dear*
Oh for Heaven's *sake!*

*(later)*

All right, all right! I'll have to use them.

**Day 65536**

There I said it. A number. The whole of human existence is endorsed by them. How old we are, what our test scores were, how much we earn, how much our friends earn, how many wrinkles we have, how many days in our lunar cycle. The universe is described by them. Mathematics, physics, probability analyses, quantum mechanics. Anything we want to know the science of numbers can tell us. It's why mathematicians earn more than ice-cream vendors.

*(later)*

In light of this admittedly bitter observation I've reached a decision. If I am part of an Axis experiment I have to control my relationship to it. I need information. At the moment I'm stuck in the ultimate solipsistic trap. I need to get objective. And fast. I need to think outside the box.
Ready? Here we go then.

**Day 131072**

Okay. Think I've cracked it. I'm going to work out when I am. I'm going to work out what's real here.

*(later)*

Someone took almost everything from the labs. There's nothing
Hang on.

*(later)*

Whoopee! Success! A Carbon Dating kit!
(For all you carbon based life forms still looking to hook up with your perfect partner!)
Now all I need is a cooperative exhibit and a handy information card to compare dates with, and
You know what?
The hell with it.
Later for infodump. For now, on with the great enterprise!

*(later)*

Damn.

*(later)*

*No wonder I can't see the sun.*

## Day 262144

History 101
Once upon a time there was a
No.
In a universe that has no matter or energy, that doesn't even have a state of *potential,* there can be no time, so that doesn't work.

*(later)*

Let's go back.
In the beginning the universe was a superdense lump of, well, call it protomatter. It was infinitely dense and infinitely small and all around it there was *nothing.* Not even a state of potential. All the potential, you see, was locked inside that tiny superdense singularity.
Then the singularity changed state.
In a fraction of a second almost too small to measure every scrap of matter and energy that will ever exist in this universe came into being. The singularity was no longer big enough to contain what it had become.

It exploded.
The universe was born.
For a long time the universe expanded. And we all thought that one day, when all the potential energy in that explosion had been used up, gravity would drag all the matter back into another superdense lump and there would be another explosion and the whole thing would start over.

The cyclic universe. It was a comfortable theory for immature minds. It was a universe of light. A universe in which rebirth was a fundamental operating principle. One in which it was easy to create God.

Now we know it's not true.

There's not enough matter. Gravity isn't strong enough, not to make a Big Crunch. We live in an open ended universe, in which only the first, tiniest fraction of time contains burning stars, heat and light, energy to fuel life as we understand it. For the rest of its life – literally eternity – the universe will expand, growing colder and darker as it does so. On and on. For ever. No light. No heat. No stars. Just clotted lumps of matter that will eventually become black holes as big as galaxies.

There is no God here. No resurrection. No afterlife.

No cyclic behaviour of any kind.

And that time, so far in the future, it's like all the grains of sand on all the beaches on all the worlds that ever were compared to *that single shiny grain glued to the sweat on the tip of your finger*, that place is

*(later)*

it's

*(later)*

That place is where I am *now*.

### Day 524288

There are still questions though.
*How?*
Perhaps more importantly,
*Why?*
All your Old Favourites.

*(later)*

I still miss Peter.

*(later)*

Maybe that's the most important thing of all.
   I have to believe that's what makes me human, what keeps me sane.
   Otherwise all I am is just an echo, just an impression of self awareness, lingering, way past its shelf life.
   An accident.

*(later)*

It's time.
   There's nothing else left now. I have to know what's inside Irving Braxiatel's inner sanctum.

*(later)*

Then I can let go. I can finally

*(later)*

Why can't I say the word? It's just a word, meaningless now when held against the infinite darkness that's all the universe has left to offer.
   Suicide.
   Such a simple word. Surely I can say *that*.

*(later)*

I'm going to

*(later)*

I'm

*(later)*

it's just that it's an idea, you see, Diary Dear. Yes, even *that*. It's a concept. A symbol, in a universe where all such symbols are long dead.

*(later)*

I'm such a *coward*.
   I'm going kill myself. I'm going to take a look inside Irving Braxiatel's Private Inner Sanctum and then having discovered the last secret in the

universe, I'M GOING TO BLOODY KILL MYSELF. ME. DEAD. BERNICE SUMMERFIELD. BY MY OWN HAND. REST IN PEACE. THERE. I SAID IT. YAY FOR ME!

**Day 1048576**

How many more entries before the numbers become meaningless? Just Rice Krispies in a box? Everything's changed now. Heaven, how it's changed.

*(later)*

Let's go back, Diary Dear.
I know, I know. Me too. But this is the last time. I promise.

*(later)*

I got the acid. I got the crowbar. Never mind the door, the age, the journey. It was all meaningless now.
I just wanted in.
What was inside?
So simple.
Peter.
Peter was inside.
He spoke to me.
I cried.
Hell, I broke down.
I tried to kill him.
I tried to kill myself.
I couldn't.
I'm not real.

*(later)*

Diary Dear, you're the only one who really listens. I know you're just inanimate, no spark in there. I know you'll be gone soon. When I don't need you anymore. But in the meantime you're such a comfort.

*(later)*

So...

*(later)*

I saw Peter.
 My dead son Peter.
 Dead for a billion millennia.
 He talked to me. Told me the last secret of the universe.
 Hands up anyone who recognises the only important sign of paranoia and delusion?
 Ah, you at the back. Splendid. Full marks. Gold star.
 Three gold
 *(if only there were any)*
 stars.
 Where was– oh yes.
 I can be paranoid. I can be delusional. But the ideas. The ideas can still be intriguing. Can't they?
 All the time I'm here to give them meaning?
 I'd thought the Axis were looking for an artefact, part of the Collection. Or Brax's timeship. Something they needed in their wars, anyway. Why else invade what essentially was little more than a museum?
 What if it wasn't an artefact they were searching for?
 What if it was something else? Something more sophisticated than a mere object.
 What if the thing they sought was a *pattern*, an energy state created by the relationship between several or even all of the pieces in the Collection? What if by their very occupation the Axis changed the relationship between these objects... altered forever the balance of potential energy between them? What effect might that have? On me? On the universe?

*(later)*

Listen. You can almost hear it happening. The universe outside this room is winding down. A clockwork toy and no child to play with it. The last light in the universe fades to a tired glimmer. The grey nothing encroaches. The fountains dry up... stone cracks... metal rusts... entropy *creeps,* a universal slow-burn, flooding inward towards the Last Place. The Last Potential.
 That's me, in case you were wondering, Diary Dear.
 (Don't worry about any typos. It's beginning to affect you, too, now. The matter you're made up of is old, tired, held in stasis only for my benefit. You're nearly over. But don't worry. It won't hurt. Even pain impulses can't travel when the energy state of the universe is so flat.
 There's just one more thing I need to tell you. Quickly now before the light goes. The last light in the universe. It's about my son. Peter.
 He's not actually my son, of course. I'm sure you've guessed by now.

He told me about himself.
He's Mind.
Not *a* mind. But *Mind*.
Consciousness itself born from the last molecules of matter in the universe... orbiting in tracks measuring billions of light years... thinking thoughts whose duration can only be measured in aeons. The logical consequence of an open-ended universe, he could only evolve in a universe without light and heat, where entropy has all but eroded the normal energy-curve to a flat line. But he *does* exist, and he *does* have self awareness, and like all life he asks questions. Who am I? Where do I come from? What is my purpose?

No, no, Diary Dear, it's okay. Really. You'll be gone soon. You won't see the last matter in the universe sucked into half a dozen galaxy sized black holes. But thank you, my dear friend, thank you for all these long years of hope. I'll miss you.

One thing before you go:

The Consciousness – my son – is composed of the only matter left in the universe. There are no new things now. All the interesting civilisations have died, without the power of suns to fuel their butterfly lives. I'm not real. Just a memory, *made* real by one of the artefacts in the Braxiatel Collection because the Consciousness – because *Peter* – is bored.

He knows he'll eventually die, when the last of his molecules are sucked into those ever-hungry black holes... but until then he wants – not a toy, not exactly – a... playmate. Someone interesting to distract him from inevitable destiny. He's been protecting the Braxiatel Collection from entropic decay almost forever, long enough to use the artefact to make real the perfect memory, the perfect distraction – in other words *me* – before finally allowing the Collection and everything in it to fall to dust.

You remember I wanted to kill myself?

I couldn't. That's why. I'm just a memory. Imperfect. Flawed. Entertaining. I'm friction in a universe without coefficients, where the only maths is trending towards zero and all bets are off.

Peter's worried about me. I would be too, I suppose. He's given me a choice. I can live in full knowledge of the truth of my situation, or be intellectually cushioned.

'How can he do that?' I hear you cry.

It's easy. Peter can use the artefact to create a structure of additional memories for me to experience as if they were real. I can have my life back, and I'll never know the difference, never know what or when I really am.

And that's why I needed you, Diary Dear.

You helped me to choose.

You see, one choice felt like running away, the other well, that would inevitably lead to madness.

Thanks to you I found a compromise.

I suggested Peter and I entertain each other. A kind of double-Scheherazade. We could tell each other stories... stories of my life... stories of the life of the universe... until the end finally comes.

And that's why we don't need you any more, Diary Dear.

Peter and I'll have each other for the rest of forever.

Mother and son.

Amen.

*Dear diary*

Today I asked Peter to tell me a story. He said he didn't know how. I laughed. He had so much to learn. I told him I'd go first. But where to start? That's the thing. There's so much to choose from. Booze. Boys. Ice-cream... Love. Hate. Truth. Lies...

Every human life is a battle. We're born in pain and we die in pain. And everything in between... it's not always peachy. So here's what: I'll tell you a story of love and hate, truth and lies, booze and boys and ice-cream.

I'll tell you a story of life during wartime.

# Acknowledgements

Thanks to: Finn Clark; Neil Corry; Mags Halliday; Alison Lawson; Caroline Symcox; Mike Tucker; everyone who pitched a story that didn't make it into the book; everyone on the Yahoo DownAmongTheDeadMen mailing list, especially those who entered the short story contest.

Out now from Victor Gollancz, check out Paul Cornell's science fiction novels: *Something More* (ISBN 1-85798-959-7) in paperback and *British Summertime* (ISBN 0-575-07369-1) in trade paperback, with paperback to follow in February 2004.

*A unique and powerful novel. Cornell's imagination ranges confidently across time and space and the human heart... Wildly epic and beautifully intimate all at the same time.*
**Russell T. Davies *(Queer as Folk, The Second Coming)***

# Other Books Available From

# BIG FINISH

## Doctor Who

*Short Trips: Zodiac* edited by Jacqueline Rayner
(ISBN 1-84435-006-1)
*Short Trips: Companions* edited by Jacqueline Rayner
(ISBN 1-84435-007-X)
*Short Trips: A Universe of Terrors* edited by John Binns
(ISBN 1-84435-008-8)
*Short Trips: The Muses* edited by Jacqueline Rayner
(ISBN 1-84435-009-6)
*The Audio Scripts* (ISBN 1-84435-005-3)
*The Audio Scripts: Volume Two* (ISBN 1-84435-049-5)

**COMING SOON...**

*The New Audio Adventures - The Inside Story*
by Benjamin Cook (ISBN 1-84435-034-7)
*Short Trips: Steel Skies* edited by John Binns
(ISBN 1-84435-045-2)
*Short Trips: Past Tense* edited by Ian Farrington
(ISBN 1-84435-046-0)
*The Audio Scripts: Volume Three* (ISBN 1-84435-063-0)
*The Audio Scripts: Volume Four* (ISBN 1-84435-065-7)

## Professor Bernice Summerfield

*Professor Bernice Summerfield and The Dead Men Diaries*
edited by Paul Cornell (ISBN 1-903654-00-9)
*Professor Bernice Summerfield and The Doomsday Manuscript*
by Justin Richards (ISBN 1-903654-04-1)
*Professor Bernice Summerfield and The Gods of the Underworld*
by Stephen Cole (ISBN 1-903654-23-8)
*Professor Bernice Summerfield and The Squire's Crystal*
by Jacqueline Rayner (ISBN 1-903654-13-0)
*Professor Bernice Summerfield and The Infernal Nexus*
by Dave Stone (ISBN 1-903654-16-5)
*Professor Bernice Summerfield and The Glass Prison*
by Jacqueline Rayner (ISBN 1-903654-41-6)
*Professor Bernice Summerfield: Life of Surprises*
edited by Paul Cornell (ISBN 1-903654-44-0)
*Professor Bernice Summerfield: Life During Wartime*
edited by Paul Cornell (ISBN 1-84435-062-2)